THE APPROACHING SUN

S.D. Hildebrand

Outskirts Press, Inc.
Denver, Colorado

Chapter 1

The mission had been called off. The word had been passed to every ship in the fleet and every man from the lead admiral to the lowliest oiler on the lowest deck of the farthest ship. The word had been passed for everyone to know. Just hours before what would have been the greatest naval mission in the history of the world, the mission had been called off.

Many of the hands below deck were unaware of the course of events; they only knew their individual jobs. Most didn't know which side of the international date line they were on or the even exact time. Seaman Second Class Hashani Nagami was a loader for one of the main guns on the heavy cruiser *Okhotsk,* assigned as an escort ship on the mission. The ship was one of the newest vessels built by the rapidly developing Japanese Imperial Navy. Hashani's job did not take him above the main deck. He had no opportunity to attend the Imperial Naval Academy. As a child he had enjoyed riding with his grandfather in a swift boat on the lake near his village. That was his first contact with the water. He did not have the education to work above deck and he didn't have an understanding of the complicated job of navigation. It didn't matter in his job, lifting and loading the huge packs of gunpowder and shells for the fourteen-inch guns of his assigned turret. He wondered if it were still December 7 because they were traveling east across the international date line.

The announcement threw everyone into a state of disbelief. Morale quickly plummeted. When they had set sail, everyone in the fleet knew they were on a mission of great importance. They were going to attack the lowly and filthy Americans. The Japanese Empire was going to show its superiority and force the United States out of the Pacific. Japan was going to take its place as the ruler of the Orient and the entire Pacific. The nation was going to bring its people to the ranks of global greatness. Now that the action had been called off, the military leadership knew the forces would be thrown into a state of complete devastation. Everyone would feel as if they were returning to their homeland in shame. It was the way of the Samurai to be victorious or else not return. The seamen and airmen had no control over their destiny at this point. They could not continue to guide ships toward the American islands of Hawaii. They had to follow the directions of their leaders and trust that the decision was for the best.

There was much questioning. Admiral Yamamoto was livid when he received the order. When the first report was transmitted to his flagship, he was contacted in the wardroom near his spacious cabin. He barked at the timid-looking lieutenant who had handed him the message transcribed on paper. The lieutenant was initially honored to go to the supreme admiral's cabin but didn't realize he was holding the order that would change the course of world events. Yamamoto crumpled the paper in his hand and threw it on the floor. He glared at the boyish-looking officer, thinking this was incompetence on the part of the radio operators and interpreters. He thought that it had to have been a mistake. The admiral ordered the young officer to correct the mistake and have the right message transcribed. The ship sent a request to the Japanese naval command to confirm the message: "Please confirm, cancel attack, return home?" The message was confirmed over and over. The attack wouldn't be carried out. The entire fleet was to return home without doing anything. None of the airplanes would take off. No seaman or airman would be allowed to do the job he had been ordered to do, that he had dedicated himself to complete at all costs.

The admiral wondered why. Since mid-autumn he had been involved in planning the operation. Everything had been discussed and directed to the smallest detail. More than a hundred surface ships and submarines had sailed. Hundreds of aircraft with tens of thousands of tons of ordinance were ready to obliterate the American fleet at Pearl Harbor. This was to be a glorious victory and now he was to just turn the fleet around and go home without even seeing the enemy? He was to run like a cowardly dog? Yamamoto would return to Tokyo, prepared to resign out of sheer indignation. To have at his fingertips the most powerful and well-prepared naval air attack in the history of combat, and he was told to simply stand down. He started pacing in his cabin, walking off the anger, each step pounding the fine carpets of his cabin and only making him angrier. He was filled with emptiness because he would not achieve victory and not have the opportunity to disgrace the inferior American Navy. He wanted answers from the military command. He demanded answers.

Whatever the reason, Yamamoto would reassemble his forces. He would build their strength again. Everyone would be more determined. This great arsenal of war that he had sharpened to a razor's edge would not just be put on a shelf. He would find his victory or die the honorable death of the Samurai.

Admiral Yamamoto had not left his room. He had walked a line back and forth for half an hour before sitting at the large steel desk near the door. The military issue desk was in stark contrast to the finer amenities he had added such as the carpets, drapes, and thick, padded chairs. He leaned back in the squeaky chair and turned toward the window. It was dark on the great expanse of ocean to the east. Yamamoto was always formally dressed when anyone arrived at his door. The lieutenant who had delivered the message earlier had met the admiral while he was wearing one of his many finely adorned and pressed, olive-colored uniforms. He had just now loosened the button at the neck of the stiff, wool topcoat. Even in the heat of the steel fortress the admiral always displayed himself in truly distinguished military attire.

The trip had been spectacularly made thus far across nearly four thousand miles of the North Pacific, undetected. He had plotted the entire course and was mentally preparing for the coming attack. He could see the blood spilling from his enemy. He could hear the cries of death in the stillness. He could taste the glory of victory—but it was not to be on this day.

The fleet continued to travel south for a short while before he resigned himself to the facts. He gave the order. It was passed to every ship. "Sharp turn to starboard. New heading of two-eight-zero. Return home." The fleet turned west/northwest. The last rays of the setting sun were visible. He would see the sun rise again. He would see the sun of Japan rise in greatness. The world would witness the rising sun.

Chapter 2

It's a dangerous and changing world. Armies and navies led by fanatical tyrants travel where they please. They take what they want and destroy what they don't choose to have. Nearly half of the globe is involved in war. America sits in peace, observing from a distance what mad men are doing.

The date is June 20, 1940, in German-occupied Paris. The train is exactly on time. Metal squeals and the brake shoes give a pungent, nearly overpowering, odor as the train comes to a gentle stop in the station. The train had to be on time considering the passenger. The train had left from Berlin the night before on a single mission: the transportation of Adolf Hitler to Paris. Troop and supply trains had to take a siding while the Nazi leader's train gently rolled forward through the cities, forests, and fields of neighboring countries. Most of the scenery was a beautiful display of old-world Europe. Everything near the train's route had been sanitized and polished for the führer. Everyone wanted him to see the attractive areas now under his authority. He never saw the death and destruction in the toppled cities and obliterated villages, caused by the short war in France.

Hitler's military forces had moved into France a month before and the entire nation was now under German occupation. From the beginning of the Blitz there was little that stopped Germany, and Europe was struck with fear. More nations fell, and now England stood alone.

The führer was completely drunk with power when he arrived. As he stepped off the rear of his private railcar he nearly jumped for joy to the platform below. The private car was built especially for him. He used it often to visit his generals in the field after a battle. The outside of the car was a dark, military gray, but the inside was built like a palace: dark, wood paneling; glass reliefs; fine drapes; and carpet. It was built for luxury and the führer used it as part military compound and part palace. The train would be polished, inside and out, awaiting his return. For now, Hitler wanted to see Paris. His polished boots clicked on the concrete as his personal aids and officers followed him. The short man was ready to take a merry, little stroll down the Champs Elysees and go to the top of the Eiffel Tower. He was ready to celebrate this victory and plan for more to come.

The German people respected and admired their leader. He was a man of the people, a wounded hero of the First World War. He had brought the German people out of post-war depression. He was an energetic man who thought himself a great military planner. His generals who were experienced officers from the Great War knew he was not. After nearly a year of military operations, Hitler's inner circle—Goering, Himmler, Jodl, Keitel, and Hess—had learned how to handle him. They were learning how to make their ideas his.

Europe was ablaze in war. Southeast Asia and the Pacific were overrun by the Japanese military.

Emperor Hirohito had succeeded to the throne of the Japanese Empire in 1926. He had adopted Showa, enlightened peace, as the official designation for his reign. The political leaders of Japan believed military aggression was the best course of action for their nation. From the moment Hideki Tojo was made minister of war, he maintained the strong, military stance of the nation and pushed the Japanese occupation over much of the Pacific and Southeast Asia.

Nazi generals soon realized that the advancing military leadership in Japan meant changes in the Far East. The two nations had never been allies, but the Nazis thought it would be good to have friends that had such pride, power, and military determination. Adolf Hitler had no respect or concern for the Japanese. They would simply be a nation he could use. He was prepared to use whatever and whomever was necessary to achieve his goal of victory and worry about the consequences later.

By the time Hitler walked the streets of Paris, Rudolph Hess was walking the streets of Tokyo. Hitler had appointed his longtime friend and second in succession to the Reich to travel and meet with the Japanese emperor, military, and political leaders.

Hess was very different from Hitler. He was a tall, thin man, quiet spoken, with piercing, dark eyes. Hitler spoke often of the superior race of German people, but not many of his military command fitted the profile he described. Hess and Hitler had been together since the beer halls of Bavaria and they knew one another well. Hess was the one man with the intellect and finesse who could persuade the Japanese. Hess would meet many times that summer with General Tojo. He would meet Emperor Hirohito once in the Great Palace of the Sun. He was greeted in the Orient with wine, women and song—saki, geishas, and lute music. Hess thought the small, yellow people were strange. They seemed backward compared to the technologically advanced nation of Germany. He realized the strength and courage of the people implied great potential. He had been entrusted to make a deal that would ultimately change the world. He didn't take his task lightly. By mid-September the Third Reich and the Japanese Empire had entered into a formal diplomatic agreement. With it, Hitler was able to continue his conquest of Europe, Western Asia, and Africa, and Japan could take as much of East Asia and the Pacific as it chose. The United States was the only world power not yet involved in the global conflict. The stage was set for the creation of a very different world.

Chapter 3

Not everyone knew yet that a world war was inevitable. Mechanized armies and powerful navies were capable of circling the globe and causing destruction at lightning speed and efficiency. There were only a few aggressive nations and they were led by insecure and greedy men in the Orient and fanatical tyrants in Europe.

By the summer of 1941, Japan had been at war with China for nearly five years. The Japanese navy was being built up with fast fighter aircraft and enormous ships. The army was growing each month with thousands of young men who had been drafted or who responded to the call of duty by volunteering. One young Japanese man who was initially fearful of military service was Yoshi Iwanami. He had been drafted into the Imperial Japanese Army that summer. He was not aware of his government's plans in other parts of the world. He assumed he would serve in the advance into China and have the Bushido honor of serving his emperor and homeland. From the first day of army basic training, the lean and exuberant young man was taught that from even the time before the Shogun, every Japanese male was born with the instinct to fight. Yoshi's sergeant looked him squarely in the eyes and told him the fighting instinct was in him and he would serve aggressively and with honor.

Yoshi began to realize that he had those qualities.

By mid-1941, Germany was possibly the most advanced and powerful nation on the face of the earth. It too was made up of men prepared to fight at all costs for the fatherland. The German navy did not control the surface of the Atlantic as their Japanese allies did the Pacific, but the German navy did have a fearful and potent weapon in its fleet of submarines. The German navy had been continually building its fleet of U-boats since 1934. To be a part of the Kriegsmarine was possibly the highest honor in the navy. Men capable of making officer on a surface ship would pass up that chance just to serve as enlisted men on a U-boat. Johan Kurz had joined the Nazi Party in 1936. He could see it would help him and he took a job as a worker in a new machine factory in Rostock the following year. In the fall of 1939, after the Blitz of Poland, Kurz left the factory to join the German military. He insisted on being sent to the navy and fought until being allowed to join the Kreigsmarine. He continued to work hard and was commissioned as an officer in the summer of 1941. He didn't know what the future of the world yet was, but he was ready to begin his part in helping Germany shape that future.

After Hess had carried out his political mission to Japan and signed a formal alliance, Nazi military officials stayed in Tokyo. They stayed as advisors and envoys to keep close relations during the advancing military operations taking place on separate sides of the supercontinent. The Japanese leadership, always hesitant to accept outside influence, was not very keen to have the Nazis present in the capital city. Some Nazis, however, won the trust of the imperial military inner circle.

Stephen Burkhalter was an SS major serving the fatherland in Japan. He had joined the Schutzstaffeln in 1936 and had quickly risen through the ranks. Burkhalter fit the Aryan mold perfectly, being tall and broad with blond hair and blue eyes. He did his best to maintain his appearance with calisthenics and always wore his hair close-cropped. His black SS uniform was always clean and pressed and proudly displayed his medals. He was dedicated to the Nazi Party and the führer and was fanatical and brutal like the rest of the SS. Burkhalter was commissioned as a lieutenant in the summer of 1939 and was involved with the first invasion forces in Poland during the Blitz. Because of his talents and dedication to the continued expansion of Germany, Burkhalter became a recognized name in the upper echelon of military command. He was trusted and chosen by Rudolph Hess as German military attaché to the Japanese Empire. Burkhalter arrived in Tokyo in October 1940.

Burkhalter became a trusted aid to General Tojo and he was allowed to freely travel anywhere within the Japanese military command. When Burkhalter first learned in the late summer of 1941 about a possible attack on the United States, he reported without delay to the SS command in Berlin. The information passed quickly around the leadership of the German military. It was forwarded to what was considered the capital: the Reichstag.

The highest levels of the German military command met in the Reichstag in Berlin. This was the seat of power for the military state of Germany. Adolf Hitler considered this his personal government office and even his informal residence. All of his personal staff and the highest generals commanded from the Gothic brick and mortar building.

The führer allowed one area of the top floor to be used solely by his closest commanders. The top military strategists were allowed to speak undisturbed in this section.

The large room in the farthest western section was more like a gentlemen's hunting club than a military conference room. It had rich, oak paneling; an ornamental, plaster ceiling; and deep-hued, Oriental carpets. No metal office chairs appeared in the room, but ornate, carved, wooden chairs sat in front of the black marble table near the door. The only indication that this room was in a military headquarters were some colored maps on the walls and the armed SS guards on constant watch outside.

It was the middle of the business day in the busy capital of Berlin and the business of the German military was taking place in the conference room. Japan's possible attack on the United States was being discussed. Five men sat in soft, oversized, leather chairs near a fireplace with a polished-marble surround. There had been no fire in it for months and it had been swept spotless of its ashes. The men were behind closed doors and had no appearances to keep up, so their uniform jackets were unbuttoned. Two smoked cigarettes and all sipped drinks from heavy glasses. The magnitude of their allies' plans weighed on everyone present.

Alfred Jodl was the military chief of staff and personal assistant to Hitler. Any information for the führer first went through Jodl. He was the first to speak about the possibility of an attack on Pearl Harbor. "I believe the führer will be thrilled. He doesn't care about the Americans. It's known that his view of the New World is one of the United States being merely a pest, like a flying insect." He sat back in his chair, relaxed and took a sip from his glass.

Wilhelm Keitel was the German supreme army commander. He was in his gray, field uniform with broad, red stripes on his pants that disappeared into tall leather boots. He had stripped off his jacket. He spoke next. "Japan can be a valuable ally in the fight against the Soviets." He had had little time to relax. Germany had invaded the Soviet Union the month before. German forces advanced with the Red Army giving no indication that it could stop them. Keitel had always been concerned about a two-front war. "Our armies in the West must still occupy France and keep the British across the Channel. Now we must concentrate on the eastern front also. If the Japanese were to attack the Soviets from the east, we could easily continue from Western Asia."

Herman Goering was a reserved man. He was tall and heavy and never spoke until he believed the moment was right. He raised his hand slightly and paused for a moment. "The Japanese have a strong fighting spirit and can be a great asset to the Reich if they respond in the way we need them to." Goering was first in succession to the führer. His word was respected all over the nation as well as in this room. "If Japan attacks the United States, how will the Americans react? We know they appear to avoid the war. They only stand by and offer assistance to other nations. They have no stake in the war now, but what will they do if they're drawn into the war by our associates in the Pacific?"

There was never any attempt by these men to impress one another. No one would jump into a conversation here as they did when Hitler was present. All of these men truly loved their homeland and loved the power of their command. Each was concerned about the nation and course of the war and wanted to plan the best possible course for ultimate victory. They sat and thought seriously about the future.

Reinhard Heydrich sat in one of the wooden chairs nearby. He slid forward to make his presence known and spoke in a low tone, "The Americans can benefit our enemies." He was the commanding admiral of the German navy and was respected as a fine military leader, but was not always liked by his colleagues. He was the brashest of the group. "As our fight continues we are weakened with each passing day of war while England and Russia are strengthened by American support. The support is much to deal with. We do not want to face the United States military also."

No one spoke for some time after the admiral made his comments. The only sound in the room was the tick tock of the clock on the fireplace mantel. Sensing that he needed to continue with something positive, Heydrich said, "We want to deal with the Americans, but we should keep them out of the fight until we can deal with them. We knew a two-front war would be a lot to handle. We should keep the Americans out at all costs." He looked at the faces of each of his colleagues as he continued. "We can destroy the Soviets and occupy their country. We can destroy the British and occupy their country. We cannot face the Soviets, British, and Americans."

Jodl was always the positive voice for Hitler and the military. He was still properly dressed in his full uniform and polished accoutrements, including the large black and silver Iron Cross hanging around his neck. Traditionally the cross was prominently displayed on a chain around the neck or on the left breast pocket of dress uniforms and was large compared to other decorations. The cross was supposed to be a high honor, but every general, most officers, and a significant number of enlisted men possessed one.

Jodl spoke again, "All other nations are inferior to the military might of Germany. The Americans cannot provide sufficient support to any other nation to stop our advances. The American army is small, weak, and disorganized. They have no quality leadership. They could not possibly assemble any type of capable military force before we have gained more than they could counter." He sat forward in his chair and his voice level rose just like Hitler's when he gave a speech. "Our submarines can cripple any ships they attempt to send across the Atlantic. They could not possibly launch any type of successful land attack against Europe. The nation's people are lazy, stupid and don't care about a fight in another part of the world."

Heinrich Himmler shook his head. "They are capable people." The room remained in silence for a moment while the comment sank in with everyone. The clock on the mantle continued keeping its beat, oblivious to the actions of the men present. No one wanted to admit weakness, but generals like these did not rise to high ranks without being pragmatic.

The men faced Himmler and waited for his comments. The slender man wore round glasses on his round face, which made him look a little like a beaver. Although his general appearance didn't always garner fear in those who met him, his leadership within the Geheime Staatspolizei did. He was the relentless leader of the Gestapo and was as dedicated to the führer and the Reich as anyone. He continued, "We can call the Americans an inferior people, but these people can rise to accomplish great things. Everyone knows their military history. They gained their independence through war. They entered into the Great War at the opportune time and by combining with the French and English. Our beloved armies of a generation ago were defeated."

Jodl turned his head away from Himmler and pressed out his cigarette in an ashtray. No one wanted to hear the words, but everyone knew Himmler only spoke for the good of the fatherland. Himmler continued, "The United States is a rich nation. It's rich in resources, technology, and determination. Whether it's recognized or not, they are a world power. They are contemptuous and should be disposed of." Everyone in the room nodded in agreement. "They can be described as slow, stupid, and useless." He raised his finger like a schoolteacher in front of a class, "These are words that can describe a sleeping giant."

Everyone sat silently as his words sank in.

Just as on the battlefield, Keitel responded at the right moment. "We will deal with the United States. It is a necessity and inevitable." The group rumbled in a positive tone. Keitel continued, "It's important we deal with the United States because they support the Soviet Union and they are the only lifeline England has. Prudence would dictate that we respond to them, respond before they are able to respond to a world war,"—he looked at Himmler—"before the giant awakens." His tone was one of sarcasm, but his words were those of a thoughtful, military planner.

Goering was a well-educated and intelligent man. He was wise because he knew that reflection was better than pride. This open discussion with the nation's leaders could only be beneficial. Hitler himself was the only detriment to the Reich. As much as he had built up Germany from the ruins of the First World War, he had taken away from its military objectives. His goals were great, but his plans were faulty.

Goering raised his chin and took a deep breath before speaking. "We must admit that the United States can be a threat to the Reich and the Japanese Empire if not dealt with properly. The United States feels comfortable in its vast, rich landscape. It is bounded by weaker and friendly nations to its north and south and protected by oceans on each side. Like the martial arts that our allies in the Pacific teach, opponents' strengths can be used against them. All of these factors that now appear to be assets to the United States could easily become areas of threat."

Confused faces appeared in the room. All of the military leaders present knew that England was safer just because of the English

Channel. The United States was too far to mount any type of large-scale attack and it could not be done while Germany was still engaged on the eastern front.

Goering continued looking toward the ceiling as he spoke, as if he were thinking out loud. "We must look in the long term. We can deal with the United States." He stood prepared to end the day's discussion. Everyone stood in response. Goering concluded, "We can allow them into the war while at the same time keeping them away." He looked around the room at the German high command. "Gentlemen, we can have ultimate control of the world if we correctly direct the führer and the Japanese Empire."

Goering walked behind the chair where he had been sitting as everyone else collected their things and shuffled out of the room. The seeds of thought had been planted in the minds of the greatest military leaders of the Axis. The field marshal would retire to his house outside the city for several days to think about the future of the world.

For now, he poured more brandy into the thick glass he had been holding and walked to the window on the west side of the room. He looked down on the capital city. The streets and sidewalks were busy with the day's activity. Everyone was active, not concerned about the war raging less than a thousand miles to the east. Between the buildings the shadows were just beginning to appear as the sun began to dip in the midday sky. All was quiet in the West that day. The sun was beginning to turn to the west over Germany and was just beginning to approach the United States. Goering thought to himself that just as the sun can quietly approach the United States, so can the war.

Chapter 4

Yoshi Iwanami wanted to stay busy. Little physical activity could take place in the cramped quarters below deck. Every area of the ship was filled with young Japanese soldiers ready for the first direct invasion of the enemy's homeland. Yoshi wanted to exercise to be in top physical condition for the next day's attack, but there was barely any room to move, much less do calisthenics. The men were not allowed on the deck after dinner. In the small quarters where Yoshi was assigned to sleep there were over a hundred soldiers who had made the journey from Japan. They were all spending their last evening on the ship in different ways. Some just sat where they could find a place and read or wrote letters. Many played games with cards, dice, and checkers. Many of the dedicated ones checked their uniforms and gear and even polished boots. Yoshi wanted to stay active to be ready to hit the beach, but that was not going to be possible in the cramped area. He decided he would do the next best thing and check his rifle one more time. He had checked it two dozen times during the trip and completely cleaned it twice, but he would check it once again. If he could borrow a whetstone again, he would also sharpen his bayonet. His rifle and bayonet were going to be in perfect condition for the attack. They were going to be the greatest extension of his body. He was the weapon and they were the tools.

Yoshi Iwanami was a twenty-year-old corporal in the Imperial Japanese Army. He had been conscripted into the army in the summer of 1940. After he entered the service he wondered why he hadn't joined on his own. He fit perfectly. He was motivated, dedicated, and obedient. He was promoted to private first class as soon as he was eligible. After just a brief time at that rank he was made a corporal. He was promoted by his superior officers because of his enthusiasm. He wasn't liked by his fellow soldiers. They saw him as overzealous and dangerous.

Yoshi wanted to play his part in raising the Japanese Empire to world greatness. Since his military service began, he had seen Japan's growth. He was happy to be a part of this expansion and wanted to do his part, whether that was occupying Pacific Islands or driving into mainland Asia. He was as dedicated as the military leadership who said, "Damn the consequences or those that stand in our way. Japan wants and deserves more." Yoshi was a true and loyal soldier to Emperor Hirohito and the empire. He was prepared to fight for both with honor.

Yoshi hadn't known about the planned attack on Pearl Harbor until the previous spring. His army group had begun training for a large invasion by sea. The troops didn't know until just before sailing that an earlier attack had been called off and they were now to attack the United States mainland. This was a direct stab at the enemy and it was to happen in glorious Samurai fashion. The navy would deliver the army to the enemy's shores. The air corps would support the ground forces. All of the Japanese military would work together toward one goal: to attack the United States.

Everyone on board knew that with everything ready, the next day would be the day of glory. Yoshi felt that the fleet had been guided to America by a divine wind that had come all the way from the shores of the homeland and would follow them onto the U.S. beaches and inland to the enemy's filthy cities. This wind would breathe life into the imperial army and help to smother the Americans.

For all the smiling faces in the cabin, Yoshi could see that most of the men were scared. It was natural to feel that going into battle. Even those who didn't display fear probably felt it. He would do his part in leading his squad. Yoshi told himself he would never show fear. He would first prepare himself and then each man, for death if that were necessary. Victory was expected at all costs. Each man should prepare to die for self and country, and always be determined to carry on with the fight until death. Their orders were simple: attack and do not stop.

Yoshi was a low-ranking, noncommissioned officer who didn't know the details of the mission. He didn't know where they were landing or how to proceed. They didn't have an immediate goal. Each man had little to carry so they could move quickly. They were not to stop and engage any enemy soldiers, just avoid battles, destroy any property in their way and keep driving east toward the middle of the country. They were told that when they left the ship the entire navy would be behind them and many more soldiers were to follow.

The excitement of the day to follow was nearly too much for Corporal Yoshi Iwanami to handle. He was determined to fight fiercely. He would have little sleep this night. His uniform was folded neatly and he used it as his pillow. His boots, belt, and pack were beside his feet. His rifle would be beside him all night.

Chapter 5

C orporal Yoshi Iwanami was angry with himself for not being awake and ready to go. The time was 0400 hours and the entire ship was awakened. Yoshi had wanted to be the first out of his bunk and ready for battle, but he didn't awaken as he had hoped before klaxons sounded all over the ship. When the horns buzzed and the speakers squawked, the large cramped room jumped to attention in response. The entire ship seemed to lift a bit and settle in the ocean because of the hundreds of men on board jumping out of their bunks before hitting the deck.

After falling behind, Yoshi dressed quickly. He was perfectly fitted for the coming battle. He had prepared his gear weeks before and had looked after it exceptionally well. After dressing in his dark-green battle fatigues and brown leather gear he stood at attention by the passageway hatch, waiting on his fellow soldiers. Yoshi took pride in the two stripes on his sleeve, and he wanted to lead by example as much as by order. He stood, rifle to his side, as still as a statue. He stood there until others came to stand beside and behind him, other young faces and old faces, those that had served in the army for many years, and those that had served less time than he. Everyone assembled and one of the lieutenants walked to the doorway. Lieutenant Hato was a fine young officer who had served for many years in the army and fought in China and Manchuria. He had been with this regiment since training had begun many months before. Hato stopped, looked over the platoon. His eyes were wide as he smiled a broad smile of joy. He had trained hard himself and had proven to the men he was ready to lead them to greatness.

Hato drew a long breath. "Men, with strength we charge at the enemy. There is pride in victory; there is honor in death during battle." He moved his head forward a little and looked at the men with an intense expression. "There is only shame in defeat." Every soldier in the room seemed to raise his chin at Hato's words. "Choose your destiny . . ." he raised a fist and yelled, "and fight the noble fight!"

With this, everyone cheered, tapped riffle butts on the floor and clanked canteens and anything they could do to make noise and show their emotion. The fleet was still some forty miles off the coast of Oregon, and Yoshi wondered if the noise they were making could be heard inland. Even if it couldn't, they would make their noise in just a couple hours when their battle cries sounded and their guns cracked.

All over the ship soldiers quickly filed through lines to get breakfast. Each received a proper breakfast for the coming attack: a piece of beef tenderloin and rice on a piece of brown paper. When they finished this they assembled on the deck of the transport ship.

With each step the excitement grew for Yoshi. He knew with each passing minute and mile he was getting closer to the attack. He was getting closer to his destiny and the noble fight. Whether he would live or die, he would strike the enemy and fight to his last breath.

Yoshi looked around the unnamed ship and had the opportunity for the first time to see all of the other soldiers. It seemed there were many hundreds on his ship. He looked out onto the dark ocean and could just make out the silhouette of other ships just like his. He had met so many other soldiers while in training and he was happy to be advancing with them. Each was to be a part of the invasion of the enemy's homeland.

On the deck soldiers were standing shoulder to shoulder. A naval supply clerk walked down the ranks with a basket and began handing each man a small porcelain cup. After this other sailors walked down the lines pouring sake into each man's cup. The soldiers waited with cups in hand to see what was to happen. The regimental colonel walked down the line dressed in his own dark-green uniform with formal gold braids on the right shoulder. His belt held a pistol on one side and small sword on the other. His heavy steps were followed by the quiet scuffing of a Shinto priest wearing an orange robe and carrying a palm leaf. The two stopped about twenty feet past Yoshi. The priest spoke in a hushed tone, but loud enough for the men to hear. Heads were bowed. He offered the men a blessing and words of encouragement and swung the palm leaf forward several times.

The colonel was handed a glass of sake and raised it. "Men, to country, to the emperor, and to the death of our enemy!" He drank it quickly and threw it on the deck causing it to shatter. Each man followed his lead and hundreds of small cups smacked the deck. The colonel yelled, "To the boats!"

Nothing was spoken. All that was heard was the sound of hundreds of boots pounding on the wooden deck and the movement of guns and gear. There was no order to load the boats that would take the men to the beaches. Each company assembled with its captain who directed which soldiers went where. Army captains fought one another because each wanted their group to be first. It was quickly obvious that the few wooden boats could carry no more than a hundred soldiers at a time from each ship. Only about twenty men could fit on each boat. Yoshi found his way to the railing and saw his lieutenant, Lieutenant Hato, stiffly salute the company captain and motion to the men to start moving down the net. He began tapping shoulders to count them as they pushed forward. Yoshi was eager and made it onto the first boat.

The boat was full of soldiers. One sailor sat at the rear, handling the wheel and throttle. Yoshi looked the men over and saw a sergeant among them. Yoshi was not the ranking man on the boat, but he would still be a leader.

As soon as he sat down, Yoshi felt a bit weak but not from fear; he felt nauseous from the rocking of the boat. He hadn't felt it on the large ship, but now he felt the ocean and was sick. Yoshi had grown up in the mountains north of Shinjo, and until two weeks ago, he had never been on a boat. Even in training, although they were near water, they had not boarded a boat. He wouldn't let this affect him. No matter what, he wasn't going to vomit. He would not let anyone see that happen and he would continue to lead and set an example.

The boat sped away from the ship. Yoshi still could not see around the dark ocean. He caught glimpses of water splashing up nearby from other boats. He wasn't sure how many boats there were, how many ships there had been in the armada, or how many trips there would be. They had their orders and each regiment, company, squad, and individual soldier would continue the fight no matter what happened. The small boat was bouncing along on the dark ocean.

Yoshi looked down and concentrated on breathing in through his nose and out through his mouth. With this he was determined not to be sick. He didn't know how long the trip would take, but he knew they would not move ashore in the dark. Sunrise was possibly an hour away. He had nothing to do but reflect on what had led him to this day. He was happy he had been chosen for military service and was disappointed in himself for not volunteering. His army group had been chosen and trained specifically for this mission. They had been training for months. They had been traveling on the ship for at least ten days. Those ten days had been filled with a full range of emotions. They had all culminated on this day.

Yoshi was feeling somewhat better. He rose up and let the wind hit his face. It was early morning in the North Pacific and cold. The boat was traveling quite fast and was nearing the enemy shores. Yoshi reached down and put his hand on his bayonet scabbard. It was ready just as he was.

Chapter 6

As the sun began to rise, so did the temperature on what would most likely be a lovely spring day on the Pacific Northwest coast. Early birds were catching worms in the little burgs and towns up and down the Oregon coastline. The early workers were up and headed to work on this Monday morning on foot, by automobile, and some by horse and wagon. Breakfast was cooking in most homes with chimneys smoking and lights coming on all over the countryside.

Finally on its way through the surf was the Japanese invasion force. The fleet still steamed slowly in from about thirty miles out in the ocean. The first small wooden boats transporting the soldiers had been on the water about an hour, fighting their way through the choppy waters. The soldiers dipped water out of the bottom of the boats, which, after many minutes on the ocean, were fast becoming full of seawater and vomit. All of the soldiers on the first few boats were cold, wet, and eager to get moving.

In the last hour Corporal Yoshi Iwanami prepared himself mentally and spiritually for the coming battle. He had spent more than a year in the army and months in training. He was not scared; he was steady and prepared.

Yoshi only heard the sound of wind and the whining of the

motor skipping through the surf. He looked forward and saw that the beach was fast approaching. There was no activity there. He looked around the boat for the first time since leaving in pitch blackness. He could clearly see other boats just like his. Men were moving around, holding on so as to not fall, gathering items and preparing their weapons to jump off the boat.

Yoshi's hand was cold but steady as he reached down to take his razor-sharp bayonet out of the scabbard. He slid it down the end of the barrel of his rifle and snapped it into place. The engine slowed. The front of the boat eased up a little as it hit the sand on the beach. When the boat came to a stop everyone stood at the same time and jumped forward. The sound up and down the beach for possibly a hundred yards was the movement of hundreds of men pounding through the water and onto the sand. Nothing was said. Everyone knew his duty and no orders had to be given. Yoshi was in the crowd of a couple dozen from his boat. As everyone headed up the beach onto the land, groups slowly started to form up. Yoshi's squad began gathering as they continued forward. A few hundred soldiers came in the first wave, along with the regimental flag. The white with red showed brightly on this clear morning. The flag of the rising sun was on American soil.

No one knew their location. Yoshi suspected that the colonel and possibly the majors had a map of the area. He didn't even know where they were or if they had made it in the first wave. It didn't matter. Their orders were clear enough. They had to move inland and destroy everything in their path leaving nothing for the enemy. They had done fairly well as they moved off the beach. The movements of a few hundred, anxious soldiers left their mark on the vegetation. They moved at a fast pace. They had spent many days on a cramped ship, but they were energetic because they were excited to be the first of the invasion forces and the first to have the opportunity to kill the enemy. They didn't care about leaving the second boat of soldiers behind. Everyone wanted to be the first: the first to burn, the first to shoot and the first to capture. They wanted to attack and not stop. It seemed the further inland they moved, the faster they moved.

After Yoshi had moved about half a mile from the beach, his throat tightened when he saw the small, clapboard house with fading paint in a grove of trees. There were a few lights visible in the windows and a line of white smoke curled up from a chimney at the back. Yoshi would never make it to the house because others were already running forward.

Several soldiers surrounded the house as the rest continued inland. As he passed the house, Yoshi heard the first sounds of war: two rifle shots, things breaking, and a scream that was quickly silenced. He passed by and as he looked back, he could see the soldiers coming out of the house. He could see flames flickering inside, and black smoke beginning to curl from the eaves.

Another house became visible in front of him as the group of soldiers found a dirt road heading east. The same tactic was used as before: men ran ahead and surrounded the house. Another attack left more death and destruction. There was no expression of emotion on Yoshi's face. He just concentrated on moving quickly forward.

The sun was up over the horizon now and the landscape in front of him was clear. The first soldiers to hit the beach moved inland toward a small community. They encountered houses and set them ablaze, leaving the occupants dead. Now they were on a paved street with larger buildings ahead. Because Yoshi had not made it to the head of the group, others were getting to the buildings before him. He thought that once they made it into the center of the town there would be many buildings for the group to spread out over, and many people to find.

As the soldiers stormed down the paved road, their footsteps were loud. They approached a small service station where two men stood at the pump beside a pickup truck. One appeared to be frozen as if this were the first time he had seen a soldier, much less a soldier of the Imperial Japanese Army on the shores of America. One of the lead soldiers came to a dead stop in the road. Just as he had been trained to do, the young man in green dropped to one knee, put the butt of his rifle stock firmly against his shoulder and fired. The man who had been frozen at the gasoline pump fell straight backward to the ground without another movement.

The man who had been standing with him ran behind the truck and into the building. Soldiers moved slowly toward it. The man came out the door and pointed a pistol at the advancing soldiers. He fired just once before being shot himself by the bullet from an Arisaka rifle. The middle-aged man stepped backward, wincing from the pain. He stepped back against the doorframe and started sliding and falling. He grabbed at the door as another soldier charged toward him screaming, "Saikoro!" The soldier's bayonet plunged hard into the man's chest, driving him backward onto the ground without another sound.

The few hundred soldiers had moved into the small town. The main street was paved and dirty because the side streets were dirt. Men moved down those streets, headed to houses. The smell of smoke was beginning to grow in the air as more structures were set on fire. The main street had stores of all types on both sides. There were bank buildings, churches, and a town hall with a clock on the top. Gunshots were heard more rapidly now. They would echo for some distance down the streets and screams were heard more often. There was a commotion of people running, buildings being broken into and torched, a few cars trying to avoid attack, and a bell ringing. The sounds of attack continued to grow and a bell clanged away somewhere.

Yoshi stood in what appeared to be the exact center of the town. He could see straight down the four streets for possibly a mile in each direction. Soldiers were running just as they had in training, attacking and breaking anything in their path. Yoshi realized he hadn't done anything yet. Soldiers walked confidently around, unopposed. One soldier stood on the sidewalk, reloading his rifle calmly, not as if he were in the heat of battle. Other soldiers threw things out store windows and laughed at one another. They held up fancy clothes and women's dresses as if they were modeling and carrying away merchandise. Soldiers took silly things that they would never be able to keep as they advanced, such as silver candlestick holders, stacks of books, plates, musical instruments, and a radio. The men were drunk with their first spoils of war.

The street was littered with debris, and smoke poured from buildings. Yoshi saw a store nearby that appeared to have been untouched. He walked over and looked in the front window where he saw baskets of fruits and vegetables. He decided he was going to take advantage of the enemy, carry out his orders to destroy, and get into this battle. The corporal walked to the glass front door and smashed it in, using his rifle. The store was light enough for him to look around. He saw shelves of boxes and canned goods, mostly in the middle aisle, and baskets of fresh fruits and vegetables filling the front window. He was actually disgusted for a moment. He had grown up in a small mountain village and had then gone into the army. He had never tasted some of the items he saw before him now. He counted eight different varieties of apples, several types of pears, plums, citrus fruit, and vegetables by the bushel. He wanted to take one of everything, but realized he wouldn't be able to carry it all. He picked up an apple and began eating as he walked along, grabbing items and putting them in his pockets and pack. He felt a certain power from being the first person to find the store and take it at will.

He arrived at the back of the store and turned to the other side of the aisle. The vegetables, he thought, would last him for weeks. When he had picked over the center of the store, he looked at the counter to see if there was anything there that he wanted to inspect closer. When he turned, his right ear caught a sound. He dropped what was left of the apple and faced the back of the store. He stood still for a moment and tried to slow his breathing. The noise sounded like wood popping. This was a two story building. So, there had to be steps behind the door at the back of the room.

He told himself that he was a soldier and had to be brave and dutiful. He quietly took his rifle off his shoulder and raised it in the direction of the door. The butt was fixed firmly against his shoulder and he lowered his head to take aim. He tried to decide if he should stand there and wait or walk toward it and investigate. There was no further sound, but as he was about to take a step in that direction, he heard another noise at the door. It was the sound of the doorknob turning. He saw it turn and the door slowly started to open.

A man's head appeared. He looked toward the wall on the side of the store Yoshi had first walked down. The man, apparently the storeowner, living upstairs, had come to see what the commotion was about. He continued to open the door and turned toward Yoshi who had his rifle at the ready. The man's eyes locked on Yoshi and he stood still. Yoshi drew in a heavy breath when he saw something shiny at the man's right side. Yoshi jerked the trigger and the 7.7 millimeter round from the rifle struck the man on the upper left side of his torso. The man leaned back against the wall without making a sound. Yoshi knew the man wasn't dead and was still a danger. He charged forward, ramming his bayonet into the man's stomach. This caused the man to groan with pain. He fell to the floor.

There was a whimpering sound from inside the doorway. Yoshi quickly pulled back the bolt on the rifle's action and chambered another round. He was going to make one quick motion, and he raised the rifle barrel and jumped around the corner of the doorway. He saw the person in the poorly lit stairway, and he fired once into the center of the silhouetted figure, which fell straight down onto the step, the legs sliding out in front. The body slid down several steps into the light where Yoshi could now see that the person who was in a bathrobe was a young woman with long dark hair. Her eyes were the color of her hair and they stared blankly up toward the young corporal.

Yoshi stepped back through the doorway and looked down at the man on the floor. The bodies apparently belonged to a husband and wife, living above their small shop. The shiny object in the man's right hand was a frying pan, probably the only thing he could grab at the moment.

Yoshi felt something touch his right hand. He looked down and saw the blood from his bayonet dripping onto his hand. It was warm against his cold hand. He wiped the blood from the blade with his fingers and looked at the bright, red liquid on his pale skin. The moment seemed surreal. He cleaned his hand on the front of his green shirt and it became sticky.

Corporal Yoshi Iwanami felt the burn of gun smoke in his eyes and nose, the blood, and the heat inside him, driving him into the fight. He was now a soldier.

Yoshi walked to the front door of the business without looking back. His boots crushed the broken glass as he stepped on it going through. He was going to find his squad and order them to continue their mission.

Chapter 7

It was a warm and beautiful spring day. The blossoms on the famous cherry trees had passed their peak, but all of the trees in the city were turning dark green. The business of the day was well underway as the politics of the nation were discussed on Capitol Hill and people went about their daily routine.

It was not yet known to anyone in Washington DC that the Japanese Consulate had been vacated over the weekend. All documents had been burned. Communications equipment had been destroyed, and all of the personnel had been removed from the city. Everything had been done quickly and quietly in preparation for June 1. Talks had been going on between U.S. and Japanese officials for well over a year. People from all ranks of American government—politicians, diplomats, and military personnel—had been in and out of the brick building on Virginia Avenue and had had meetings at the State Department, the Executive Mansion and several fine hotels in the city. Everyone got scared when the talks suddenly stopped in early December 1941, but things seemed to progress in early '42. On this occasion, the office building had been stripped to the bare walls and not a member of staff would be found in the country afterward.

By mid-morning, eastern daylight time, the War Department

had learned of the activities on the West Coast. Reports were coming in from several locations. The messages were not even understandable at first. Japanese landing crafts? How was that possible? There was not even news of a fleet, and now landing craft?

What analysts could not comprehend at first was soon understood: Japanese landing craft had hit the beaches in Oregon and Washington. Troops had stormed ashore with no warning, and enemy soldiers had fired at whoever stood in their way. Japanese warships had been seen in dozens of locations just miles off of the West Coast. Japanese carrier-based planes were making sorties against locations inland ahead of an apparent invasion. What had begun as a routine Monday morning, reviewing information from the weekend, quickly appeared to be turning into Armageddon. What was never believed could happen was happening. The Japanese Empire had begun an invasion of the United States. Hardened military men first froze in disbelief at the news, then reacted to what some had known was inevitable. The United States was now at war.

Information streamed into the military intelligence section of the War Department from more and more sources. It began slowly and with confusion. It quickly progressed to overwhelming amounts of data and sheer terror. Veteran servicemen screamed through telephone communications. War was beginning for the United States and it was on American shores.

The intelligence was quickly compiled and forwarded to ranking officers. Colonel Nathan Farb was writing as fast as he could. Information was coming in bursts and was difficult to keep pace with. Intelligence officers were sticking red pins on the large plotting map that was the centerpiece of the room. It didn't take long for Colonel Farb to understand the operation. The Japanese military was beginning an invasion of the United States.

"Lieutenant Lenoiran," the colonel yelled at a young, West Point graduate. The under-officer was an eager soldier, but he looked back at the colonel with wide eyes and a pale face. He didn't even speak. The colonel stepped quickly and grabbed his arm just to focus him. Farb's voice was even and calm. "Contact General Marshal immediately. Then establish an open line to the house." Farb didn't even seem to take a breath, "Then go to the Department of the Navy building. I'm sure they're getting the same information, but make contact with the ranking person in naval intelligence. Tell everyone to meet at the house as soon as possible—that's where I'm going now." Farb grabbed up several folders that he had been writing in and took his hat off the rack at the door. He turned and took a last look at the map. From a short distance he now got a look at what seemed overwhelming. The colonel glanced at Captain Stillman who stood beside the map. They made eye contact and Stillman tipped his head as Farb headed out the door.

The "house" that Colonel Farb referred to was the White House—The Executive Mansion—and that's where General George Marshall, the chief of staff of the U.S. Army, regularly briefed the president on the war. The action had been in Europe and Asia until just moments before. Now they would need to report that the war had come to America.

Colonel Farb ran to an awaiting car as other officers ran to their duties. The army and navy were in two different buildings. That had always made things difficult for those two branches of the armed forces. A new, big, five-sided building was under construction near the Potomac River, but for now they had to make do.

The car, a four-door Pontiac, painted the standard, drab olive with a white star, took off as soon as the colonel got in. The driver, a sergeant with three stripes up and one down, maneuvered the morning traffic as best he could and was liberal with the horn. There were a few tricky intersections and a traffic officer slowed them down and gave them a mean look, but waved them through as the sergeant continued blowing the horn.

During the trip Colonel Farb planned how he would deliver this news to the president, a man he had never spoken to before. He was mad with himself for not wearing his class A uniform.

Within minutes the car screeched through the main gate at the White House. The marines who guarded the entrances were caught by surprise. The colonel didn't slow down as he went through the doors to the West Wing. He had been there before and knew his way. He made a right just inside the front door and headed west to the newest part of the old building.

He reached the Oval Office to find the door open and no one inside. "Where's the president?"

The president's secretary looked up, startled. "He's in the treaty room on the third floor."

"Great," Farb said to himself. "All the way through the residence and up to the top floor." The colonel was not out of shape, but he breathed heavily, partly because he had run and partly because of his anxiety at the impending war. He was the man who was going to deliver the news of world-changing events to the president of the United States. He marched back through the doors of the West Wing, rounded the corner and started up the steps back at the main entrance. His shoes slipped as he maneuvered the thickly carpeted steps.

The president was quite comfortable at the table in the treaty room. In President Lincoln's day the room had mostly been used for cabinet meetings. With the addition of more formal offices on the west side of the house, the room became the president's private area and those who were allowed there were very few. He finished reading a report from the Department of Agriculture, put it down on the table and put a cigarette in the ashtray.

His valet, a white-haired, black man, came into the room with a silver pot on a tray. "Would you like some coffee, sir? I just made it myself." His voice was always hushed as if he were ashamed to interrupt the man he had personally attended for over three years.

"Thank you, George."

Colonel Farb came through the door with such force he nearly knocked over the old man with the tray. Farb gave a salute, as was proper. "Mr. President, the Japanese army has begun an attack!"

The president was used to interruptions and they never bothered him His tone was calm as usual. "Where?"

"The Northwest. Japanese soldiers are reported coming ashore in Washington and Oregon."

The calm appearance of the president suddenly changed. "They're attacking the United States?"

The army officer nodded once.

The president continued to look up without moving. His eyes were fixed, as if he were staring a thousand yards. Even though the temperature was rising along with the sun, the president felt a sudden chill. Although he didn't yet have details, he knew the war had come to the United States, which had helped on the other side of the globe and had so far avoided the fighting. He'd believed the country was safe. The death and destruction that had been happening elsewhere for so many years was here. War had begun.

Chapter 8

L ife in Washington, D.C. was pretty much the same as usual around lunchtime. Most people were still at work and oblivious to the action several thousand miles away. Not until a convoy of cars and trucks converged on 1600 Pennsylvania Avenue did anyone take notice.

Within the first hour of the first report some forty men packed themselves into the large conference room of the White House's West Wing. They included the vice-president, some congressmen, the major members of the cabinet, and more generals and admirals than had ever been assembled at the White House. The room was at a fever pitch with men talking and moving chairs and papers, and no one could hear anyone beside them, much less across the room. The table was spread with maps, notebooks, and papers. Two telephones were set up at one end of the room, each manned by officers of the army and navy. Each man had the receiver to one ear and a finger plugging the other to block out the noise in the room. They were writing as fast as they could.

There was constant activity outside the room too as people moved around. At every door leading into the room were two armed marines. The house, which normally had eight or ten soldiers guarding the doors and corners, now had an army platoon surrounding it. A staff person also verified and recorded every person who walked in and out of the building. A stenographer sat in one corner of the conference room. She hadn't yet typed a word.

The men inside were animated. Some stood and pounded the table to be heard. When an outer office door opened, it took several seconds for the room to turn silent. Chairs squeaked and scuffed the floor when everyone stood and looked toward the man rolling forward. President Roosevelt was wheeled into the room by his valet who pushed the wheelchair against the head of the table. The dutiful valet retired from the room.

"Gentlemen, be seated, please."

Sliding chairs and shoes made a sound as everyone sat and adjusted themselves. Every man sat in a dignified manner and awaited the president who surveyed the room. Seated on each side of him were the vice-president, Henry Wallace, and the president's chief of staff, William Leahy. Five cabinet members were present: Cordell Hull, Henry Stinson, Frank Knox, Harold Ickes, and Francis Biddle. Seated behind the president was J. Edgar Hoover. Military leaders included Army Chief of Staff George Marshall and Navy Commander in Chief Ernest King. Other Commanders were U.S. Army Air Corps Henry "Hap" Arnold and Commander of the Pacific Fleet William F. "Bull" Halsey. Their technical bosses were Carl Spaatz, chief of staff of the air force and Chester Nimitz, commander in chief of the Pacific Fleet. It had to be a unique and devastating event that had brought all of these men together. The president recognized several other faces including those of Dwight Eisenhower who was the commander of the War Plans Division; Admiral Raymond Spruance, and General Omar Bradley. They were fine and qualified men, known and trusted by President Roosevelt.

Each ranking official had two or three men with him, and the crowded room became hot, even before noon.

The president didn't speak in a concerned voice. In a normal, conversational tone he said, "Gentlemen, please tell me the situation."

Everyone had been railing before his arrival; now the room sat quiet. General Marshall spoke first. "Mr. President, the Japanese military began an invasion of the United States at about 7:00 a.m. Pacific Time. It began with landing crafts coming up on beaches," he said, pointing to red arrows drawn on a U.S. map on an easel behind him, "just north of Hauser and south of Charleston, Oregon. Troops have also landed at Seaview, Washington, on the north side of the Columbia River. We are also receiving reports that troops have come through the Queen Charlotte Strait and are now on the Canadian mainland, east of Vancouver Island."

President Roosevelt continued gazing intently ahead.

"The soldiers of the Japanese army were landed by a Japanese naval fleet of unknown size. Japanese ships have been seen in several locations along the West Coast. Some have fired on U.S. ships and also some land positions." General Marshall again pointed to the map and black Xs. "Japanese submarines have also fired on U.S. warships. The Japanese naval forces include at least one carrier because planes have flown to targets inland and fired on military positions."

Military people were still moving around the room, writing and handing notes to one another. General Marshall attempted to be timely with his information. "Japanese soldiers are currently moving off the beaches and heading inland."

The president continued gazing intently ahead and said, "Where are these forces moving to?"

Marshall consulted the map again. "We don't know, sir. Soldiers of the Imperial Japanese Army are driving quickly forward, destroying what's in their way."

"American citizens are being killed?"

Marshall hesitated. "Yes, sir. They are killing anyone they come into contact with."

The room was deadly silent now. President Roosevelt lowered his head. He spoke again. "The Japanese are invading this nation. What defenses are in place? What are we doing to stop them?"

General Marshall looked around the room. He didn't have a good answer. Admiral Nimitz spoke up. "Sir, most of the Pacific Fleet is …well …there, in the Pacific. We have a large contingent near the Hawaiian Islands, but its focus is between there and Malaya. Our concern with the Japanese has always been the outposts of the South Pacific."

The president raised his voice. "And they are not attacking outposts now; they are attacking the United States proper. What are we doing for those in the northwestern United States?"

"Ships from Seattle to San Diego are steaming and preparing to sail. Every ship within a thousand miles of the mainland has been contacted and is coming toward the country. Sir, sailors all over the Pacific are ready to defend the nation." Nimitz looked around the table, as if seeking relief.

After several seconds General Marshall spoke again. "Mr. President, every soldier in the western United States is being dispatched to the area, but it will take time for any sizable force to arrive."

"Wouldn't you be able to stop these foot soldiers with tanks and cannons and air-force bombers?"

Marshall didn't look directly at the president, "Yes, sir, but it takes time to move heavy equipment. We aren't prepared to move sizeable military pieces toward a quickly advancing front. Soldiers are traveling by train, truck, and foot to the invasion forces, but . . ."

Roosevelt squinted at him. "But?"

There was a pause. "But we don't know where they should be sent. Japanese forces are coming ashore in three locations in the United States and at least one in Canada. We don't know the size of these forces or their objectives. This could be the spearhead of the invasion, or a distraction to land a larger force at a different location." The men stared at one another as Marshall continued. "The hounds could be sent to the hunt only to find they have chased a rabbit and let the fox slip past."

The president sat against the table in his wheelchair. He pressed down on the table with both hands. His fingertips were white. "How many Japanese soldiers could be attacking us?"

"Sir, there could be as many as a hundred thousand Japanese soldiers in the country in a week."

There was a murmur in the room while that sunk in. Everyone present knew the combined forces of the entire U.S. military numbered less than three hundred thousand. People began talking more openly now. The generals had already been talking and the consensus was that all army forces should be dispatched west. General Marshall spoke with several generals. The noise in the room began to increase again.

"Gentlemen." The president waited for the noise to subside and repeated, "Gentlemen, when do we stop this attack?"

General Marshall had been keeping his chin pointed toward his chest. He'd only raise his eyes toward the president to speak. "Sir, as the Japanese army moves east, they will definitely be slowed by the mountains."

"You're saying that's all that would stop them at this point: the terrain and not our military?"

"Sir, our best course of action is to stop the forces cold in the plains. Our forces will be better concentrated and prepared, and the Japanese army will have exhausted their provisions and won't develop a supply line that distance."

"General, am I to understand you are prepared to simply give up on several western states and meet the enemy in the middle of the country?"

There was again silence. Generals looked at the map so as to avoid eye contact with the president like a school child who does not know the answer and avoids the teacher.

Secretary Stinson spoke up. "Mr. President, the U.S. military will respond with all possible might and vigor. Everyone will do what is necessary to stop this invasion. The nation needs to respond immediately with fighting men." Many in the room nodded their heads. "We should increase the draft of young men."

"How many young men should we respond with?"

Marshall and Ernest King spoke simultaneously. "Three million."

Roosevelt looked surprised. "We need to draft and train three million men?"

"Yes, sir," Marshall spoke. "That is immediately necessary for the defense of the nation. It would be immediate and intense training to stop the Japanese advance."

Stinson continued, "We need to begin immediate production of war materials. We don't have three million rifles." The room became an open discussion again. "We need trucks and tanks to move men and stop Japanese forces. Fighter planes and light bombers are needed to support our ground forces. The Coast Guard needs to be turned over to the navy and we need destroyers and battleships."

Secretaries began speaking back and forth. The president could only understand the occasional phrase in their loud conversations. He heard the secretary of state say, "We'll need bonds for immediate cash and we need funds from every government department. The nation can't produce that quickly. We need assistance from other nations."

The room turned to chaos until the president yelled to be heard. "No other nations can provide assistance." The room became silent again. "We have assisted other nations. Every industrialized nation on the face of the earth is involved in this conflict. We are the last world leader to be at peace." He looked around the room at each face at the table. He had anger in his voice when he asked, "Gentlemen, how did this happen? How did the Japanese Empire land on American soil completely by surprise?"

"Mr. President, the Japanese have been continuously involved in actions around the Pacific. It was never thought they would engage the United States, and especially not by direct invasion."

President Roosevelt pushed himself back from the table and everyone rose.

"Men, it is our duty to lead this nation out of fear and to be safe from attack. We will defend this nation at all cost."

His words were not necessary. Every man present knew his duty. Every soldier would fight for the nation even without commands.

George came into the room and turned the president's wheelchair. They headed to the hallway and on toward the executive office.

It was a short trip, just going through one outer room to the Oval Office. As George stopped the chair at the huge mahogany desk, he asked, "Mr. President, sir, can I get you some lunch?"

The president had not thought of lunch. His only thoughts

were of men and women in the western states being killed by enemy invaders. He thought about the fears of everyone who saw enemy ships off the shores and heard Japanese planes flying over the United States. His thoughts were thousands of miles away as he sat in his wheelchair, unable to respond.

Chapter 9

The sun was well up into the sky in Middle America by the time Japanese forces began approaching the shores of the West Coast. In Omaha it was one of the last school days of the year. Workers in the plants and factories were already hard at work. Stores and banks were beginning to open for their day's business. As usual, Earl Frankton was one of the first people to arrive to work at the downtown branch of First Grainger's Bank of Nebraska. As the vice-president, he was always early to arrive and late to leave.

No one could have known that less than two thousand miles away to the west, enemy troops were starting their assault on the United States and Canada. No one had yet seen ships of the German navy patrolling the East Coast some twelve hundred miles away. War was raging in Europe and the Pacific. In this part of the world all was quiet. Everyone was satisfied with their lives and their nation and most were content to stay out of a war that was not their own. Little did they know the war now was theirs.

The day progressed as a normal, early summer day. Just before lunch time the news began to be known. It began first as a trickle of information about military actions in the Pacific Northwest. The war was on the other side of the globe and no one suspected in the least that the enemy could come to the United States. As the invasion in the west of the nation progressed, so did the reports. Military installations all over the nation were put on instant alert. Law-enforcement personnel and every area of the government were made aware. When the media found out the information, it began to spread quickly around the town and across the nation.

The first reports came out in anxious bursts. Radio broadcasters scraped the needles on records in their hurry to switch to news. As the earliest reports came out, people found radios and hovered around them.

Omaha newspapers began collecting information from telephone reports, telegraphs, and whatever sources they could find. They began running an extra edition at just past noon with the news they did have. Young butcher boys would be on the street corners by mid-afternoon, screaming out the headline: "The United States is under attack."

As the day progressed more information came in about the invasion of North America. Japanese forces were coming ashore in an unopposed, full military attack. Numerous ships of the Japanese navy were seen in the immediate vicinity, both transport ships and gun ships. Waves of soldiers were coming ashore, followed by tanks. They ruthlessly attacked, causing much slaughter and destruction.

Initial nervousness in Middle America quickly turned to full panic. Schools were dismissed early. The youngest schoolchildren didn't understand what was going on. The oldest were truly frightened. Christopher Frankton, the sixteen-year-old son of Earl Frankton, was one of the many high-school students who could not believe the news. No one believed the crazies in Europe and the Pacific could possibly attack the United States. Young men and women actually debated whether the news was true. They wondered if it were just a big hoax. In the brief amount of time it took for information to get out and for young men to realize a war was taking place, many were ready to go to the nearest recruiting station and sign up right away. The war that was taking place in other parts of the world had been brought to the United States. Americans were being killed. American property was being destroyed. American soil was being occupied by enemy soldiers. Not since the Mexicans had been pushed out of Texas more than a hundred years earlier had the United States been occupied by enemies. Hearing the report of what was taking place thousands of miles away, young men punched one another and yelled at and cursed an enemy they hadn't even seen. Many of them were ready for blood.

Just in the short time that the first reports were made, panic started. Department stores and hardware stores were cleaned out of guns and ammunition. Canned food and medical supplies were purchased just as quickly. Citizens readied themselves for whatever might take place.

Police officers responded all over the city to fights and attacks. They opened their own armories and patrol cars now carried shotguns, rifles, and submachine guns.

Activity began at lunchtime at First Grainger's Bank just as it did at every other bank in Omaha. People came in to withdraw money—lots of money. The initial response turned into a throng of people who nearly caused a riot by 4 p.m. All of the gold coins in the bank were gone by 2:00 p.m. The silver coins were gone by 2:30 p.m. Some people cleaned out deposit boxes and some filled them up. The bank couldn't handle the business and at 4:15 p.m. Earl Frankton closed the doors and called for the police. The bank was empty by 4:30 p.m., and he started sending the employees home. The building had been a madhouse for several hours and then it became as quiet as a church mouse. He planned the next day's business because the bank, which regularly held around one hundred thousand dollars in cash in its vault, now held about three thousand dollars.

Earl sat in his small office. It had a glass window that looked out onto the lobby floor. He could have had an upstairs office, but he had come up through the ranks behind the counter and he wanted to stay close to it. It was dark in the building because the blinds were closed everywhere and the lights were off. He sat in isolation to collect his thoughts. The heavy-set, middle-aged man who always wore a vest and high collar leaned back in his chair to get a breath. The bank was closed down as if it were the end of the business day although it shouldn't have closed for another hour. The tellers had all gone thirty minutes earlier. The regular office staff in the two-story building had gone. He had a dedicated staff, but they worried about their homes and families. So, he sent them home. There was still a lot going on outside. The evening rush hour seemed more frantic than usual. People were out front, knocking on the bank door. The sound of the occasional police siren went down the block. Earl was worried himself, but knew he couldn't withdraw his funds. Surely the Federal Banking Commission would step in within the next several days and bring some sanity to this run? Earl took twenty dollars for himself and sealed the vault. He checked the building again and then waited by the front door until everyone left before walking quickly to his car and heading home. There were lots of people on the street, walking, riding bikes and riding in cars. People appeared to be running around without purpose, and they all seemed to be carrying something. They seemed intent on possessing property, as they had when they withdrew money from the bank. The country was under attack and people wanted their property. Earl had read the stories of Jewish people being rounded up and sent to concentration camps in the heart of Germany. There were people all over Southeast Asia who had been captured by Japanese troops and sent to work camps. All of them knew they were headed to certain death, and everyone took their property. Those who could only carry one suitcase or a pack on their back loaded it with items. Families took jewelry, silverware and dinner services that had been in their families for years. People took furs and books. Some even tried to carry small pieces of furniture. Everyone who entered a Nazi concentration camp or a Japanese prison camp had their possessions taken from them. They would fight for their items, even to the death. These things were theirs. They belonged to their family. They were what they wanted to have and live with. The sad scenes from other parts of the world seemed to repeat themselves on the streets of Omaha. Enemy troops were hundreds, if not thousands, of miles away and people took their things with them.

Earl maneuvered his way home in the rush. His typical twenty-five-minute drive turned into forty, but he was still forty-five minutes earlier than usual. He parked in the drive and saw his wife looking around the curtain in the kitchen window. As he walked toward the side door he peered across the lawn toward his neighbor's house. His neighbor's car was parked in its usual location. All of the curtains in the windows he could see were closed. Everything seemed quiet. He began to question whether his neighbor's car had already gone when he had left for the office that morning. Earl felt fear now.

He walked through the side door and closed it quickly. That door faced the neighbor's house. He locked it and closed the curtains. His wife, Edith, stood at the sink, motionless. Her face seemed void.

"Where are the boys?"

"They're upstairs." She walked slowly to him and they embraced. "What's happening, Earl?"

"I don't know yet, but we'll be fine." They just held onto one another.

Chapter 10

It had been a typical, hard day of work for Gerald at the plant. He, like so many others in the town of Harbitsburg, worked at one of the local cheese plants. Just as areas of West Virginia were coal-mining towns and areas of Texas were oil towns, Harbitsburg, Wisconsin was a cheese town. Gerald was satisfied with the work. The young man with bright, blue eyes was a year out of high school and was happy with what he had. The job was decent and just like coal and oil jobs, it offered security.

The whistle blew at 3:30 p.m. and the people on the primary shift shut down the machines that weren't needed and closed up shop for the day. The day was Monday, June 1.

As he walked out the front door with the eighty or so other people who worked in the plant every day, there seemed to be something different about the office. The front office where the attractive, redheaded receptionist would always be the first smiling face anyone would see, was empty. He slowed his pace a bit to see through the windows and further back into the office area. Several of the office staff were gathered in one room. Gerald didn't think much of it. This was the head office, and he didn't concern himself with that.

He continued through the parking lot and down the street

toward home. As he headed down the roadway, he thought there seemed to be fewer cars around. That was fine with him because with no rain the past week, cars kicked up a lot of dust. It was quitting time on a Monday. Cars were leaving his plant, but not many others were around.

Gerald's walk home was only about two miles. It took him straight through the middle of his small town and as he made the turn north onto Main Street, he realized something was different. No one was on the sidewalk in front of him and only one car traveled slowly down the street. He walked past the fire brigade building. The front door was open, but the big red truck was still inside. As he approached Central Avenue, he could see a large crowd gathered near Siegler's Department Store. He stopped at the intersection and looked around.

There was no big sale going on at the store. He couldn't put his finger on what was different, but he noticed something odd about the group even without looking at their faces. People seemed fidgety. There was either complete stillness or the inability to be still. That's not a buying crowd; that's a nervous crowd, he thought. A similar crowd had packed into Mull's Barber Shop next door. Gerald's nervousness made him cross the street.

Gerald walked toward the front door of the department store and like so many others, he couldn't get in. People in front of him stood on tiptoe. So, he took a couple of jumps and saw the crowded main floor. People seemed to be focused on the wall where the appliances were.

He tapped the shoulder of a man in front of him. The man who seemed more his type was dressed in overalls and a straw hat. "What's the excitement?"

The man didn't look in Gerald's direction. He kept his focus straight ahead. "We're under invasion!"

Gerald furrowed his brow. The man still didn't look in his direction. "Who's under invasion?"

"The whole country! Those Japs is bombing the coast and coming ashore!" the man said in simple, backwoods dialect.

Gerald's confusion turned to plain disbelief. He had heard about this before when somebody had thought it funny to play a fake radio broadcast and get a laugh, or maybe it was an odd sighting that had been blown out of proportion, and people thought the country was under attack. From what he had read in the paper he knew the Japanese were fierce, little devils, but there was no way the Japanese army and navy were attacking the United States.

There was a lot of talking. Gerald heard people saying many bad things about the Japanese people and the country. Men cursed and tried to one-up one another, saying every Japanese soldier would be killed before they got a certain distance inland. They wouldn't make it more than thirty miles. They wouldn't make it more than twenty miles. They wouldn't even make it ten miles. Men made murderous statements. Gerald noticed the woman beside him was quiet, pale and had tears in her eyes. He still wasn't able to comprehend what was going on. It didn't make any sense.

This is just madness gone too far, he thought. There's no way any war would come to the United States.

Gerald crossed back over the street and headed in the direction of home again. It was an easy fifteen minutes to the little house where he lived with his parents. As he drew closer, he noticed his father's Chevy station wagon already in the drive. That was odd for the time of day, just before 4:00 p.m. Too much seemed wrong. Something was going on.

He ran through the front yard and jumped onto the porch.

He darted through the screen door. His father, John, stood with crossed arms in the middle of the parlor floor, looking down at his feet. His mother, Ester, sat on the sofa with her hands on her lap. She also looked down, and neither of them looked up when Gerald came through the door. A harried announcer was broadcasting on the radio, which usually wasn't turned on until after dinner.

"What's going on?" Gerald asked in a weak tone.

His father looked up angrily. "The war has come here. We're under attack by the Japanese."

His mother didn't move.

Gerald smiled skeptically. "It's just some joke or misunderstanding. The Japanese can't make it to the United States. They're not going to attack us." Gerald spoke with confidence, but was also trying to convince himself.

John spoke in an even tone. "It's true, son. The Japanese army has landed on each side of Coos Bay in Oregon and on the north bank of the Columbia River in Washington. They think they're in Canada too, somewhere north of Vancouver Island, and Japanese navy ships have been spotted all up and down the coast. They're shooting and killing on the shores. The war has come here too."

The war has come here? The war was on the other side of the world. It was in Europe, Africa, Asia, and in the Pacific. Maybe it came here because this was the only part of the world that wasn't involved yet. For whatever reason, the war was here.

Gerald took a breath and spoke reticently. "What's going to happen now?" He hadn't been prepared for anything like this. He didn't know what to say. He noticed his mother's head drop a bit.

John perked up some. "Nothing much to worry about. Those Japs might have tried to sneak in, but they won't make it very far. Uncle Sam's army will take care of things."

His father's attitude seemed much different from that of the radio reporter who was speaking in a quick and terrified voice. He didn't know what to do for his mother. She was motionless beside the radio. His father's stiff tone and expression softened as he walked around in a small area. "Why, whatever Japs made it ashore will wish they hadn't got off the boat. They'll be lucky if they stay alive until the army gets there. Any fifteen-year-old with a squirrel gun could take care of your average Japanese soldier."

John walked directly to Gerald and slapped his hand on his son's shoulder. "I'm an old man and I could take care of one. So, I know you would have no trouble at all."

Ester stood up without a sound and walked into the kitchen. Gerald watched with concern.

"Don't worry about your mother. She's just a hysterical woman. That's how they are and it's up to us men to protect the women and our country."

Gerald walked toward the kitchen as he tried to assemble his thoughts.

"It's in your blood, son," his father said, raising his voice as Gerald stopped and turned. "Your grandfather was a Rough Rider. He rode with Teddy Roosevelt. It goes back before that. There was a Flaghart with General Washington all the way to Yorktown." His father looked into his eyes. "There should be a Flaghart to help push them dirty, little monkeys back into the ocean."

Gerald started back toward the kitchen. His father continued as Gerald walked out of the room, "This war is for brave men!"

Gerald thought, "America will respond how it needs to." His father was right; the Japanese army would be stopped fast enough. This could still be some mistake. The United States wasn't at war with Japan. Why would they invade?

Gerald had read about the war in the rest of the world. It was run by mad men. He had learned about the evils of the Japanese and Germans who were apparently trying to take over the world. Could there actually be an occupation of the United States? No, it would never happen, he told himself.

Gerald dropped his lunch box on the counter and headed toward his bedroom. The house was a simple, clapboard structure with two bedrooms. His bedroom was at the back. He wondered what the next few days would bring. The war had come to America and the country had changed in just a few hours while he was at work making cheese. Gerald felt a little insignificant at that moment. A war had started without him even knowing it. Soldiers and sailors were fighting and he was just making cheese. America will do what it needs to, Gerald thought. It would never have to involve him—no fighting, anyway. The Japanese army was tough, but it would never make it far. The war in Europe had gone on for nearly three years. The Japanese had been fighting in Southeast Asia for a decade. That would never happen here. That was a different part of the world. He would never be sent to fight. It would be over before that.

Gerald closed his bedroom door. He took from underneath his bed the wooden box that held together the homemade radio. At night he could always get it to work by the window if he strung the antenna wire just right. He turned on the radio and tuned it as best he could. The news was still the same. The war had come.

Chapter 11

After the planned December attack on Pearl Harbor had been aborted, the Japanese Imperial Navy returned to its homeland. All the men felt shame. They had sailed with great expectations, prepared for a great victory against the Americans. Upon their return, they felt as if they had disgraced themselves, their families, their emperor, and the entire nation.

The mood of the armed forces was one of sorrow. The fleet that had sailed for the Hawaiian Islands had been ideal. The sailors and airmen stayed close to their stations for the months that followed. They became lethargic. Other imperial forces made great strides all over the Pacific and Asia. Japanese bombers struck the British colony of Hong Kong, causing huge damage and winning a glorious victory. Japanese soldiers invaded Thailand. The smaller nation was just too weak to stop any kind of attack. It surrendered within hours of the invasion and joined forces with Japan in the world war. Japanese troops finally took control of Hong Kong and began whittling away at British control of the region.

From Thailand imperial forces soon moved into Malaya and Burma. The British military, thought the Japanese troops couldn't move through the thick jungles of the Malay peninsula and fell prey to them. Soldiers poured through the jungles and quickly overran the peninsula. By late January Japanese forces had pushed the feeble British troops back to Singapore. In early February imperial forces continued their pursuit of the Brits and assaulted the island. It fell in only a week. This included the capture of eighty-five thousand British troops. This was the greatest loss for the British in its military history and the greatest victory for the nation of Japan thus far in the war. The Japanese nation expected more great things.

A large part of the naval forces stayed at Kushiro. Others traveled to the petroleum-rich Dutch East Indies that had been protected by U.S. and British naval ships. To avoid direct confrontation with the U.S. Navy, Japanese ships only made their presence known. There were no battles. They wanted to keep the U.S. fleet occupied and not provoke a fight . Not yet. Japanese troops began making small attacks, slowly gaining territory in the Dutch East Indies. They continued their unrelenting advance into Burma. China assisted British troops, but neither China nor Britain were any match for the imperial military.

Because of those glorious victories and the large span of control won by other Japanese forces, the forces left on Hokkaido felt discouraged. They felt pride and respect for the forces of victory and great sadness for those who had been lost. Hashani wondered why they had been left to do nothing while the rest of the military advanced all over the Pacific. Seaman Nagami sat idly, along with many men in the other fleet. He wondered when they would be allowed to attack and find their own glory.

In early April the forces remaining at Kushiro were told their opportunity was at hand. They would be assembled and would sail from there in May and strike the Americans. They erupted with jubilation. They were to have their mission. They were to achieve glory along with the rest of the forces.

It was June 1 and the war was underway. Japanese forces had landed to begin their attack against the United States. The job of the cruiser *Okhotsk* was to attack the U.S. Navy and support the Japanese landing forces. Ships would stay behind at the immediate location to continue bringing forces and supplies to shore. Most of the fleet had sailed on. The *Okhotsk* was one of them. It had sailed south. Some naval groups had specific missions and some were simply given orders to harass and confound the enemy at all costs. No sailor questioned the phrase, *at all costs*. It was simply part of his duty to die if necessary. *Okhotsk* was one of the ships ordered to just deal with any enemy vessel they came across. The commander of the ship, Meki Hatsoto, was a longtime seaman and well respected by the crew. He was seen as the emperor of the ship and therefore his word was law. Every crewman knew he was in dangerous waters, sailing at times within twenty miles of the west coast of the United States mainland. The crewmen knew that they could sail completely freely in the waters of the North Pacific, possibly for several weeks before incurring the full response of the U.S. Navy and Navy Air Corps. They would make the most of that time. Hatsoto's orders came down that they would attack any vessel they happened to meet. They would fire indiscriminately into coastal cities. The continuous parade of Japanese ships sailing along the coast could level many areas. The firepower unleashed onto the U.S. homeland would devastate the Americans and lead to a quick victory as in so many other parts of the Pacific.

Seaman Second Class Nagami was one of the proud crewmen of some sixteen hundred Japanese sailors on the *Okhotsk*. The ship had been on alert since sailing across 140 degrees west longitude. The crew knew they were approaching the enemy and all were ready to do their duties to the death if need be. To die gloriously for the sake of self and nation was the greatest honor. The *Okhotsk* sailed behind several other warships of the navy, which attacked enemy ships. By mid-morning on June 2 the *Okhotsk* had not yet fired a shot and the crew became anxious. They had been ready for battle for months. With the exception of the designated ships, every ship was free to sail wherever it desired. Hatsoto was ready for action also.

The commander sat in his chair on the bridge and appeared to be enjoying the ride through the big ocean. With his binoculars in hand he looked east and asked, "What is our current position?" Hatsoto didn't give direct orders. He just called out the command and the appropriate officer gave the answer within seconds.

The lieutenant commander, a young naval-school graduate, named Fitsu Nicora, checked with the navigator. "Currently 46 degrees, 15 minutes north longitude and 129 degrees, 2 minutes west latitude, Commander."

Hatsoto walked to the navigator's station and consulted maps, first looking at navigational charts, then land area maps. Nicora was standing at his side. Hatsoto pointed and said, "Lunar City, at Point Saint George. Plot a course."

Hashani Nagami lay in his bunk. It was the one, small place a crewman could call his own on a Japanese warship. It was Hashani's place of refuge. He rarely participated in the gambling games the other men played. He mostly kept to himself. All of his prized possessions, which were usually kept in the small locker beside his bunk, were now in front of him. The bunk was typical of a Japanese naval cruiser: six feet long, two and one half feet wide, and a little less than three feet from the top of the thin mattress to the bottom of the bunk above. In this small space Hashani could mentally shut out the rest of the activity in the room and focus on his own thoughts. Today he was writing. He had written a letter to his parents and had enclosed most of his month's wages in it. He only needed a small amount for himself. After sealing the envelope, he opened his writing journal. It was small enough to carry in his hip pocket, and he usually had it with him. He wrote a lot about the crew, the ship, and the honor and glory of serving his emperor.

"The attack has begun against the Americans and victory will soon belong to all who are humble and gracious," he wrote. Writing his thoughts in the pages of the journal consoled him.

After a brief few hours the cruiser arrived at its destination. Fifteen miles off the coast of Point Saint George, Commander Hatsoto ordered battle stations. When bells all over the ship abruptly struck, Hashani reacted slowly as he came out of his daydream. By the time he had collected his thoughts and belongings and made it out the door, everyone else had already left the bunkroom. The trip to the number-two turret was a short run and just one deck up. He ran to his station as the ship erupted with activity. Orders were being given over the loud speaker and everyone soon knew they were to begin their first action.

Hashani found his way into the number-two turret of the *Okhotsk*. He was the last to arrive and was yelled at by the petty officer in charge of the guns there. "We are prepared to attack," he said, "and you have delayed the actions of this battery! Those who are last bring shame to themselves and for this you will report to me after the engagement! Stand by your station." The skinny, noncommissioned officer slammed the hatch closed, gave one last scowl and climbed into the gunner's chair.

Hashani was embarrassed. He would take what punishment was meted out, but he would work harder to prove himself worthy. He was ready to begin the fight against the Americans. Hand-powered elevators began cranking the high-explosive shells from the magazines well below the water line of the ship. No job firing the guns was safe, but the seamen were especially carefully with these awkward projectiles. One wrong move could cause the round to detonate. Everyone inside would be vaporized in less than the blink of an eye. The turret would be lifted off the deck. The magazine below could be ignited, causing the ship to be cut in half by the explosion. The death of the sailors inside the turret would be a loss, but their deaths would not be as shameful as causing the deaths of their shipmates. They would be haunted in their afterlives by such a dishonor.

The shells came up one at a time and each was tamped into its barrel before the next one arrived. There was little room to work, but the sailors practiced their duties over and over. Each man performed like a machine. After each shell arrived, the powder bags quickly followed. The men in the magazines were told how many bags to send and the barrel loaders knew how many to ram. The command and control center (CAC) gave the orders, depending on the type of shell used and the distance to the target. Much like tamping a muzzle-loading cannon from behind, the men pushed the shells and powder bags into each barrel before closing the breach. One man delicately twisted the primer into the breach of the huge guns, cocked the firing pin, and then moved out of the way.

On the bridge Commander Hatsoto looked toward the coast. No one on the ship knew what lay inland. The ship would begin its attack by firing at what the map showed to be the center of the town and expand its fire from there. As far as Hatsoto was concerned, any city of the United States was hostile to Japan. Any city was capable of providing troops and goods to the war effort, and therefore a preemptive strike to serve the Japanese nation was acceptable. The men in the CAC of the *Okhotsk* found the distance and trajectory to the estimated center of the city. They calculated the degree of distance to the target in relation to the ship's position and the elevation of the guns. Each gun chief, a ranking NCO, threw levers to start the electric motors that moved the behemoth turrets. Every man stood at attention after readying the guns for the first shots. Hashani, like most other men on the ship, beamed with pride. Only the men on the bridge and in the CAC knew what was targeted. The men in the rest of the ship only knew their duties had taken them to the enemy, and they were ready to begin the attack.

The word came from the ship's commander to the CAC. "Commence attack!" The CAC ordered "Fire!" and the nine guns of the ship fired simultaneously. The sound was louder than thunder. Clouds of thick black smoke covered the left side of the ship. The recoil of the guns, forcing a total of more than eight tons of shells toward the unsuspecting city, pushed the ship back several inches in the water. Commander Hatsoto continued holding his binoculars to his eyes as the ship listed, and he rocked a bit on his feet to keep his balance. The shells landed on their targets in just over fifteen seconds.

By this time of the morning most people in the town of maybe a thousand were going about their everyday lives. They had not realized a war was on their shores. The community was not a threat to the Japanese Imperial Navy and Army. The only thing it could provide for the war would be lumber and a couple dozen, able-bodied young men. Most of those men would not have a chance now. The sound was one that most people had never heard before. It was a brief whistle followed by an enormous rush of eighteen-hundred-pound shells splitting the air at more than seven thousand feet per second. No one had time to look up. The shells hit very close to their intended target: the center of the little community. In a second an entire block of the town was leveled. Most people near the blast who could move panicked and ran in complete disbelief. No one immediately understood what was going on. Those near the first explosions were torn apart and thrown indiscriminately across the landscape. Large pieces of buildings and cars and trees were tossed like pebbles. Those that were far enough away from the blasts not to be hurt still had to pick themselves off the ground. People staggered around in complete confusion. What was happening? What was causing these explosions? Like birds thrown around in a hurricane, no one was sure of where to go or what to do. They recognized danger, but didn't know how to react. Terror and panic was the only thing most of them knew as those who were unhurt ran to assist. There was little to assist with. The blasts decimated an area of several acres. Only rubble was left in its place along with scattered clothing and personal property. None of the buildings in that spot were recognizable. Straight and level roadways, headed toward the center of town, just disappeared into a mass of debris.

All that was known was that some horrendous act had taken place and help was needed. The bells at two nearby churches rang for assistance. The sound of the bells and harried voices could be heard over the summer breeze. Just as people were regaining their senses and beginning to respond, the sound could be heard again: a second salvo of fourteen-inch shells fired from a Japanese Imperial Navy cruiser. The second round fell over a wider area, causing much the same damage. More people were torn to bits. The small town on the coast was being blown apart.

On the ship the proud warriors were continuing their duties in the fight against the U.S. homeland. Crewmen did their duty because it was expected, and because they desired to strike at the enemy. The United States was a land of unimaginable wealth. The sailors knew the richness of the land was exploited and its people were selfish and lazy. Japan was a great nation and deserved recognition for such. They were prepared to force the white men out of Southeast Asia and the entire Pacific so as to not be infected by their filthy and deviant ways.

Hashani continued working hard at his station. He didn't know what was happening outside, if the ship were under attack, or if they were attacking a warship. He only focused on his duty to load the gun. To call the job difficult is an understatement. The interior was cramped and it was difficult to load the large shells and powder bags, but the men were well trained and they worked together like a choreographed ballet. Everything about the job was miserable. Their bodies soon weakened and ached from the heavy work. No matter what the outside temperature was, the interior was sweltering hot. It heated up even in cold weather from the combined body heat of the crewmen and the firing of the guns. After a couple rounds had been fired, any bare skin that touched the gun barrels would be burned off. Clouds of acrid smoke burned the eyes and lungs and bore into pores. The forced recoil of the guns rattled every bone in the men's bodies. As horrible as the job was physically, it was a joy and a great honor to perform.

After about twenty minutes the cease-fire order was given. A cheer arose over the ship. The *Okhotsk* earned its first decoration of battle and each man felt joy.

Hashani was as elated as the rest. After the battle stations were cleared he would report to the petty officer who had scolded him and then return to his quarters. He had performed well and was proud of his job. He would collect his thoughts writing in his journal.

Smoke cleared from the ship and rose from the land. The war of Europe and Asia had come to the United States with a community destroyed and American lives gone forever.

Chapter 12

He ached to get his first kill. From the moment he was given command of Unterseeboot-432 and given his assignment, he physically ached to take a shot at an enemy target.

Captain Johan Kurz was a man who could make Hitler himself proud. He was an unrelenting and forceful leader, and a man who wanted to kill. He had a small, round stature, salty hair and a bushy mustache. He was easily angered and accepted nothing less than immediate action when he gave a command. He was young to be a submarine skipper. At thirty-two years old he had shown great spirit and determination in the German navy. He was just old enough to remember the soldiers returning from the Great War and one of his first understandings of the world was that of defeat. He grew up during the economic depression following the war and was quick to follow the ideals of the Nazi Party. He truly believed in the fiery and virulent leader of the party. After Hitler took power, Kurz wanted to be a part of the powerful German war machine and prove himself and his nation worthy. When he had the opportunity to join the Kriegsmarine, he jumped. Perhaps he saw some comparison of the boats to himself. They were small and less powerful than surface ships, but they could sneak up on their prey from underneath and strike fear in the hearts of their enemies. That is what Kurz wanted to do: destroy and make the enemy afraid.

Kurz was given command of his boat in April 1942. He was eager to get out and start doing his part for the war: sinking supply ships on the routes between the United States and England, terrorizing war ships around the continent, moving into the frigid waters of the Barents Sea to support the advance into Russia, or sailing to the warm Mediterranean to help the German advance into Africa and the Middle East. It made no difference to him; he just wanted to make his first kill.

Kurz was picked as a captain because of his strong character and eagerness. He was one of the captains to be picked for a special service to go to the shores of the United States. He could hand-pick his crew. He could write his own mission. He could advance and attack at will. He was to be a small part of a mission that was to change the world. His moment in history had arrived.

U-432 sailed in early May, completely loaded with supplies and munitions. It was on a mission of undetermined length, skippered by a maniacal, little man, bent on destruction. His orders were simple: gather intelligence without being detected until June 3. At that time he would be free to roam the entire eastern seaboard of the United States and strike at will. Anything that was of strategic military importance to the U.S. was a potential target. He could fire on anything without provocation. He could advance as closely to any ship or land area as necessary and withdraw if necessary.

Captain Kurz was not aware of the entire strategic purpose of the mission. He knew he had been hand picked by Admiral Vanziger of the U-boat command for "a mission of the utmost importance." Kurz was not given written orders. Very little in the German high command was put on paper. His meeting with the admiral was brief. He left only with the most current maps and diagrams of the western Atlantic. His time had arrived to show himself worthy and to inflict losses on the enemy. He would do so to the best of his ability.

As was standard practice, U-432 sailed submerged by day and surfaced only at night. Submarine service was not as glamorous as many thought. Because the selection process was rigorous, the jobs were coveted, but once sailors came aboard the little boats, they were ready to go stir crazy. The submarines were damp, dark, and cramped, and the combination of smells in these small metal tubes could make a man sick to his stomach. A sailor had no room to call his own, yet there was a camaraderie that was unparalleled in any other crew in the German navy. Everything that sailors hated about the little tin cans only fed Kurz's passion for the boat. Whether he was made for the U-boat command or whether the U-boats had been built for him, he lived for this duty.

Kurz turned further south than the normal convoy lanes of the North Atlantic. He knew he could probably have sunk several cargo ships on his way, but he had no desire to give up his location. He was not even required to report to his fleet command, only to go and fight in close quarters with the American forces. He was on a high-speed course to arrive on the east coast of the United States and begin his job. He wanted to be the first to draw blood in the Americans' front yard.

It was June 1 and Kurz, along with his crew, was feeling anxious. They had been floating in their smelly boat for three weeks. Their only contacts with friendly forces were a refueling vessel and a supply ship. Each action took most of a day after they rendezvoused some hundred miles due west of the Bermuda Islands. Kurz was ready to get his food from American ships that he had overrun like a pirate. He wanted to get his fuel oil directly from pumps at refineries on the Gulf Coast. He was deluded enough to believe that one day he could pull his boat up to a dock and pump his own diesel fuel.

Upon its arrival on the coast, U-432 patrolled undetected between South Carolina and Georgia. Kurz had viewed Jekyll Island through his periscope. This is a resort for the lazy Americans, he thought. After the war he would lounge on the beach.

He knew there were friendly U-boats lurking in the waters from the southern tip of Greenland, past Cuba to Texas. When the date arrived, Kurz was going to be ready to release the wrath of his small but potent war machine. Whatever crossed his path would be obliterated.

Kurz had been given very ambiguous orders. Beginning on the third day of June, he could attack at will any and all targets that could assist the United States in any possible war effort against the Third Reich or its allies. He secretly rode up and down part of the East Coast, quietly looking and listening. He silently sat outside the ports of Charleston and Savannah, studying the shipping activity and deciding how the American military would react when the navy of the Reich attacked.

At the beginning of his naval career he had been on U-318 in a North Atlantic wolf pack. He so enjoyed the activity. They could simply pop up, target a transport ship, sink it and disappear under the chilly waves. As much as he enjoyed his duties there, he loved the fact that he was assigned his own ship. Kurz wasn't in a hunter group; he was a lone wolf now. The lone wolf was more dangerous and feared. That's how Kurz thought of himself: dangerous and feared. He was ready to become the Red Baron of the submarine fleet.

On the evening of June 2, Kurz retired to his cabin early. His small room was very Spartan. His entire life revolved around the navy and he had no use for any items that were not government issued. Service on a U-boat was generally informal. After intense training and entry into the select group, men relaxed on the boats and enjoyed camaraderie. This was not the case on U-432. Kurz was very strict with the crew. He demanded that they appear and act in true military fashion at all times. Kurz polished his boots to a high gloss. He prepared his formal dress uniform to include the small, decorative sword.

The ship surfaced and the crew carried out routine maintenance, preparing for a long dive the next day. Everything had to be ready for early light. Kurz laughed a bit knowing the war with the Americans was going to begin the next day, and they didn't know a thing about it. He sipped a cup of tea and sat in quiet contemplation. He slept without making a sound all night.

Captain Kurz was up at 5 a.m. He methodically dressed and ordered only toast and black coffee from the galley. By 5:30 a.m. he was in the conning tower asking for a status report on the ship and crew. After receiving the report, he looked at the chief of the watch.

"Where, may I ask," he said in a cold tone, "is my chief of the boat?"

The lieutenant had been in charge of the ship since 9 p.m. the previous night. He was tired but didn't dare respond glibly. "He is probably still in his bunk. It is only five thirty in the morning, Captain."

Kurz turned with a look of contempt. His words were given staccato. "That is an odd place for him to be at this time. He is aware, is he not, that our attack will begin at the first opportunity? The sun will be up very shortly." The skipper looked around the tower. His voice got louder. "This boat will be prepared for this day's activities in five minutes. Sound the alert. All crews to their work stations. Commander Gruber is to report to me immediately." He had an intense look on his face much like Hitler nearing the end of a speech. "The war begins now!"

The chief of the watch was not physically or mentally prepared for the captain's activity. He was tired and ready for sleep, which he now knew was not going to come soon. He took a bit of pride in knowing they were going to be a big part of history, and he knew the skipper was to be an auspicious part of it. The chief did his job immediately and exactly as ordered. He looked at the watchman and commanded, as he was supposed to, "Sound alert 3; open 1."

"Sound alert 3; open 1; aye, Chief."

The horns in every compartment blasted three times in quick succession. Their sharp timbre was agonizing. The voice of the chief on duty came through the loudspeakers all over the ship. "Attention, all crewmen. Attention, all crewmen. Report to your duty stations. Commander Gruber to the con."

The entire ship came to life. Lights came on and crewmen rolled out of their bunks and grabbed pants and boots. No time to brush teeth and wash faces. The day was at hand, and the captain was ready to begin the battle. Men rubbed their eyes to look at their watches. They moved quickly and quietly around the ship. They shifted past one another in narrow passageways as they went to their posts. The kitchen crew had already begun their day. Now breakfast was going to change from a hot meal to a cold meal on the run. The night crews realized there would be little sleep for them that day.

Commander Gruber stumbled his way into the conning tower. Half of his shirt hung over his belt and he ran his fingers across his hair to straighten it. Franz Gruber was much older than Kurz and well respected by the crew. He was in the Kriegsmarine service because it was his duty. He did not aspire to glory and had no personal agenda. Gruber was an excellent tactician and could have taken command of any boat in the German navy, but he didn't have the desire. He had only gained his rank because it had been forced on him. Gruber respected Kurz because of his rank and recognized Kurz's energy. He did not have the same fear for Kurz as most of the crew had, but he did fear Kurz's desires. Kurz had vigor that brought danger with it.

Kurz spoke in an even tone. "I am happy to see you well this morning, Commander Gruber."

Gruber knew Kurz meant to be sarcastic. He never engaged the captain in petty remarks and would never do so in front of the crew. "Good morning, Captain."

The captain tipped his head to one side. "The war awaits, Commander."

"Aye, Captain." The full staff was in the tower now, each man preparing for his assignment.

Kurz had made a perfunctory scan of his maps. He knew exactly what he was going to do that day. He had thought about it for days. "Boat Chief, set your depth at sixty meters, speed at eight knots, and heading at zero four zero and report all contacts."

"Aye, Captain. Set our depth at sixty meters, speed at eight knots, heading at zero four zero, and report all contacts, aye." The message was repeated all the way down the line from the captain to the dive officer. Everything was always duplicated because the captain wanted absolutely no mistakes.

The room and boat churned with activity from the exuberant activity in the engine room to the silent vigilance in the sonar man's chair. The crew was excited. Even though it was early morning and most had not yet eaten breakfast, the ship's crew was exhilarated. All of their previous activity was going to be put to the test in this, their first act of war against a new enemy, the United States.

The engines rumbled and the ship groaned a bit as it sunk farther into the ocean, and everyone became more anxious.

The day was well along and there was only quiet activity on the boat. Captain Kurz was silent, but moved and fidgeted like a caged animal. He was impatient. He wanted action. He started to question his plan for the day because U-432 had been traveling in a northeasterly direction at a steady eight knots for nearly three hours with no contact. He was some fifty miles off shore and wondered whether to aim directly at a port. He could find any number of naval ships at Charleston, but he knew that would be dangerous. Any attack near a military installation would bring an immediate response from the navy. Kurz continued contemplating this. He had driven his boat up and down the coast for weeks, completely undetected. He could attack a ship and slip quietly away without the enemy knowing what had happened. He could sail his ship into the entrance of the harbor and wait for the perfect moment to attack any big ship. He was hungry for a kill and just like a wolf, was ready to search for his prey rather than wait for it to find its way to him.

Before plotting a new course, he asked, "Chief of the boat, what contacts do you have?"

Commander Gruber walked to the sonar station and quietly inquired. There was a delay, followed by conversation.

"Captain, small craft approaching directly ahead."

Kurz rose from his chair. "All stop. Raise the ship to five meters."

"Aye, Captain. All stop. Raise the ship to five meters."

The ship sat silently in the warm waters off the Georgia coast. The captain's face had a certain glow to it. "Periscope up." His voice seemed to quiver. He was in his black, full-dress uniform and had turned his hat backward to lean against the periscope. Searching the distant horizon he found his target. It was a small, wooden boat moving slowly in his direction.

"All ahead, slow."

"Aye, Captain. All ahead slow."

The U-432 passed to the boat's port side and would come into better view.

"Twenty degrees to port, then all stop."

"Aye, Captain. Twenty degrees to port, then all stop."

"Boat Chief, sound battle stations."

Gruber watched for a moment. The captain didn't turn away from the periscope. "Aye, Captain. Battle stations."

The horn now sounded a staccato blast, which vibrated in every area of the ship. Every heart jumped. Every crewman ran to his station. When they received a call to battle stations, the crew didn't immediately understand the facts of the situation; they only had to be prepared to react. The feeling on the boat was one of excitement. The crewmen knew this could be the fatherland's premier attack on the United States. Kurz was thrilled that this was his stealthy war machine's first chance at a kill. This was his first opportunity to show his authority and ability. He hoped he was the first ship of the German navy to shoot. The con was quietly sounding its response to the captain's orders. Kurz turned the periscope, never taking his eyes off the approaching target. He could feel tension in his hands as he held the scope. He had to concentrate on drawing breath into his lungs. The morning sun beat down on the small craft on the water. It moved slowly. He could see it perfectly and knew he could send a shot into its side with no problem. He would maneuver a bit, leading the nose of his boat a little more. The target would pass within a hundred and fifty meters of his boat. This would be textbook. He would send a torpedo directly into the center of the boat. Its crewmen would be dead before they even knew what had hit them. They would have no opportunity to call for assistance. His mind raced. He would draw blood first and not be detected. His boat could continue to cruise unobserved and he could attack relentlessly.

"Ten degrees port, load torpedo tube one."

"Aye, Captain. Ten degrees to port. Load torpedo tube one."

The conning tower breathed a collective sigh of anticipation. This would be the first real military action that most of the crew had been involved in. The boat made its subtle and silent adjustment and seamen in the torpedo room loaded a tube. It took a bit of muscle to move the projectile, which weighed more than the two seamen, into the tube on the left side of the boat. It was cool and damp in the small room. The physical activity didn't take long, but the men sweated and breathed heavily. The highest-ranking man, a petty officer, turned a valve and cold, ocean water could be heard rushing into the large, metal cylinder. Another crewman began quickly turning a wheel to open the tube door. The petty officer pulled back a handle to set the trigger and the torpedo was ready to head to its target when the order came. The petty officer turned and spoke into a metal mouthpiece. "Tube one ready to fire."

On the bridge Commander Gruber spoke in a steady voice. "Torpedo tube one is ready to fire, Captain." He walked toward Kurz. His job was to assist the captain with everything from plotting a course to plotting the trajectory of a shot.

Kurz quickly retrieved a slide rule from the side pocket of his chair. He wanted to make his first shot the only shot. Ammunition was precious in the middle of the Atlantic Ocean. It was going to be textbook. He estimated the speed of the target and distance and he was going to put his shot directly in the middle.

Gruber, not knowing what Kurz planned to do, walked to the periscope. He took a quick look and focused on the approaching ship. He took a more thorough look back and forth on the horizon and saw nothing else. "Captain, the ship appears to be to a civilian fishing vessel." After he had said that, Kurz's angry look was palpable. Gruber looked around the tower and noticed that everyone was focusing on their duties rather than on the two officers. They had heard what was said, and were aware of the captain's rage. They were afraid to look up.

"Commander Gruber, I see a ship flying an American flag. We do not know its destination or purpose. My orders are to attack anything that is of possible military significance." His jaw was clenched. "That is what I am doing."

Gruber had felt uneasy about his captain before. Now he felt fear for the first time. In a voice not much more than a whisper he said, "Aye, Captain."

Kurz took heavy steps back to the periscope. Not a sound was to be heard. He looked again into the scope and said, "Prepare to fire."

Gruber repeated in a placid tone, "Aye, Captain. Prepare to fire." He picked up the brass mouthpiece and repeated the captain's words, "Prepare to fire."

The petty officer in the torpedo room took a deep breath and placed his left hand on the firing handle. He had a smile on his face, knowing he was about launch an attack against the United States.

The captain still stared into the periscope. The boat about to pass in front still trundled along. Its crewmen were not able to see the periscope barely sticking out of the water less than two football fields away. They were unaware that a German sub was targeting them. Kurz could see men on the deck raising the net on the boat's port side. His only thought was that the net shouldn't rise too close to the side of the boat and deflect his perfect shot. Several people in the conning tower looked around to see the commander's face and the captain standing at the scope. The men could see the commander's lips moving with his count, *"funf . . . vier . . . drei . . . zwei . . . eins, Feuer!"*

Gruber snapped his head forward as he repeated into the mouthpiece.

Petty Officer Stunn gasped, and his arm twitched forward. The torpedo made an almost musical sound as metal hit water, and it left the tube and began its trip. The whole submarine, everyone inside, and the boat itself remained still and silent. The torpedo made it to the surface of the water at a distance of about fifteen meters in front of U-432. Once it had found its draft, only a fraction of the projectile was out of the water. Its wake was barely visible. No one on the fishing boat saw it.

The explosion was heard by the entire ship. U-432 didn't even move in response to the concussion. Everyone yelled jubilantly. They had struck at the enemy.

Kurz was disappointed. The explosion made by his torpedo completely destroyed the fishing boat. The forty-foot long, wooden boat was reduced to splinters, which fell flat onto the water. There was nothing left to sink as there would have been with a larger, steel ship. Kurz's first act of war was a bit disheartening. He though that the next kill would be better.

Kurz slammed the handles up against each side of the periscope. "Down periscope." Excitedly he ordered, "Chief of the boat, dive to thirty meters. Set our course at zero three five, full ahead. Report all contacts. I will be in my wardroom."

"Aye, Captain." Gruber didn't want to say any more.

Chapter 13

The activity in the room was even more frenzied than on Monday. The circumstances seemed even more extreme than two days before. Many of the same people were present, only the room was different. The meeting now took place in the map room of the mansion. This was a large room on the ground floor, full of wood and leather furniture. It faced the large back lawn of the White House and was below the level of the main entrance. The president was comfortable there. He had often used it to chart the progress of the war during the previous three years. The room was directly off the center corridor and government and military officials could easily arrive and leave at the back of the residence. Now the room was packed with a lot of boisterous people whose discussions were not about the war in distant locations, but within the United States.

The president was wheeled into the room. All conversation stopped and, as was the standard practice, everyone stood. His valet rolled the wheelchair to a sofa against the west wall where he stopped and locked the wheels in place. The president lifted himself, gripping the arms of the chair. An army officer, General Hampton Wade, stood nearby and nearly moved over to assist the president. He thought better of it and stood simply looking in the general direction of the crippled man.

The president was steady on his feet. He turned around and sat down on the sofa. His valet nodded and wheeled the chair out of the room.

Everyone stood in silence, waiting for direction from the president.

"Be seated please, gentlemen."

President Roosevelt surveyed the room. He always took notice of details when he attended a meeting. The entire room was filled with maps. Some, showing activities around the world, had always been there. Lots of new maps, detailing military movements in specific regions had been added. Men walked in and out the door leading to the center hallway and delivered notes to various people in the room.

The president looked around. "Gentlemen, what news do you bring?"

Admiral Ernest King was the first to speak. "Mr. President, German warships have been seen in the Atlantic near the U.S. coast."

Everyone in the room with the exception of the president had known and been prepared for the news. The president's expression changed only slightly to that of shock.

King continued, "A ship believed to be the pocket battleship, *Admiral Sheer*, was seen approximately sixty miles south southeast of the eastern tip of Long Island. It was apparently alone. The heavy cruiser, *Admiral Hipper*, along with two smaller ships, was seen a hundred miles due east of Portsmouth, Virginia. All the ships were seen sailing south at top speed."

People seemed to shift a bit in their chairs when that was announced. Everyone realized the close proximity of Washington, DC to Chesapeake Bay. The British had burned the White House in 1812. The Germans might have an easier time a hundred and thirty years later.

Chief of Staff Leahy looked at the president. His first concern was for Roosevelt's safety, but he was probably also concerned for his own safety. "Sir, perhaps you should be relocated."

President Roosevelt looked in anger at him. "This has been the nation's capital for over a hundred and forty years. That will not change."

"Sir, the capital would not need to move, but prudence dictates that you be relocated for your own safety, for the continued safe functioning of the government."

Soldiers were not supposed to be scared; it was their duty to face the enemy. Some feared an invasion of the nation's capital would be the ultimate blow.

"The business of the nation rests here with me, the elected officials, and the military." Roosevelt's tone was direct and clear. "This is where I will stay."

The president looked down in thought. The admiral drew his attention again. "Additionally, U-boats off the U.S. Atlantic coast have begun actions, firing on a military supply ship and sinking two civilian vessels."

"They're firing on civilian ships?"

Admiral King blinked slowly. "Yes, sir."

"My God, what is happening in this world?"

Secretary of the Navy Frank Knox spoke up next. "Mr. President, the fact that these surface ships didn't initiate fire and were hundreds of miles apart may mean there will be no East Coast invasion."

"Secretary Knox, these ships are within a hundred miles of the nation. They are traveling in the same direction and U-boats have sunk ships. This is surely a prelude to an attack."

General Dwight Eisenhower spoke for the first time. He was not new to the city, but new to the ranks of the military council that was assembled there and new to the War Department. He was working his way up the ranks. He had been to France in the First World War and was currently stationed in Panama. He had been first in his class at the Command and General Staff School and was a graduate of the U.S. Army War College. He had made his way from chief of staff in the U.S. Third Army to the War Plans Division. He spoke in a low, raspy voice. "Gentleman, I should interject. We are now intercepting communications from the Atlantic and Pacific theaters. The commonly heard phrase in the Pacific is *ni heika*. The words commonly heard from the Atlantic are *zwei Klingen*. They translate as *two swords*."

The room broke out in noise. Everyone jumped to the conclusion that both Japan and Germany were attacking the United States. The two swords were Germany and Japan, one sword on each side of the country. General Marshall said out loud, "This was well planned and executed. The Japanese strike from the west and the military responds in that direction. Then the Germans sweep in from the east." Secretary of War Stinson replied that the nation would now lose more land in the west before stopping the Japanese invasion.

The room continued buzzing. Men talked about the extreme situation and the immediate need for millions of men in uniform, and equipment that could be used in the field immediately.

The discourse in the room continued. President Roosevelt simply looked down, shook his head and said to himself, "Madness, sheer madness."

The men noted the president's response and looked at him. He looked up, "Madmen are attempting to rule the entire world."

General Marshall continued, "Mr. President, Japanese forces appear to be moving further into the Pacific. Japanese warships are moving on Guam and Wake Island."

The faces on the men in the room showed nothing but fear.

"How is this possible? How are these evil nations able to occupy so much land, and still attack this nation?"

Marshall responded, "Sir, the Japanese military is fanatical. Germany is the same and technologically advanced. These nations' leaders are apparently prepared to attack and sacrifice much to set the world in flames. The Germans are still advancing east into Europe and the Japanese are continuing to spread out from their homeland."

"Call MacArthur back from the Philippines." The president's words were short.

"Sir?"

"Call General MacArthur and all troops back from the Philippines and all troops from Iceland. All U.S. forces are needed here."

Eisenhower spoke again. "I believe General MacArthur would be opposed to that and a retreat from the South Pacific would need to be discussed before being carried out."

President Roosevelt looked perturbed.

Eisenhower continued, "Gentlemen, if the Japanese were to gain control of everything in the Pacific from Singapore to Hawaii, they would become too powerful to respond to. I believe we must gain at least a small foothold somewhere so as to not allow them the entire Far East. They will need to be dealt with and if we give up now, we can't respond later."

Roosevelt spoke again. "Gentlemen, there will be no need to protect U.S. territories if the mainland is overrun. The world seems to be crumbling around us and we must first defend this nation to the end." He struggled as he pushed himself to his feet. "Good day."

Men filed quickly out of the room as George came in with the president's wheelchair. George was dedicated to the president and always a welcome sight, a small comfort in that uncertain time.

Chapter 14

The quiet conversations in the Chamber of the House of Representatives were as important as the loudest debate ever held there. Only standing room remained and armed soldiers stood at each door and on every corner of the building. Just as the clock struck noon, the sergeant at arms entered the back of the Chamber and walked forward. His voice was clear and loud when he announced, "Mr. Vice-President, Mr. Speaker, the president of the United States!"

The room erupted in applause as everyone stood. President Roosevelt entered from the side near the speaker's desk. He walked forward with the assistance of two canes. Two men walked directly behind him to assist him if he began to fall. The applause continued and he climbed to the podium. As was the accepted practice, no cameras could be used until he stood behind the podium. Then, flash bulbs began going off.

The president placed both canes out of sight and removed the pages of his speech from his coat pocket.

"Mr. Vice-President, Mr. Speaker, Members of the Senate, and of the House of Representatives, within the past few days the United States of America has fallen under the sudden and deliberate attack of military forces of both the Empire of Japan and Nazi Germany.

"This nation has seen the violence perpetrated by these two vehement nations upon the rest of the civilized world and have yet rested in peace knowing that we have been spared their wrath. The atrocities that they have perpetrated around the globe are now being repeated on our shores.

"In the early morning hours of June 1, 1942, soldiers of the Imperial Japanese Army came ashore in the sovereign states of Oregon and Washington, and began killing innocent men, women, and children. All those who are dead were citizens of the United States and as such should be mourned, and their deaths vindicated."

The audience, which had sat in quiet respect, now clapped in response to this call to arms. When the noise subsided, the president continued.

"Ships and airplanes of the Japanese navy performed operations against coastal areas of the western United States. These operations began after the Japanese consulate was secretly vacated, as if by a thief fleeing in the nighttime.

"Two days after the unprovoked attacks on American soil by the Japanese military, ships of the German navy made their presence known to this nation, and began attacks that have cost the lives of Americans on the high seas.

"These direct and obviously coordinated attacks indicate that those two nations have worked through collusion. The actions of these governments' militaries make it clear that those nations have commenced plans of attacks and the actions have constituted acts of war against the United States of America.

"Attacks against American property and interests by the Axis nations continue. This nation will not bow to the evil and villainous actions of its enemies. We will do all that is necessary to respond and fight valiantly until we are completely victorious. No enemy will threaten, intimidate, or destroy that which this nation has resolved to protect, defend, and hold sacred.

"As commander in chief of the army and navy, I have directed that all measures be taken for our defense. With confidence in our armed forces, with the unbending determination of our people, we will gain inevitable triumph, so help us, God. I ask this Congress declare a state of war against the Empire of Japan and the German nation."

The president stepped back from the podium and the chamber erupted. Men bounded to their feet with cheers and applause. To increase the level of noise and show their support, men beat their fists on tables. The noise continued at that level for several minutes as the president retired from the chamber.

Chapter 15

What remained of the regiment continued to fight its way inland. It hadn't faced very much military resistance. It was disorganized and had broken apart in the rapid charge inland. It had been the first to land on American shores more than a week earlier, and had hit the beaches completely unopposed, to the surprise of the U.S. nation. The tenth regiment of the second group of the Imperial Japanese Army, the regiment of squad leader Corporal Yoshi Iwanami, had been the first to attack the United States. It had begun its murderous attacks from the very first morning and continued to attack as it went. The regiment was now some seventy miles inland. It had passed over the coastal ranges and had begun to climb the Cascade Range.

Yoshi could not help but note the fact that his group still had no specific target. The soldiers had terrorized towns, obliterated small communities, brushed by and harassed cities and still didn't seem to be going anywhere in particular. Whatever the reason, whatever their duty, the group would fight on to a bloody end.

After the first week of the war, the soldiers of the Tenth Regiment hadn't seen any more soldiers from the Imperial Japanese Army. They knew they were the first wave and would most likely outrun the second wave. Yoshi wondered if they were lost and had missed the war. After the first two days they did meet up with a half company from one of the primary attacking groups that had come ashore several miles south of Yoshi's group. On one northern trek, as they headed down toward the southern tip of the Willamette Valley, they saw a couple tanks ahead in the valley. The tanks came under attack, as did the soldiers traveling with them. They weren't seen after that. On the third day of the invasion Yoshi's troops heard artillery fire behind them, but they weren't sure whose artillery it was, and they continued their advance without investigating. They were told prior to the day of the attack that they would be supported by soldiers following with tanks, cannons, and other small arms; carrier-based planes; and air drops of supplies. They hadn't seen any of this. Were they in the wrong place? Was there no support as they had been told?

The fight hadn't been the glorious charge against the enemy that Yoshi had expected. His regiment had done its job of destroying property so the enemy couldn't use it against Japanese forces, but they had seen few enemy soldiers. They hadn't tracked down the enemy as Yoshi had believed they would. It seemed as if, when they came near any enemy army unit, his regiment had turned away.

"This is not the Bushido way that I have learned," Yoshi said to himself.

After destroying an area, a Bushido soldier moved on. He didn't wait on the enemy. He looked for the enemy. Yoshi's regiment had taken a zigzag course through the mountains of Oregon in what seemed to be a mission of avoiding the enemy.

Corporal Iwanami was fast becoming physically tired and disillusioned. It was not the place of any soldier to question his military leaders. No one had spoken out loud, but it was evident on the faces of the young men of the regiment that they had questions. The days had passed with no sight of support. There were no orders of what to attack or where to go. Each day parts of the regiment faced isolated attacks and men died. There were no huge losses because there had been no major action against enemy soldiers. For those who died in the fight there was honor and glory, but for what end? They had not yet taken the battle to the American military. This was not what they had trained for: precision attacks and valiant charges. They were here on American soil to stab at the heart of the enemy.

The sun set on another day of the fight. The regiment was well in the cover of the mountains and would be safe for another night. It would soon camp, and Yoshi would have a moment to contemplate the activity. He knew that the fight would continue. He would lead his squad and they would wholeheartedly follow their military leaders, their emperor, and their nation to its glory and victory.

Chapter 16

The United States began right away building for war. Every night citizens were glued to radios and read newspapers for news of that day's events in their country and around the world. The Axis nations advanced on every front around the world. In the United States the Imperial Japanese Army seemed to be swarming into the Pacific Northwest, but the U.S. Army and Navy had slowed its advance. In the east the German navy demonstrated its presence up and down the coast. It seemed that Nazi commandos were preparing for an invasion.

Gerald Flaghart continued his daily routine. He would listen and read intently each night to hear the progress of the war. He was scared just like everyone else in the nation. Battles were taking place in each ocean. Combat was taking place on the West Coast, and the east was hunkered down in anticipation of invasion. Gerald was scared of war in general. Just as the enemy armies had marched across continents in other parts of the world, they could march all the way to Wisconsin. Even though that event was unlikely, Gerald still feared war in his own country. It had been foreign to the United States for years, only an afterthought on the evening news, but now enemy forces were here and fighting on American land. Gerald wondered what his place was.

He had a lot of time to think and decide. He maintained his job at Northern Valley Cheese Company and just days after the outbreak of war the primary shift was extended to nine hours per day. On the weekends Gerald found odd jobs around the house and neighborhood. On this Saturday he sawed up a tree that had fallen across his neighbor's fence during a spring storm and had lain there for a couple months. It was a small tree from Deloris Meeker's yard, behind his house. She was an older widow who didn't have the ability to do it herself or the money to have it done. Gerald decided it was the right thing to do, to get it out of the way and to give her some firewood for her parlor fireplace that winter. He didn't announce to anyone that he was going to do it; he just got a saw and an axe and started after breakfast. He would have it split and stacked at her back door by sunset.

Gerald's father, John, was back from a morning trip to take care of errands downtown. He made his way to the backyard carrying a glass. Gerald wasn't sure what was about to happen. He doubted his father had come to help and Gerald didn't want help anyway. One of two things would happen, based on his experiences of the previous couple weeks: a fight would start or they would go their ways in silence.

"Your mother saw you working and wondered if you wanted lemonade. I told her I knew it was hard enough work and you'd probably like some." John handed over the glass and Gerald accepted it without a word. He didn't want to say anything that could lead to a confrontation and just nodded his head. He took a large gulp and thought his mouth was going to turn inside out.

"That's pretty tangy." He squinted as his eyes started watering.

John tipped his head down, covering a smile. "I know. I had a sip inside. You know why that is?"

"Because mom doesn't know how to make lemonade?"

"It's because she only used a couple teaspoons of sugar because of the rationing that's started because of the war. Everybody is doing their part, and cutting back on sugar is important."

There was no need to respond to his father's hint.

"I took a walk by the fire brigade building when I was in town. That's where the army guys are recruiting again today. People are still signing up."

Gerald looked down and gently shook his head. He knew where the conversation was going. It was going the same place it had been for their last five conversations. Gerald pushed back his sweaty hair.

"You know your cousins Jerry and David both went down together last Saturday. They were there early and still had to wait in line. They're headed out together for boot camp on Monday morning."

"Yes, Dad, I know. You've told me that about six times already this week." Gerald put the glass down on the grass and turned back toward his work.

His father squinted and turned his mouth down in a look of disgust. "Sorry to take up your time." His tone was typically sarcastic. "I'm headed back in to find the news on the radio at noon. I want to hear what kind of beating we're giving the Japs and Huns. Them boys will hate it if they ever tried to set foot on this ground."

Gerald went back to sawing the limbs into fireplace-sized pieces. His father was headed back to the house. "Oh." Gerald knew his father would have to say something else. "Since you're so hard at work on this tree that's been here for a couple months, I'll tell your mother you'll just take your lunch out here, and she has plenty of that lemonade. I guess somebody has to take care of that tree before the winter that's coming in five or six more months."

Gerald didn't acknowledge the comments. He continued with his work. His only thought was that he had work to do. There was work for him to do in his job at the plant. A lot of men were volunteering and the draft was in full force. The workforce at the processing plant was being stretched thin, and he needed to be there to help it survive and produce cheese for the nation. There was plenty of work around town and he was an able-bodied young man who could help and earn money and do what he needed for the home front. Somebody had to stay behind. That's what he believed and what he thought was his place, no matter what was said. There was no shame in chopping wood and repairing fences and tending to gardens. He told himself that he would work that much harder to do his part.

There were so many young men in town, and he was sure that with men all over the nation going to fight the war, he would never be needed. He picked up the pace and was determined he would have the tree gone and the firewood stacked by dark.

Chapter 17

The city of Omaha seemed to have regained its sanity. In the few short weeks of the war the entire nation had responded. Once people had come to terms with the fact that this was truly war and it was taking place, not on the foreign soils of Europe or the islands of Asia, but in the United States, the nation responded. It was no longer a question of assistance to other nations fighting tyranny and greed; it was a question of defending an attack against the United States.

Each evening the nation gathered around radios to hear the news reports. Panic changed to anger. The reports on the radio and the newsreels shown in the movie theaters described the destruction and despair suffered by those in occupied regions. All over the nation people lived in fear of "the big invasion" that could come at any time at any location. The government spoke of spies "living among us." Every citizen had to be constantly vigilant against potential saboteurs.

The news also reported the courageous response of the nation's military. In short order the peacetime forces that had numbered only a few hundred thousand had grown to nearly one and a half million. Every young man was encouraged to do his part for his nation and join Uncle Sam in the fight for freedom. Not only had young men signed up for military service, but all over the nation common citizens were also doing their part for the war. Several members of the Frankton household took note of this news.

Peter Frankton was always present for the evening news. The younger of the two Frankton boys, he asked a lot of questions as he tried to understand the events that were happening in his country. His life had always been a good one. The tall young man with light blonde hair and subtle freckles across his nose and cheeks had never known violence in his neighborhood. He didn't understand the war being waged by foreign fanatics in distant parts of the world, and now he didn't completely understand that it had been brought to the United States.

"Dad, how far is Washington from here?"

Earl sat in the armchair with his shoes off. He stared at the radio. Edith sat quietly on the couch, staring at the floor as she listed to the news. They had never spoken directly to their sons about what was taking place. Peter knew his older brother, Christopher, understood what was happening and wanted to do something about it. Peter wanted to understand too.

"It's a long way from here."

Peter lay on the floor. He rolled over to face his father. "How far is a long way?"

Earl was taken a little by surprise. He didn't know he was going to be quizzed by his ten-year-old son about the war. "Peter, where this is happening is three states away. The nearest fighting is over a thousand miles from here. The closest any soldier or sailor can get to us is about a thousand miles."

"But they're moving inland, aren't they? The military said they didn't know how big the first attack was or how many of them were already in the country. Couldn't they move in pretty fast?"

Earl turned his head toward Peter with raised eyebrows. Peter's blue eyes could always penetrate deep into his parents. They were a child's eyes, full of innocence, but they had started to reflect wisdom. Now Earl was even more surprised. His youngest son was definitely paying attention and beginning to understand what he was hearing on the radio. "Well, General Pershing, maybe you need to come out of retirement and let them know how to fight this thing."

"Well, there's Japs up and down the West Coast and Jerrys all in the Atlantic."

Earl suppressed a smile. Such odd things to hear from an elementary school kid. "Well, young man, I believe the U.S. Army and Navy can handle things despite what you may think. We are right in the middle of an enormous country. There are no enemy soldiers who can get to us. Any Japanese soldiers will be stopped long before they get here, and I don't think we'll see the *Bismarck* sailing up the Missouri River."

Peter crossed his arms and looked seriously at his father. "Dad, the Brits sank the *Bismarck* last year."

Earl crossed his arms and smirked in response. "I'm sorry. I wasn't aware."

He waved his hands to have Peter come to him. Peter climbed on his father's lap. "Peter, you shouldn't worry about it. The Japanese and the Nazis may think they can pick on us like they picked on the rest of the world, but they're not going to do it. We're completely safe and we don't have to do anything about it."

Peter looked up, still inquiring, still trying to understand. "What about the Masukos next door?"

Earl and Edith looked at one another. They were concerned about their son's questions. He understood more than they had realized, and they didn't want him to live in fear. Also, what kind of answer could they give since they too had concerns about their neighborhood? The Masuko family had moved into the house next door the previous summer. They kept themselves very isolated. The government had said the invasion had been planned for weeks or months, even while the Japanese government continued peace talks. Earl had wondered about his neighbor. He didn't know any more than the fact that the husband worked as a salesman at one of the meat packing plants and the wife stayed home. Their daughter was a year younger than Peter and spoke excellent English. They seemed like the perfect little family. Maybe they were just too perfect.

"Peter, our government is doing everything they need to do. Don't worry about the Masukos."

Peter sat straight up in his father's lap, "Maybe they have a short-wave radio and send signals to Tojo! They could be building a tunnel under their house to get troops from other places to here!"

Earl rolled his eyes. He and Edith knew Peter was just trying to act silly. Peter spoke faster now and exaggerated. "The old man could be building a bomb or have a machine-gun factory in his garage!" He fell onto the floor, holding his arms as if he were using a gun and starting spouting, "Rat-tat-tat-tat-tat-tat!"

The dog didn't like that and ran in from the kitchen. He barked and started pawing at the floor in front of Peter. "We're under attack. Send reinforcements!" He fell against the dog and acted as if he were fighting for his life. The brown Labrador, which always stayed near the family, obediently played and barked with joy.

The two wrestled on the floor for a few seconds until Edith said it was time for bed. Peter moaned and fell flat and the dog barked and sat up. Both knew the meaning of the phrase.

"Go on, and I'll be upstairs in a minute."

Peter begrudgingly headed toward the steps and patted his leg. "Come on, Jake." The dog ran to his side.

Earl stood up, ready to head to the kitchen. "No, no. The dog goes outside."

"Ah, but Jake needs to be inside to protect us from the damned Japs."

Edith jumped up. "Peter Conrad Frankton!"

Peter froze and said to himself, "Uh, oh, the dreaded, three names."

"You need to have your mouth washed out with soap," she said as she pointed at him.

Peter stood with a shy look. "But that's what they are, aren't they?"

Earl spoke up. "You just need to watch your mouth and put the dog out."

Peter turned to comply. Earl continued just so Edith could hear. "The dog can watch the damned Japs from out there."

Edith gave him a cold stare. "He learned that from you."

The family divided up for the evening. Peter took the dog to the back door and put him on the porch. He could sneak his old friend upstairs in a little bit. The young man was full of innocence. He learned a lot from watching and listening. He wanted to understand life. He wanted to figure out what war was all about.

Chapter 18

Things advanced rapidly in the nation. Even with enemy forces on each coast the nation's war machine rapidly developed at a powerful tempo. There was a certain energy, even in the little burg of Harbits, Wisconsin.

Gerald Flaghart worked hard, putting in more than forty-five hours per week and helping occasionally on Saturdays. Government people had been to the plant several times in the past month. The plant had received a contract to supply products specifically for the war effort. It would provide items for soldiers in the field and on ships and bases all around the country. Gerald considered himself one those who worked behind the uniform. When he wasn't working at Northern Valley Cheese he stayed busy around town with odd jobs.

It was Friday and it had been a long week. With storm clouds moving, in Gerald believed he wouldn't be able to get much work done that weekend. It would be the perfect night to watch the summertime storm while sitting on the front porch with a cold cola.

As he walked down the main street, Gerald could see how the town had changed. The usually quiet, narrow street was busier with walkers than it was with automobiles. Most of the stores displayed red, white, and blue banners and flags. In several of the yards along his route home trees had yellow ribbons tied around them. Before the war had started, people he knew lived in some of these houses. They included young men with whom he had gone to school but who were now active soldiers. Older men had also gone off to war. Women were starting to take jobs at the plant and one woman even volunteered with the fire brigade. Nobody thought very highly of her doing that job until she became one of the first to arrive with the truck at the burning building behind the hardware store. She dragged a three-inch hose to a hydrant more than a hundred feet away and manhandled—womanhandled—the hydrant open to get water flowing to the truck.

People in the town were doing things, different things, big things—whatever they could. Mrs. Brackage who lived farther down on Simmons Street, was a widow. She had lost one son in the Great War in Europe. Hers was the smallest house on the street. She had more flags and banners on her property than anyone in town. People started to notice that she kept hauling in canning jars of any size she could get her hands on. For weeks it went on until one day a three-axled, army truck, painted standard, OD green, pulled up in front of her house. Two soldiers in fatigues and an officer in uniform walked up to her front door. After they loaded it, which took about a half hour, the truck pulled away with dozens of boxes of jams, preserves, and sauces, which went to three, different, military camps around Lake Michigan. Mrs. Brackage's story appeared in the newspaper after a general sent her a letter of commendation.

Gerald made it home as the wind in the gray sky stirred through the trees. The Chevrolet wasn't in the drive and the front door was locked. His parents had gone somewhere. The sky was already darkening as he walked into the kitchen and turned on the light before heading to the sink to wash up. Two things sat on the table: a plate of food covered with a towel and a letter. Gerald looked down to see his name and a Washington, DC postmark. He realized what it was even before opening it.

The return address on the page inside was the Department of the Army and the letter began "Dear Mr. Gerald Flaghart." It wasn't written as a friendly letter. It wasn't a "you are cordially invited." It cited some government regulation and Congressional mandate number and stated, "You are hereby ordered to report for duty."

Gerald had little reaction. There was nothing to be said or done other than report for embarkation at the county court house by Wednesday of the following week just as the letter ordered. The inevitable had happened.

He decided he was going to get a cold cola out of the icebox and have it on the front porch along with his meal. He grabbed a plate, drink, napkin, and fork and headed to the front. The screen door made its typical groan, and he opened the door to a breeze. The first drops of the evening's shower had started to fall.

Chapter 19

From the first attacks on American soil it was said that the U.S. military would respond and root out all of the enemy attackers. Every threat to the United States would be met with fierce resistance. It was now the middle of summer. The Axis powers were quickly taking over Europe and Asia, and in the United States attacks seemed to come almost daily. The American way of life had changed drastically in just over a month, and Americans were guessing what the future of the nation would be.

Omaha reacted like so many other cities. Citizens adapted to rationing. People went to work as the country geared up for what was to become a mighty, defensive strategy for the great nation. Weeks after the first attacks young men still came from all over the city and surrounding areas in response to Uncle Sam's call to service. Every recruiting office in the city opened at 7:00 a.m. and closed at 7:00 p.m. Men formed into lines that sometimes stretched around a block. The offices stayed busy all day, six days a week, and many stayed open past closing time to process every last person. So many young and different personalities were soon going to morph into equal parts of a fighting machine. Old men were turned away because of their age, as were boys, trying to enlist too young. So many were prepared to fight and defend.

This was a different war than the last one. Most of the young men ready to enlist had not been alive when the doughboys traveled "over there" to fight the Hun. There was a feeling among the young men of duty, excitement, and fear. Someone was invading the nation. The enemy was killing America's men, women, and children. Fanatical soldiers and sailors filled with anger were destroying part of the country. They were coming, and the nation would not stand for that.

Nearly every day Christopher Frankton drove by, or just walked by, one of the recruiting stations. He saw the activity and the excitement on the faces of the young men. He saw many of his friends, neighbors, and young men just like him lining up to go off to fight. It weighed on him. He wondered what was holding him back from getting in line.

He knew the biggest reason. He was only sixteen years old and he needed a parent's permission to enter the service. He was ready, but were his parents?

On this day Christopher made the trip to the local recruiter's office and got in line. He didn't immediately recognize anyone. There were others in line who knew one another. Groups of young men came together and were ready to go through service together. Men joined out of duty, a desire for excitement, and even because they were dared into joining. That was one reason a tattoo parlor had opened next door to the recruiting office. The dares could continue there. It wasn't as obvious that an insurance company had opened nearby. It specialized in life and casualty insurance.

Some men stood in line as if they were standing at attention, staring coldly and only taking one step forward at a time. Some picked and laughed at each another. Every class was represented from young men in suits and shiny, leather shoes to young farm hands with dirt under their nails and clodhopper boots.

Christopher stood in line for nearly an hour before he got inside. The room was abuzz with noise and it was much cooler inside with fans keeping the air moving. Everything was nondescript. The office furniture was basic, and a sergeant with stripes and ribbons all over his uniform sat at the main desk. They spoke briefly and the sergeant gave him the necessary paperwork and instructions. Christopher walked out of the office. He felt a bit ashamed because he went out the front door and not on into the back room with the other men. He thought long and hard, not about whether to join the military, but about how to speak to his parents about it.

Chapter 20

Contact between U-boats and friendly ships or the fatherland, while in enemy territory, were few and far between. U-432 had been on patrol in the Atlantic for months, first observing enemy activity, then attacking enemy ships and installations at will. Captain Kurz had accepted his assignment earnestly and with great excitement. He drew blood at his first opportunity, and now he wanted more.

The ship had been in a state of constant alert since the third day of June when the entire German fleet in the western Atlantic had been given authorization to attack. Captain Kurz called for general quarters regularly. He wanted to be prepared to attack a target at a moment's notice. He would avoid enemy contact only to save his ship. He wanted enemy contact to be on his terms. He wanted his crew on their toes. Instead, they were on edge.

While in enemy waters the boat generally stayed submerged during the day and surfaced at night to circulate air and recharge its batteries by running on engine power. The daytime was now dangerous because the submarine was so close to the United States. The U.S. Navy and Navy Air Corps had reacted strongly to the direct attacks. They now had ships from Greenland to Brazil. Every kind of plane in the air service was on constant patrol. There were blimps along the coastline and larger airships at sea. The nation was on constant watch for enemy activity. Kurz didn't know who else was with him. He knew the German navy had advanced numerous submarines and several surface ships to harass the United States, but there were no specific assignments. He wouldn't know if he would meet another German sub until the two had passed one another.

This didn't matter. Kurz was ready to fight for führer and fatherland, even if it meant being entirely alone. He was confident in his ship and himself. He enjoyed being able to attack with complete stealth from underneath the waves. He was confident that he could put fear into the hearts of Americans.

He sipped coffee in his chair on the bridge. All was quiet after his lunch of canned meat, a vegetable, and bread. At this point in the trip there was nothing fresh anymore. Most food came out of cans and boxes. The captain always got the best and the lowest-ranking crew got leftovers, but the best wasn't much and the leftovers were barely better than garbage. On the bridge each man was quietly going about his duties when the sonar man blurted, "*Achtung*, Chief of the Boat." All heads turned as the lieutenant at the console concentrated on what was coming through his headphones. "Possible enemy contact, surface ship, bearing two zero zero."

Kurz gulped the hot coffee from his mug, which jolted his body. He stood and replied, "Direction of travel?"

The lieutenant hesitated a moment to confirm his information. Better to delay information to the captain than to give him the wrong information. "It's traveling toward us, closing at possibly fifteen knots."

"Chief, raise us to five meters. All stop. All crews to their duty stations."

Dutiful officer that he was, Commander Gruber snapped his

response. "Aye, Captain. Raise the boat to five meters. All stop. All crews to their duty stations."

Fatigue from the continual alerts began to wear on the crew. When the horns sounded, they didn't realize that this time they would actually be involved in an attack.

The ship was at its station in about two minutes. It usually responded more quickly, but fatigue was taking hold, and bodies and minds were becoming lethargic. Captain Kurz was at the periscope, watching for the ship on the horizon. He always wore a hat outside his cabin, and it would typically be turned backward on his head when he was at the periscope. As he scanned the horizon and focused, he caught sight of the ship about three miles away. He could clearly see that it was an American cruiser. Its relatively slow speed meant that it was just out on a patrol and not going anywhere in a hurry. Its slower speed also meant it would be easier to hit.

Kurz called out the estimated speed, and direction of travel and distance to the target. "Contact the torpedo room, have them load both tubes and be ready to fire."

By now everyone on board knew that this was an actual attack. The crew was excited. The ship began its slow maneuver to get the best possible shot while the torpedo tubes were readied.

The American cruiser, the USS *Austin*, was about ten years old and had no reliable radar or sonar. It was entirely unaware that a German U-boat was sitting just a couple thousand yards off its port bow. The twelve-hundred-man crew of the light cruiser was going about its daily business. The observers on the ship didn't see the top of the periscope sticking less than a foot out of the water.

It was stuffy in the conning tower of U-432. Captain Kurz was sweating, but it wasn't from heat. This, he thought, would be his best victory yet. With precisely placed shots, he could easily sink this ship. He continued giving commands for delicate adjustments to the sub and the surface ship came closer. He was lining up the sub so the American ship would sail right into the torpedoes without even knowing. Every command was repeated as the captain remained perfectly still, watching and waiting. "Prepare to fire." The entire ship was silent. Kurz could hear his heartbeat. He suppressed his breathing to stay focused through the scope. He waited until just the right moment. "Fire, fire!"

The boat seemed to lurch in response to the several hundred pounds of explosives that were hurled at the target. Kurz watched intensely for the hits. His stomach tightened in anticipation of the nearby explosion. A small smile, not visible to anyone else on the bridge, appeared on his face

On the *Austin* a petty officer lookout on the port side near the bridge saw the two, faint, ominous trails of the torpedoes headed directly for the ship. They were only some eighty yards away when he spotted them. He didn't bother picking up the telephone headset; he simply turned and began yelling and waving his arms. No one on the bridge failed to understand what the petty officer was trying to communicate. Everyone knew it was danger. The officer at the ship's wheel began to turn to starboard. He was only able to make one turn of the wheel when the first torpedo found its mark. The *Austin* reeled in response to the explosion at its water line. The ship hadn't yet stabilized from the first shot when the second one hit. The ship still traveled forward, which caused the second torpedo, just several feet behind the first, to hit nearly the same spot. The two hits together tore a hole in the hull large enough to drive a Jeep through.

Everyone on U-432 heard both hits and broke out in cheers. Captain Kurz kept his eyes on his prey. He could tell by the explosion's size and location that the American ship would go down. He adjusted his course to move beside the already listing cruiser and the submarine began to move forward at five knots.

The American ship was taking on water at an astonishing rate. There was nothing to do but abandon ship. About two hundred of the crew near the explosion were killed instantly. Some six hundred more would not be able to make it out in time. Around four hundred men scrambled to the deck, most still in shock, not really knowing what had happened. The men were in various conditions: some were wounded, most missed shirts or shoes, and hardly any had life preservers. At least two, large, inflatable rafts were thrown overboard in the evacuation. Men jumped into the water from all over the ship, swimming away as fast as they could and knowing more men would be coming into the water behind them.

On the bridge the captain had no orders to give. He watched as men jumped. Some were thrown into the water. The ship quickly rolled over to the port side. As it did, men on the deck lost their balance and began to slide into the water.

In the conning tower of U-432 Captain Kurz ordered the periscope down and the ship to surface. He wanted to crawl out of his sub and see his victory first hand.

On the bridge of the *Austin*, the captain struggled to keep upright as the ship began to roll over. The ship continued to tip over until the superstructure fell into the water and the captain was thrown against the now horizontal wall. He was able to stand on the wall as if he were standing on the floor, but only for a minute. Water rushed in and pinned him against the ceiling. He only had seconds to think about the moment. He had been sunk by a German submarine, unable to fire a shot in defense of his ship or nation. Hundreds of American lives, the lives of good young men, would be taken to the bottom of the Atlantic. As he floated toward the corner of the room he closed his eyes and accepted his fate.

The *Austin* was afloat on its side for what seemed like a minute. Men in the water struggled to find one another and safety. Injured young men were pushed into a circle for safety. Others retrieved the large rafts and whatever they could that floated.

The ship sank under the waves, stern first. It rolled over entirely so that most of the hull was out of the water and hardly any of the deck was visible. Men moved away from what remained of the ship, which sank farther below the water, and as it did, it straightened. About ten minutes after being hit by the two German torpedoes, the ship sank below the surface of the ocean some fifty miles due east of Charleston, never to be seen again.

The German submarine splashed to the surface a hundred yards from where the ship had plunged. Several men stormed out of the two hatches on each side of the conning tower. Some of them were armed with machine guns. The men in the water knew the U-boat was there, but could do nothing. The small, enemy ship couldn't rescue the several hundred men in the water. The German sub hadn't enough life rafts and even if it had, the crew would not have offered them. Some of the *Austin*'s crew believed their injured might be taken prisoner. They thought they would have to wait for another American ship to arrive.

On top of the conning tower Captain Kurz stood beside Commander Gruber, surveying the damage. Men in the water struggled to help others and stay afloat. Debris floated on the ocean's surface and water still bubbled from the sinking cruiser. Kurz looked over at Gruber and gave the unimaginable order: "Shoot them."

Although Gruber was a navy veteran, his jaw dropped. The expression on Gruber's face was response enough.

Kurz repeated the order. "Shoot them. We are facing the enemy. Use the shoulder arms and the deck gun and shoot them."

Gruber had nothing to say. If he had spoken back to the captain of a submarine involved in military action, he would have been charged with treason. He looked down the ladder to the officer below and relayed the order. Within seconds ammunition was hauled up and fed to the guns. An officer yelled at the men on the front and back of the surfaced sub to open fire. Thousands of rounds of ammunition started coming from half a dozen German submachine guns. The deck gun, a twin, twenty-millimeter cannon, designed for the aircraft of the Luftwaffe, began firing indiscriminately into the water at a rate of over eight hundred rounds per minute. Those who had survived the sinking were torn apart by the guns of the submariners. There was nothing anyone could do to survive in the water. Some tried to dive under, but they were either hit underneath the water, or they were shot when they came back up to breathe. Some swam away, but they were shot when the German sailors began fanning out with their fire. Hundreds of American sailors had survived the sinking and had been bobbing in the ocean, and hundreds were now dying, screaming in pain, fear, and anger.

Kurz looked on, unwilling to stop until there was no more movement in the water. The guns slowed. The sailors on the deck reloaded but were ready to stop. They heard the same sounds their captain did. They watched the ocean turn red. They were sailors just like those in the water who had survived their ship being sunk beneath them and had the right to live. Some men looked up at the captain on top of the tower. His face was blank and he stood motionless, making a sharp contrast to the suffering in the water.

Commander Gruber turned away. In doing so, he saw the fast approaching ship. "Captain, enemy ship approaching from the west! Looks like a destroyer, closing fast!"

Kurz looked over his shoulder indifferently. "It looks to be five miles away."

"Sir, they can easily fire on us at that distance."

"They wouldn't dare fire on us for fear of hitting their men."

Gruber looked back at the wreck. There was very little movement in the water. Gruber's jaw was clinched as he forced the words out. "Captain Kurz, may I suggest we submerge immediately so as to leave the area and avoid what will surely be a prolonged and vicious attack from an American destroyer."

Kurz looked at Gruber indifferently. "Clear the deck and submerge."

"Aye, Captain." Gruber slid down the ladder giving the cease fire order as he descended. The last shots sounded and men secured the guns and scurried from the deck. The hatches slammed shut behind the last seaman and the horns below deck sounded the dive order.

Kurz slowly stepped down the ladder and an awaiting sailor dogged the hatch closed behind him. The conning tower was alive with activity. The men on the bridge knew an enemy ship was approaching. They didn't want to face a destroyer, and they didn't want to face the same fate as the Americans from the USS *Austin*.

Kurz gave his orders as to depth, speed, and direction. He was pleased with the day. He thought of the stories he had heard of the American Wild West when gunfighters would carve a notch in the grip of their pistol when they killed someone. Kurz thought of the sinking of the American cruiser as just a notch. He wanted more.

U-432 would circle around to the south and travel at top speed to elude its pursuer. Kurz would see another day to fight. His next kill would be bigger. He needed more to satisfy his insatiable appetite.

Chapter 21

Christopher had been waiting for some time to find the right moment. He looked at the bottom of the front page of that day's newspaper and saw the headline about military recruiting in Omaha. The article pointed out that in the first month since the war had begun in the United States, the city of Omaha had provided three thousand men for service. This number reflected the number of volunteers who had signed up. Several thousand more had been drafted during the first six months of 1942. He hoped that his father had seen that and would comment on it.

The evening at home had gone by routinely. Earl came home from work and dinner was on the table. Everyone ate and Peter went outside along with the dog to enjoy the remainder of the day until he was called inside. Christopher would normally have met friends, but most of his friends either had jobs or had gone into military service. Christopher hadn't known how to act with so many changes taking place. All over the nation people reacted to the war. Men fought and died in defense of the nation. Military and civilians alike turned the coastlines into fortresses. People went to work to make the things needed for war, and they adapted to rationing for the war effort. Even those who seemed not to be able to do anything for defense bought war bonds. Everybody was doing something, and in this small part of the world, in the Frankton household on McCabe Avenue, life continued as usual. Earl arrived home, took off his shoes, loosened his tie and sat down in the armchair to read the evening news.

Christopher sat quietly at the dinning table, not even looking at his father. He listened until he heard every page of the newspaper folded up. Then he stood and walked to his father.

"Did you see the front page?"

His father stood up, ready to walk to the kitchen. "Yes, I read every article that looked important."

"The recruiting stations of Omaha have sent probably five thousand men into service this year."

Earl's only movement was to slightly raise one eyebrow. "Is that correct?"

"Yes, that's correct." Christopher had promised himself that he was going to become a man this summer. He had been a child answering to his father his entire life. Now he was going to put his childhood to rest, and he was prepared for his father, and war. He raised his chin and said, "I'm prepared to be number five thousand and one."

Earl was not entirely surprised. He knew so many young men had blindly walked into service for the government with no experience in the ways of the world. He pitied them. He had no desire to engage his son in such an inane conversation. "I believe they only take grown men into the service."

His tone cut Christopher who didn't lose his temper and was ready for the insulting comments. "I consider myself a man, and my concern is what counts."

"If you're a man, why aren't you wearing a uniform?"

"I believe you know why." It was turning into a stare-down. "I have the paperwork filled out and ready to be signed."

Earl's response was sarcastic. "Well, good for you."

Christopher continued, "I can be processed tomorrow and on a bus the following day, headed to basic training." His tone was even and his eyes direct. "I'm ready."

Earl smirked and shook his head. "Son, your intentions are well placed, but your intelligence is well off the mark." He turned again toward the kitchen.

"I don't see it that way. Tell me one good reason why I shouldn't and I'll stay here."

"You're too young! You would never survive as a soldier. You just couldn't do it. You've had a good and simple life here, and you couldn't do the job." Earl's voice became louder. "I'm not going to approve my son for service so he can be sent somewhere to die on a battlefield."

Both stopped to take a breath. Christopher looked surprised. It seemed his own father didn't think very much of him.

"What your part needs to be is to finish school and find a decent job. That's all you need to do. I'm sorry. You're not a soldier."

Christopher was growing up. His first thought was to scream. Sensibility took over. "Do you know how many guys are going to be in my junior class this year? Not many because they're all doing their part. Guys who are smaller than me, dumber than me—they're all doing something. They're working and fighting." He held up the papers. "This is for me. This is what I need to do."

They continued staring at one another. Christopher spoke again. "You said I'm not a soldier. You're right, I'm not. When I join the army, they'll make me a soldier then."

Earl looked away. "You may become a soldier one day, but it won't be with my approval." He walked to the kitchen. Christopher stood in the same spot for a minute, then retired from the fight and walked upstairs.

In the kitchen Earl picked up the coffee pot from the stove and Edith handed him a cup. He poured and both sat down at the table. All of a sudden through the side door came a bounding young kid and his dog. Both headed straight to Earl as he protected his coffee. Peter jumped into his father's lap and Jake followed his master's lead and lifted his paws against Earl's legs.

"Hey, get off of me you dumb mutt!"

The dog put all four feet on the floor and just kept wagging his tail. The friendly animal had never met someone it didn't like.

Peter looked up at his father disapprovingly. "Who are you calling a dumb mutt?"

His mother just laughed under her breath.

"Huh? The dog. The dog is a dumb mutt."

Peter folded his arms in front of him and raised his eyebrows. "My dog is neither dumb nor a mutt. He's smarter than some people."

His mother laughed out loud.

"Pardon me. Well, you and Jake Thomas Edison can run along now." Peter jumped down and headed for the steps and Jake dutifully followed.

Peter's mother yelled, "And Jake needs to go out tonight! No sneaking him under your bed."

Peter and Jake moaned together.

Edith and Earl sat, relaxed, at the table.

"Did you hear what Christopher was talking to me about?"

She nodded her head. "I heard most of it."

"Can you believe that he's considering such a block-headed thing?"

She hesitated and then shrugged her shoulders.

"I don't know what notions he has. He says this is what he needs to do"

Edith stared in front of her. "The entire nation has been called on to do its part. This may be his."

Earl looked at her with surprise. "Did you know about this?"

"No."

"Are you saying you approve of this? Do you want him to go to war? You know your son. He could never make it."

"I don't necessarily approve of him going off to fight, but this is what he feels he needs to do. Do you know your son?"

"He answered for himself when he said so many thousand men from Omaha have already gone into service. It was silly for him to say he would be one more. He would just be one individual among thousands."

Edith continued staring in front of her. "All of those thousands are made up of just individuals."

Earl put his coffee cup down rather hard on the table.

Edith continued, "I've thought about my part also."

"What are you saying?"

Edith looked at Earl. "The old allied processing plant on Bellevue Boulevard is opening back up as a meat cannery. They're going to hire a few hundred people to work from the office all the way to the loading dock."

Earl sat with a confused expression on his face.

"And I'm thinking about applying."

"You want to go to work in a cannery? What? You're ready to punch a typewriter all day long? No, wait. You're going to work on the loading dock using hand trucks all day long, packing cases and pallets of canned goods into trucks and boxcars. Are you considering that?"

Edith pushed her chair back and stood. "Yes."

"What is wrong with this family? People think they have some type of obligation to run off and become some government conscript. I can somewhat understand the young, wild-eyed urge our son has to join the army, but what notion have you gotten to go to work in some plant? This is not our war. This is something happening on the coasts, hundreds of miles away."

She was still standing, looking down at her husband. "Some of the canned goods will be going to soldiers in the field, and some of it will be going to the war-torn areas of the country. Some of the goods that I help produce may find their way to Poplar Grove, Oregon."

Earl still wore a confused expression on his face. "What is in Poplar Grove, Oregon?"

"I'm not sure." Edith turned away and walked toward the stove. "That was one of the first places attacked by the Japanese army. Soldiers and tanks tore up the town and I don't know what is left or who is left because I haven't heard anything about it, and I haven't heard anything from my cousin Gladys."

Earl stopped, paused and said, "Isn't she your second cousin once removed you haven't seen in years?"

Edith turned back. "She is a relative I grew up with. She is an American just like us." She turned toward the stove, staring at the coffee pot, which was still steaming. "But she's not like us because she faced the Japanese army a few weeks ago, and we sit here in our kitchen, drinking coffee."

Earl said nothing more. He left his coffee cup on the table and walked outside.

At the top of the stairs Jake was lying quietly beside his best friend, Peter, who was sitting on the top step. Peter scratched behind the dog's ear and Jake began wagging his tail in response. Peter's world had changed in the previous few weeks. He had led a simple, happy life until that day and then things changed. He still didn't fully understand what was going on, but he knew what a soldier did. He had learned his brother wanted to be one. Soldiers could get killed, but they had a mighty job.

Every day after school and during the summer his mother was there. She could give him everything he needed in life. Now she wanted to go to work. He thought that maybe he could start to do for himself if she had to start helping other people.

His father had been the leader. He worked, he decided things, and he was the person Peter looked to for the answers to big questions. Now, his father didn't seem to be able to do anything.

"Come on, Jake. Time to get you under the bed. No damned Japs are going to get in tonight."

Chapter 22

Gerald was exactly on time at the courthouse. Cars were lined up and down the street, and several dozen groups of people stood near the front steps and on the lawn. Each group included someone with a suitcase. There was very little to be said when his parents dropped him off. His mother hugged him and told him to write often. Gerald and his father looked one another in the eyes, and John simply nodded his head. The bus loaded and left within minutes.

By noon of the first day, along with a few hundred other young men, he was loaded onto a Chicago, Milwaukee, St. Paul & Pacific Railroad train. Each man was handed a bagged lunch as he boarded. The men had made their way to Chicago by the evening and were offloaded from the first train straight onto a second. The same thing happened in that they were handed their dinner in a bag— no dining cars with crystal and fancy tablecloths on these trains. They were an amalgam of modern, steel Pullmans and old, wooden coaches from different railroads. Everyone was marched in line and directed onto the first car they came to until it was full. The first night was on the train.

Gerald, like many of the other men, had never been more than twenty miles from home. He happened to get a window seat, and he tried to enjoy the trip as best he could. As anxious as he was, he enjoyed the rocking of the cars and the sound. He never bothered talking to anyone in the loud group. He just sat back, looking out the window, watching the countryside go by and looking at all the freight trains waiting on sidings as the troop train passed. He fell into a serene sleep as the night approached from behind.

The next morning the train stopped at a small shack beside the track just before sun-up. Carrying their worldly possessions, the men were lined up in rows and marched several miles to Camp Hamilton, a brand new military post, named for some barely known, dead general.

When they got to the temporary, new home, Gerald finally found out he had arrived in southeastern Wyoming on the western edge of the Great Plains. This was still the middle of America and the entire Rocky Mountains were between them and the enemy. It was still difficult for him to believe that enemy forces were just a few hundred miles away and making their way east.

Camp Hamilton was one of many thrown together by the U.S. Army Corps of Engineers. The barracks were filled with bunk beds and smelled of freshly cut wood. The blankets smelled of mothballs, and the faces of the men were also new. Gerald looked over the group of about forty men and tried to decide which men he was with. Their faces showed excitement, fear, anticipation, and much more.

The men were met on their arrival at the barracks by an older man in uniform with stripes on each sleeve. He had a coarse face with dark eyes and was strangely shaped. His face was as square as a box, and his shoulders met his arms at a ninety-degree angle. He introduced himself as Master Sergeant Ashaul. They were to muster in front of the barracks in five minutes. They would march to the mess tent for breakfast before appearing before the colonel and being sworn into the United States Army.

The men slowly reacted to the sergeant's direction. Gerald looked out the window. There were dozens of buildings and several tents in a small cluster in the middle of nowhere. There were mountains to the west and nothing but flatness to the east. He thought that there was no leaving. He would simply have to find a way to survive, no matter what that brought.

Chapter 23

In the short time the war had raged in the United States, the country seemed to have got a hold on its panic, although fear was still present. The nation seemed to have been attacked everywhere, and people were not sure who to trust or where the war would move next. There were rumors that a million-man invasion by the Japanese would come through California and extend all the way to the Mississippi River. News programs discussed frightening German military technology. Supposedly Germany had planes that could fly all the way to the United States and small ships that could penetrate harbors and rivers, which could be the perfect attack on the United States. The Japanese army would move east to the Mississippi River and the German navy and air force would sail and fly west to the Mississippi. The entire nation could be overrun within a week. That was the word from the perpetuators of doom and gloom.

Peter heard this and was scared. He was old enough to understand the news and the danger. His father had said they were safe in the middle of the United States. Now experts were saying that no place in the country was safe.

Each mention of attack and destruction was countered by the president and other government leaders who spoke of strength and victory. The U. S. military had been built up in every region and was prepared for any possibility. The nation's strength continued to grow and weapons of defense were being built at an unparalleled rate. The national government was prepared for any attacks and local governments took care of their citizens. Because this was the first attack on American soil since the previous century, state and city leaders in many areas advocated the use of local militias. Just as the nation had gained its independence through local men who had volunteered for service, local communities needed to be prepared to defend themselves in the same way. Some city leaders spoke of establishing minuteman forces of those considered too old for regular service or classed as 4F. These men could train locally and be prepared to respond at a minute's notice to whatever might be necessary in the city.

Peter was excited about the local activities. He developed the romantic idea that he could become a drummer boy or bugler for the home guard. He didn't know how to play either instrument, but it was a nice thought. He wasn't sure what was involved, but he wanted to get a uniform and be a part of what was happening.

He knew that his brother and mother were trying to get involved. As a ten-year-old, Peter lived out his summer days pretty much as he always had. He played all over the neighborhood with his friends and went to the drugstore for candy or soda or to the movies when he got enough money. The only thing that was different about his ventures downtown was the city streets seemed to be more active. The shelves at the drugstore were not as full; the streets didn't have as many young men; and the movie theaters showed a lot of newsreels about fighting. They weren't like real movies; they weren't as much fun to watch. In town he occasionally saw strange cars that had no tops and were called Jeeps. He knew that they were special cars for soldiers and they had a dull paint on them. He also saw regular cars that were painted in the same dark green with a white star on the door. Officers drove them.

Peter asked his father if he was going to do something. His father looked at him angrily and said he had an important job at the bank.

The reactions to the continuing war seemed to grow each day. The Frankton family, like every other family in the United States, dealt with the effects of the war. Other countries had survived thus far with the supplies sent by the United States. Suddenly these supplies grew short. Rationing was a brand new word in the United States. A family could no longer go down to their local grocer and get exactly what they wanted. The government instituted rationing soon after the outbreak of the war, first to save on materials immediately needed for the war effort, and second to control the materials essential for a strong, civilian economy. Now families had to apply to a local control board and obtain coupon books. Rationed materials could only be bought with cash and coupons within a certain time period.

One thing that Peter didn't like at all was having to eat cereal without much sugar on it. Christopher explained to him that it was for the war.

Peter quizzed his older brother. "Why do soldiers need so much sugar? Do they eat that many cornflakes?"

"The soldiers don't use sugar like that. Sugar is needed to make molasses. Molasses is used to make industrial alcohol. Industrial alcohol is what's used to make nitroglycerin. That's what makes gunpowder, dynamite, and bombs." Peter stared up at his brother with a look of excitement. The young impressionable boy's older brother was the source for a lot of information. Even with several years' difference between them, they were close and cared very much for each other.

Peter continued to eat his plain cornflakes. He had asked his father about things and never received an answer—at least one he believed in. He stared down at his bowl and popped out with the question. "Chris, do you want to go off to war?"

Christopher hadn't realized that his little brother knew anything about enlisting. He paused a minute, not sure of what answer to give. "Pete . . . I can't tell you yes or no to that." Christopher had thought about it. Fighting was a scary thing, but he wanted to go.

"Why not?" Peter looked up with his freckled innocent face. "Is it a secret?"

"No. I just don't have a good answer."

"Is that why Dad won't let you go?"

Christopher wondered if this were something that his father had put Peter up to. No, he thought. He wouldn't put Peter up to anything. It was just between the two oldest men and Peter wouldn't understand at all. I have an answer, he thought. Dad just doesn't understand the reason I don't want to go to war. I need to go to war. He looked straight at his brother, something he found difficult to do with his father. "I have to go to war. Nobody is making me. Nobody is making most of the guys I've seen at the recruiting station. The guys are going because we're at war. The entire world is fighting and now its here. I have to do it because . . ." Christopher still didn't have the exact words.

Peter munched away as his cornflakes became soggier. "Dad said there's a lot of people doing it. Why do you need to go?"

Christopher realized his little brother was concerned for him. The questions that the young man asked were exactly what their father had been asking, but Peter had come up with them on his own.

They were questions that Christopher had already passed by in his own mind without stopping to think. He was already like a soldier. He was ready to do what needed to be done without question. He stared at his younger brother and smiled a little.

"Pete,"—the two used their nicknames with one another even though their parents had always called them by their proper names—"if everybody asked themselves, why me? there would be no one to do it."

"Dad says the fight isn't even here. He told me it was hundreds of miles from here."

"It still involves us, the United States." Christopher squinted. "You know how you got sent home from school last fall because of the fight you got into? Mom and Dad yelled at you and said you shouldn't hit anybody."

"Yes. I didn't mind. Jimmy Swarthout was being a horses butt."

Christopher crossed his arms as he rushed to make his point. "What was he doing?"

"He wouldn't leave Jennie Shepard alone. He was bothering her during class, in lunch, outside. He was just being a horse's ass."

"So, you didn't fight for yourself, you were fighting to help Jennie?"

Peter looked up from his bowl for the first time. He didn't say anything, but his expression made it clear he understood. He looked down again, finished the rest of his soggy flakes and headed toward the sink with the bowl and spoon. "Well, if you're going to fight about something, get it over with so I can get some sugar for my cereal."

Even with rationing and recycling, it was going to take a lot of effort to meet the war production of the Axis. Germany and Japan had been building their military for years. The United States had only been in production for a few weeks.

On the West Coast, the military and government law-enforcement officials were beginning to round up Japanese families. It wasn't called "rounding up" in the news; it was called "confinement of enemy aliens." The Federal Bureau of Investigation was looking into the personal lives of Japanese families living in the United States. It was thought that they might be providing information, or physical or financial support to the enemy troops. Many newly arrived immigrants from Japan were removed from their homes and relocated to secure internment camps at inland locations. The fear of Japanese residents across the country gripped the Frankton family too. They couldn't help but think about their neighbors. The Masuko family kept themselves to themselves. Not much was known about them.

In response to the threat of attack all over the nation, civil defense was set up by authority of the federal government at the local level. Boards were established at the city level and followed guidelines set up by the War Department. Their jurisdiction included everything from the construction of bomb shelters to the inspection of first-aid kits for families. Volunteers were assigned to certain areas of a city, even single blocks. They were made up of men and women of all kinds from those who did nothing more than acknowledge that they were government-designated officials to overzealous, crazy men who attempted to arrest people. The newspaper published an unconfirmed report of a public hanging that took place near Santa Fe because a man smoked a cigarette on a sidewalk during a blackout drill.

The block captain responsible for McCabe Avenue in Omaha was somewhere between inept and mad. Jacob Cranford was known to everyone on his streets as Captain Jake. There were war stories told about him, but he himself never told these stories to anyone. No one was sure what war he had served in. He was too old to have served in the Great War, and probably hadn't been born until after the Civil War. The stories were about fighting Indians and the charge up San Juan Hill, but no one really knew. Captain Jake acted like an officer in the U.S. Army. He would always wear tall, brown, leather boots and a brown, felt, campaign-style hat with a chinstrap and small, gold tassels on the brim. He had some type of metal, civil defense pin on the front of the hat for anyone who questioned his authority. That just made him funny looking, but the scary part was that he carried a revolver in a brown, leather holster on one hip and a bayonet in a scabbard on the other. He took his job seriously, and when the orders for some type of drill came out, he snapped to duty. He was quick with the whistle he wore around his neck and quick with a stiff word when someone spoke rudely to him.

The citizens of Omaha had been informed by the newspaper and radio for weeks about what was to take place during a black-out drill. With the fear of long-distance bombers from Germany or fighters from Japanese aircraft carriers attacking the United States, the nation was ready to make itself invisible. Some of the stores sold thick, dark, blanket-like material designed to cover windows. Every light in the city had to be extinguished or covered, and that was one of the block captains' duties. They had the power to turn off street-lights, and they made sure windows were covered so no light was visible. Everyone knew that when the blackout drill started, Captain Jake would soon come down the street, checking everything.

Young Peter Frankton didn't really know or care about lights being visible to high-flying airplanes. On the evening of one black-out drill, Captain Jake was making his way down the street and his whistle could be heard from a block away. Peter headed inside for lights out. It was a fun experience for him. He would help hang the blackout curtains in the living room and make sure everything was dark. He thought it was like making his house into a fortress against enemy attack. The reward was popcorn and a game on the parlor floor. The whole family would come together in the parlor because once in, no one could go out, and because there were only so many curtains that could be hung, they were confined to the one room. The enjoyment of family overcame any concern of war for the youngest of the family.

It didn't take Peter but once to realize that if his dog came inside at lights out, he was in for the night. The two could sneak upstairs at bedtime and crawl under the bed. Peter would put the blankets all around his bed to cover the light from his flashlight. There the two had their private fort. Life was simple for a boy and his dog in the middle of America while the world remained a complicated place.

Chapter 24

Attacks seemed to be taking place all over the nation. Many of the reported attacks were rumor and speculation, but still caused fear. Soldiers had been sent to all parts of the nation in response to attacks, and sightings and reports of suspicious people and actions. The entire nation was on edge. Sailors were assembled on ships and sent to sea to guard each coast and the Gulf of Mexico. The navy's orders were simple: shoot first and ask questions later.

Lieutenant Commander Ralph Stollings was the most unlikely of skippers. He was a bit too young to remember the Great War, but he had read much about it during school. He was very much a military historian. The farm boy from Iowa had been nowhere near the ocean for most of his life, but he knew he was a seaman at heart. After high school he didn't have the ability to go to the Naval Academy. After a year and a half at the University of Nebraska he knew he wouldn't go far. He joined the navy in 1933, the same year Adolf Hitler gained power.

By the summer of 1939, Stollings had been in the navy for six years. He was trying to decide whether to stay in or head home. He was a ranking, noncommissioned officer and hadn't had a spectacular career. With the outbreak of war in Europe, Stollings decided he was staying in the navy, and he was determined to have his own boat. When he finally made officer, he worked hard. War changed the young man. By the spring of 1942 he was a lieutenant commander, assigned to the light cruiser *Vicksburg*. When his ship was assigned to leave its homeport at San Diego, the commander, Anthony Scarberry, came down with appendicitis. Scarberry and the port commander were both mad. Stollings was excited and scared.

The USS *Vicksburg* had been at sea for three days, headed north. It was to take a coordinate grid of approximately five thousand square miles in an area south of San Francisco. The *Vicksburg*, along with one destroyer and possibly a battleship were to maintain vigilance in that zone. Stollings wasn't a war-hardened sailor, but he now had control of some twenty-five thousand tons of warship, eight hundred sailors, and tens of thousands of tons of firepower. He had never faced an enemy before, but now he had the responsibility of protecting his homeland and confronting with courage any enemy who found him. He hoped he was ready.

The *Vicksburg*'s mission had gone quietly thus far. They constantly received information about enemy activity on both coasts and on the continent. The command staff was scared that the Japanese troops still to be found up and down the West Coast were supported from the sea, or were only the first of a larger invasion force. U.S. Navy ships were strung from the Bering Sea to the Panama Canal. No one knew much about the Japanese military. How would it attack? Soldiers had apparently not landed in huge forces—nothing that could cause significant damage to the mainland United States. Were they going to come back? How and where and when? Would their navy come in an overwhelming force, or try to sneak through one at a time?

The only other ship that Lt. Com. Stollings was aware of in his assigned area was the Destroyer USS *Simpson*, commanded by

Lt. Commander Andrew J. Price. They stayed in contact with one another and made a zigzag pattern up and down their area, waiting for whatever might come along.

That third day at sea was the day Commander Stollings, along with his ship, would be tested. It was sunny with cumulus clouds. The puffy, small clouds made spots of shadow on the ocean, which played tricks on the eyes as the ship moved in and out of them. Everyone had been on their toes since leaving port. The ocean could be calming, but that ever-expanding body of water could also make a person feel very small and scared.

When the lookout saw a contact due west, he didn't at first know how to react. This was Seaman Second Class Steven Young's first contact with the enemy. He recognized the mast of a naval vessel and believed there wasn't another U.S. ship within a hundred miles. Seaman Young fought for a moment to get his breath and reached for the radio handset at his station. He picked up the receiver and it immediately rang to the bridge. Young turned his face to the wind to catch another breath as the call was answered: "Bridge."

His lungs were full of air, and he had to push it out. He spoke slowly, and with belabored force, "Contact, five o'clock." The line clicked dead. The staccato blasts of the horns sounded from stem to stern and were enough to make anyone's blood run cold. Boots stomped and slid across floors all over the ship as sailors scrambled to their battle stations. There was no chaos in the activity of hundreds of men moving around every part of the ship. They were like ants. At first glance they appeared to be doing nothing but running around, but a closer inspection revealed that each one was precisely doing his job.

Lt. Com. Stollings, still buttoning his shirt, walked onto the bridge in less than ten seconds. The entire ship was at battle stations in less than two minutes. The CAC center set the range and bearing on the target, a Japanese heavy cruiser, steaming forward from a distance of eighteen miles. The ship turned slightly away from the approaching Japanese ship so that it could use all of its nine, big guns. Against the larger ship, they were going to need everything they had. The radio transmitted news of the contact. Any ship in the area would respond, but Stollings knew this was going to be a ship-to-ship battle for a while. Just as in a duel, quickness and accuracy was more important than the caliber of the gun. His ship would be ready for the good fight, and fate would decide life and death.

As the *Vicksburg* directed its first shots, a second target came into view: a Japanese destroyer, tucked in directly behind the first ship. Stollings knew that his ship could handle a destroyer by itself, but now he was definitely outgunned. He knew the ships would separate and attack him from two sides. Yet, in so many battles he had read about as a child, commanders had been outnumbered and outgunned and still showed their ability. He was ready for whatever he would meet.

The *Vicksburg*'s batteries fired their first salvo down the line, aiming for the lead ship. The Japanese cruiser appeared to have been beaten with the first shots. The shells followed their path to the target, a heavy cruiser of the Imperial Japanese Navy. The destroyer would be the second concern. Time seemed to pass slowly as Commander Stollings watched through his binoculars. The two-thousand-pound shells began falling around the enemy ship, and one appeared to have hit the tip of the bow, causing a shudder on the decks.

There was activity in every part of the *Vicksburg*. The crew was prepared for this day, the first day they had faced their enemy, and they were not only ready to prove to the navy and nation, but prove to themselves that they could fight and survive. During the fight no one had time to think of his mortality. That was something to think about in the lonely times below deck. Now was the time to do one's job and think later.

The Japanese cruiser gave a hard turn to starboard, and oddly enough, the destroyer followed. The ships attempted to position themselves just as navies had since the first gun ships had been built centuries before. They wanted to face their target on one side so that the ship could fire all of its guns at its target. Each crew would work to fire more shells more accurately at the other ship. Each ship would try to outmaneuver the other. It would become a battle of attrition.

The *Vicksburg* fired a second round at the cruiser. As the shells went on their way, Stollings saw two things through his binoculars that frightened him: the first rounds fired from the Japanese cruiser, and another Japanese ship.

As the Japanese cruiser and destroyer moved parallel to the *Vicksburg*, the crew could see a second heavy cruiser continuing straight ahead. It was going to sail behind the *Vicksburg* and circle around. Stollings couldn't outmaneuver or outgun three ships of the Japanese navy. The American forces had deployed all along the Pacific, not sure when, where, or if the Japanese would attack with their navy. The Pacific Fleet was stretched thin to cover the area. The navy realized that if a lone ship came into contact with several Japanese ships, it could turn into a suicide mission. Stollings realized that just might be the case. His ship called out information to anyone in the Pacific Fleet who might be listening. He might only slow down this Japanese mission, but he would do his job to the end. Other ships in the U.S. fleet might respond too late to save the

Vicksburg, but they would never stop until the Japanese navy was defeated.

The crew of the *Vicksburg* continued firing away and began making contact with the lead Japanese ship. The turrets had to concentrate on three targets now. Stollings knew the plotters and gunners would give it their best. The ship fired rounds and adjusted its course. It would take a zigzag route through the dark waters of the North Pacific, firing and continuing to move until the battle was decided definitively. Stollings would direct as he was trained and each man would do his duty. The ships were pounding on one another like boxers in the ring. The *Vicksburg* was taking rounds from two directions now, with the first cruiser and destroyer on their starboard side, and the second cruiser moving around the stern. The commander knew that surrender was not an option. He would never lower the Stars and Stripes to hoist a white flag. He knew the Japanese navy would never accept a flag of surrender. The *Vicksburg* would continue the fight until it was no longer able.

The crew felt very alone in the big ocean as the enemy surrounded them. The Japanese rounds were finding their mark even with the ship's evasive action, and the rounds were beginning to take their toll. Men on the *Vicksburg* were hurt and dying and chunks of the ship were being blown away. Stollings decided his next move. He was looking through his binoculars at the lead Japanese ship when he saw it take a round that hadn't come from his ship. A salvo of large shells lit up the front of the Japanese cruiser. He directed his binoculars south and was able to spot the smoke from ten miles away. It was from an American battleship. He walked across the bridge to a large, fixed scope and pushed a lieutenant out of the way. He moved it and focused on the approaching battleship. He could see by looking at the water across its bow that it was cutting a wake at more than twenty knots. He could just make out the number on its starboard side: fifty-five. Commissioned and first put to sea just two months before, the battleship *North Carolina* had arrived in the nick of time.

As quickly as he could focus the large binoculars on the ship, it was already firing its second salvo. The *North Carolina* was brand new with a crew just as young as those on the *Vicksburg*. It had never been in an engagement before and would show its mettle that day.

The *North Carolina* was the most modern battleship in the navy. It had a mechanical computer system in its CAC that made it a deadly accurate predator. The second salvo was just as damaging as the first. The lead Japanese ship took its own evasive action and slowed down. The destroyer that had been behind it made a mistake and turned in the opposite direction of the cruiser. Both were now open targets. The firing rate from the *Vicksburg* had slowed and one turret was out of commission. With the Japanese ships focused on the large, quickly approaching warship, the *Vicksburg* could work more precisely. Stollings walked back to the port side of the bridge and spotted the second cruiser that had been moving in behind them. It had been turning toward them to move up the port side and have full use of its battery, but now it turned northeast and appeared to be retiring from the fight.

The *North Carolina* was much closer now and appeared to be going to thread the needle: sail between the *Vicksburg* and the enemy ships. The battleship could fire directly on the enemy and at the same time shield its compatriot from any further harm. The big guns on its deck could tear huge holes in the hulls of the other two ships. The five-inch guns on the deck could select small targets on the Japanese boats and make hits with surgical precision.

The large battleship could approach without fear. The ships would pass one another so closely that the crewmembers of BB-55 could almost throw things and hit the Japanese. Stollings didn't need his binoculars now. The *North Carolina* was close and firing at such an astonishing rate that the smoke and fire from the guns made the opposite side of the ship appear as if it were in flames.

Stollings could see the lead Japanese ship had lost power and was listing. The *North Carolina* aimed one turret at each enemy ship. The firepower was incredible to see and feel. Even inside the bridge the rumble under Stollings's feet and in his chest was greater than that of any thunderstorm. It was even greater than Stollings would have felt if he had stood next to a Sherman tank. The *Vicksburg*'s crew could concern itself with recovery and repairs while the battleship put to rest part of the Japanese navy. His view of the destroyer was blocked now, but Stollings could hear and see part of the destroyer as it was lifted into the air. The *North Carolina* had made a perfect shot that hit a magazine and split the small ship completely in two. The first cruiser was silent and sinking fast. It was no danger to anyone now. The *North Carolina* would give chase to the second cruiser, headed north. Even with the enemy ship's lead of many miles, the guns of awesome Number Fifty-five would find their mark.

Stollings looked over his ship and had the opportunity to contemplate the day's events. The Japanese had come on strong, but the military might and fortitude of the U.S. Navy had prevailed. Lt. Commander Stollings was proud of this day and felt confident that his nation could and would prevail.

His crewmembers were on the deck. Some looked toward the Japanese cruiser as it sank beneath the waves. Some waved and cheered from the stern while watching the *North Carolina* steam on.

Like a Good Samaritan, the *North Carolina* simply came and went. Stollings thought about what General Robert E. Lee had said some seventy years earlier about North Carolinian troops: "God bless those Tar-heel boys."

Chapter 25

As the sun began to set on another day of war on the enemy's soil, Corporal Yoshi Iwanami thought about food and a night of rest. What remained of his regiment was still traveling through the Cascade Mountain Range. Soldiers were spread out along a ridge headed east. The war had dragged on with no end in sight, and his military unit had been constantly engaged since the beginning of the invasion. In the desolate areas of the mountains they would sometimes go for days without seeing any sign of civilization. They continued without orders, not knowing the whereabouts of or hearing from other units of the invasion force or hearing anything about relief. Yoshi had understood that the invading forces were to move quickly inland so as to not block the forces following them. Yoshi had been proud to be the tip of the sword. He now wondered where the rest of the sword was.

As the Japanese forces advanced inland, the fighting became more severe. For many days Yoshi's regiment rolled forward with nearly no opposition, leaving a path of destruction through populated areas. The regiment stayed well fed on American food from not only the fields, but also homes and businesses. Japanese soldiers took souvenirs: weapons and clothing. They would take valuables until they became too heavy to carry. Some soldiers had read about wild Indians and developed the practice of scalping, cutting off fingers, and mutilating bodies. Every soldier wanted to show his courage and make his mark. As time passed and as they traveled farther and farther across the landscape, the young soldiers concerned themselves less with souvenirs and marking their territory and more with fighting and surviving.

As the regiment met larger, enemy, military units, it moved further into the mountains, making large, sweeping movements around open areas and staying within heavily wooded areas and behind land cover. This was not what Yoshi had believed his duty was. He had envisioned a quick and powerful stab at the enemy to achieve victory for emperor and homeland.

The regiment went days without contact with the enemy, and some days the enemy seemed to be on every side. The constant fighting was beginning to take its toll physically and emotionally on the regiment. More and more soldiers died. All were happy for those soldiers' honorable deaths but were disgusted they were left lying on the enemy's battlefield without proper burial. Yoshi believed and expected of every man that they should be ready to do what was necessary to achieve victory. He was prepared for one, last, decisive battle.

The quiet of the evening was suddenly broken by a pair of low-flying airplanes. Yoshi didn't bother to look up to see what they were; he knew they were American. He knew from their sound they were fighters, quick and nimble and just as dangerous to small groups of soldiers on the ground as any other type of aircraft. Planes flew overhead constantly and were especially dangerous because they could bomb a precise area or mutilate soldiers with machine gun fire. Planes overhead were such a common event that no one reacted and no one attempted to draw their wrath by firing at them.

The planes continued quickly north as the regiment traveled east.

Ahead, Yoshi saw a soldier sitting down on a fallen tree with his rifle leaning against it. Other soldiers paid no attention and walked past him. When Yoshi reached him, he felt it was his duty to react.

"Private Kato."

The young soldier looked up at the corporal standing beside him. He raised his eyes and stood immediately.

"Why do you stop? Fall back into line."

The young private said nothing. He bowed and turned in the direction of the marching soldiers.

"Private Kato, do you think you will need this?" Yoshi pointed to the soldier's rifle, still leaning against the downed tree.

The private turned and an expression of fear crossed his face when he realized he had forgotten his rifle. He didn't look at Yoshi. He bowed and grabbed his rifle. "Very sorry, sir. Very sorry." He shouldered the rifle and moved quickly forward to join the line.

Yoshi followed directly behind him, "Why did you stop, Private?" Yoshi didn't use a scolding tone. He wanted the soldier's respect but also wanted to show his disapproval.

"I am sorry, sir. I wanted to adjust my stocking. I have a blister on the back of my heel."

"Do you feel that the small pain of a blister allows you to fall out of a marching column? Have you seen anyone else stop because of a simple complaint?"

"No, sir. It will not happen again."

Yoshi stayed behind the private and watched him walking lightly on his left foot. He felt tired and hungry, but he would never let it be known to anyone else. He took the responsibility that went with leadership.

"Perhaps the spirits of nature and your ancestors have placed the blister there as a small punishment for your unworthiness as a soldier."

Kato faced forward and bowed his head again. "No, sir, I am most honored to be here fighting for all that is right. I will continue to fight for honor and duty."

They continued marching forward in the long line. Private Kato had first appeared in the regiment only a couple months before the invasion. He had been drafted and trained along with everyone else for this invasion and had been assigned to another squad. Yoshi outranked the private and felt a duty to deal with him appropriately.

"Where are you from, soldier?"

Kato looked back over his shoulder as he walked. "I am from the city of Niigata."

"That is a very large city on the Sea of Japan is it not?"

"It is large, sir, and a beautiful place to live. It is far more beautiful in my homeland than in this dirty country." He felt comfortable speaking now.

"What did you do there before being called to duty?"

"I cooked in a fine restaurant." He turned his head again with a smile. "That is why I believed I should have been made a cook rather than a foot soldier." He took several more steps before turning quickly toward Yoshi to say, "Not that I am not proud to be a rifle soldier. I am pleased and honored and will not fail in my duties, sir. I will work hard and will kill many more than the forty Americans I have killed thus far."

Yoshi didn't respond. He had killed perhaps half that many. He would not say any more to the private for the moment. Yoshi was a corporal in the Imperial Japanese Army and believed he must maintain himself in a superior manner.

Two planes flew over, this time from east to west. They sounded

like the plane that had flown past minutes before. As the powerful engines moved off behind them into the darkening sky, Yoshi
focused on his own feet. They had made many steps on American
soil and he continued moving them forward. The line of soldiers
in front of him had packed the soil under the trees and his boots
made a pounding noise as they fell on it. His feet seemed to feel
heavier everyday, and he didn't move them very far with each step.
The sounds of many more boots fell behind him, and he thought
about the darkening surroundings. There were no other sounds of
the night. There were no breezes and no animal sounds, only the
sounds of humans. Yoshi looked around once and continued forward. He wondered if he were going deaf because he had never
heard silence in the woods for the weeks that he had been there.

The silence of the night was quickly broken. An intense whistle
gave way to bristling air that pushed against Yoshi's eardrums. The
mortar shell landed about forty yards away. The explosion pushed
him several feet backward, and he shuffled his feet to keep his
balance.

The shell seemed to come from the north. Yoshi pulled the sling
off of his shoulder and raised his rifle to the ready in that direction.
He peered intently, ready to face the enemy. The sounds of men
screaming quickly faded, and dirt could be heard hitting the leaves
around him. He shook his head to try to relieve the ringing in his
ears. He looked around, screaming, "Dress to me! Dress to me!"
He reached for his bayonet when the second mortar struck even
closer.

Yoshi was thrown to the ground and would have landed on his
face had his rifle not been in front of him. The fire of the explosion
burned the back of his ears and neck.

He pushed himself up, not bothering to dust himself off. He

believed the men could charge toward the mortars and overtake them before the enemy could adjust its fire. "Form up and move forward!" They could easily charge down the hillside. Yoshi looked around and through the dust and smoke could see a captain farther up the line. He was motioning and yelling for everyone to move forward.

Yoshi's first response was obedience. He was not to question his leaders. He pointed in the captain's direction, "Move forward men!"

He moved back up the hill and advanced toward the captain who had turned and moved east. Yoshi ran at a pace that allowed men to pass him. He didn't know who was behind him to the west and he took the leadership role to the rear.

Another shell fell within feet of where Yoshi had stood to prepare his charge. Men were being killed by the falling bombs, and they moved to avoid them. The line went down the hill to the south, out of sight of the mortars to the north. He believed they would form to the rear of the ridgeline and then assault the enemy position. More rounds fell, but because the Japanese soldiers had fled forward, the shells were off their mark.

Soldiers still moved forward in a hunched position but had slowed their pace, feeling less danger from the mortar position. Yoshi began looking around for an officer to see what he was going to do. He was ready to attack and pulled his bayonet out and snapped it onto his rifle barrel.

The line ahead had slowed considerably. As the men prepared to form ranks, shots rang out from the south.

A barrage of gunfire opened up less than two hundred feet down the hill. The firing intensified with large-caliber rifle and automatic gunfire sailing through the trees up the hill into the line ahead. Soldiers did just as they were trained to do, standing bravely and firing in return. Yoshi couldn't see the soldiers on the hill below, only the flash of gunfire. He did as he was trained to do, concentrating on squeezing the trigger, then racking another round into the chamber. Even in the intensity of the battle Yoshi focused only on his rifle. What he had concentrated on religiously before the invasion had got a workout and was beginning to show wear. Yoshi had to pull harder on the bolt to get it to move because the oil had dried up. A spent cartridge flew out and brushed his cheek. He slammed the bolt back home, pushing another round in the chamber. He never saw a target. He just fired as rapidly as he could.

The sulfur from the smoke surrounding him burned his eyes and nose. He concentrated on retrieving another clip from his ammo pouch. He caught a glimpse of movement out of his left eye. A group ahead quickly formed into a line. Soldiers were stepping over other soldiers to prepare for a charge.

Yoshi slammed the ammunition clip into the rifle and chambered a round. "Prepare for a charge!" he yelled again as loudly as he could to get everyone's attention. He believed this was his moment of destiny, a glorious final stab directly at the enemy. He looked around to see soldiers forming a line.

The line ahead to the east charged down the hill screaming a blood-curdling "Banzai!" The gunfire from below continued unfazed. Brave young Japanese soldiers were cut down, falling before reaching their goal. Fewer and fewer progressed down the hill enveloped in smoke.

Yoshi held his rifle with his right hand and raised his left to yell his own battle cry. He heard Lt. Hato call out from behind him. He turned to see the lieutenant motioning and ordering the men to fall back. They complied immediately, moving back up the hill.

Yoshi looked back down the hill. There was too much smoke to see anyone standing. The gunfire below had died down. He could see the hillside to the east littered with bodies. Men around him were pulling back from the enemy, and what did they have to show for this day?

He turned and walked up the hill. The remaining group of the Tenth Regiment, about the size of a platoon, moved west. They stayed on the south side of the ridge and moved quietly. Corporal Iwanami was near the back of the line. He would pull up the rear. The invasion into the middle of America was going the wrong way. Japanese soldiers were dying and being left to rot on the field of battle. The death taking place around him didn't make sense.

Darkness was falling on them. There would be no more fighting this day. He dutifully followed the group and concentrated on moving one foot quickly in front of the other.

Chapter 26

It was a beautiful Saturday morning, and the problems of hundreds of miles away did not affect Omaha. Edith Frankton had walked to the bus stop to travel into the city for some shopping and Christopher had walked with her. Peter was going about his usual weekend activities in the neighborhood. Earl finished a cup of coffee and decided it was time to get out the hedge clippers and pruning saw and take care of some things around the house. He put on old clothes and headed to the garage on the side of the house next to his neighbor. As he headed down the drive toward his garage, he happened to notice his neighbor, Tetsuji Masuko, cutting bloody meat. At first Earl was startled at the sight of Mr. Masuko holding a knife and standing over a large portion of meat. Earl realized that he had stopped walking to his garage and Mr. Masuko had looked up and seen him. He became more self-conscious as he hesitated for a moment before walking over and speaking.

"Good morning, Mr. Masuko."

Mr. Masuko quickly returned the greeting.

"Lovely morning," Earl said.

"Yes, lovely morning." Mr. Masuko's accent was obvious when he replaced *l* with *r*. He stood over a wooden table with white butcher paper on it. On the blood-soaked paper were knives of different sizes, a meat cleaver, and what appeared to be an entire side of beef. It wasn't a large side, but Earl wondered how Mr. Masuko's family of three would be able to eat it before it spoiled. Mr. Masuko concentrated on his work and it was clear he didn't have the speed or skill of a butcher.

"That's quite a cow you have. It's a lot of meat for one small family."

Mr. Masuko looked up with questioning eyes and replied, "This is beef I paid for. It is to feed my family."

Earl was a bit embarrassed now. He didn't entirely trust his neighbor, but he didn't want to insult him or give the impression he wanted free food. Rather than dig any farther, he decided to keep quiet. As the seconds passed, there didn't seem to be any other subject to discuss. So, he continued, "I've never seen you with beef before." He was trying so hard that the attempt at making friendly conversation became painful. "Did you get that from work?" The man works at a meat packing plant, he thought. Where else would he get it?

Mr. Masuko continued with his work for a moment, then stopped and looked up, confused. "Have you never seen cow before?"

"Yes. I'm sorry. I just thought it interesting that you would butcher your own beef . . . here behind your house."

As Mr. Masuko spoke, he looked down at his work. "I butcher out here so I do not make mess or smell in house. I butcher beef because is good to feed my family. I butcher meat myself because butcher shop will not do for me." He slapped the knife down on the table and looked up. "Any more question?"

The two had never had an in-depth meeting before. They had spoken to one another when the family moved in. They had passed one another regularly. Earl wasn't scared, but he realized he was making Mr. Masuko mad. He wasn't trying to. He knew all of the activities of the past year and the investigations to which the Japanese in the United States were being subjected must have taken a toll on the Masuko family. His attempt to be courteous seemed to have turned into a stupendous failure. It was best to let things alone and leave.

"My employer was kind to sell me this meat." Mr. Masuko's voice softened. "I cannot go to the butcher shop. The local shop-keeper questions me and will not provide me with what I ask. I cannot go to the shop now because the local board has delayed our ration stamp book. We were nearly unable to buy anything because the FB of I took our bank account for a week."

Earl who had been looking down now looked up in confusion. "What is the FB of I?"

"They have gold badge that says Federal Bureau of Investigation. He say he is agent with the Bureau."

Earl held back his smirk, "I see."

"No, I see man with gold badge at my front door. He come in and ask me many question about my family, how I came to America and Omaha ..." Mr. Masuko's voice became louder. "He want to know how I make my money. He want to know my activities after work and weekend." He pounded the table with the fist holding the knife. "He want to know my family and my life!"

Earl listened politely and was ready to speak. "Mr. Masuko, I'm sorry that your family is suffering inconvenience, but you should understand that it is your country that attacked my country. The government is concerned about your people who are here."

"I live in this country for ten year. My daughter was just a little baby when my wife and I sold everything we had to come to this country. I work hard for what I have." Mr. Masuko went back to work on cutting the meat. "They tell me I might have to give everything I have to the government and be moved to concentration camp."

Earl knew what Mr. Masuko was talking about. He understood his neighbor more and more. "I don't believe you mean concentration camp. That's what the Nazis have." Earl knew that Japanese people on the West Coast were being relocated and had heard rumors that it would take place all over the country. "What I have heard is that for everyone's safety some Japanese people are being given alternative housing." He had tried to be as conciliatory as possible. There was no need to be intentionally rude to his neighbor, and he was still concerned about what Mr. Masuko, basically a stranger, might do.

Mr. Masuko looked down and continued his work unabashed. "I come to this country with no evil motive. I work hard. Why does United States do this?"

"Mr. Masuko, why does Japan do this to the United States? This is a peace-loving country."

Mr. Masuko looked directly at Earl. "I know your nation. You kill and take from the Indians living here. Where we stand, a peace-loving nation stood." The man looked directly at Earl. "Now those people live in alternative housing. Your country exerts its beliefs around the world. You go to far-away lands to fight and tell people how they should be. Your country travels the world like it has the given right to be anywhere it wants to be."

Mr. Masuko looked down at the table almost as if he were bowing. "Japan is a great and ancient nation with many great people with pride of self and heritage. Japan has been negatively influenced by the West. There are those who have taken power that demand much. They use military actions to take by force. I do not fight for

Japan." He again looked into Earl's eyes. "I fight for self. I fight for those who fight for me." Earl suddenly became very aware of the large knife that Mr. Masuko had been using.

Mr. Masuko continued, "America is a large and bountiful nation. There are Japanese people who see the wealth of this country and have envy, envy that did not exist in the ancient beliefs of the country."

"Japan is coming to this country to steal what we have," Earl returned Mr. Masuko's hard look. "America is fighting for its freedom."

Mr. Masuko looked down again at his work. Earl turned and stomped away. There was nothing more to be said between the two. Although they were both working husbands, fathers, and neighbors, they seemed very far apart in their beliefs.

Earl thought that Mr. Masuko was a confused and angry man. No one in Omaha was a threat to him, and Earl told himself that he had done nothing to the Masuko family.

Earl walked through his back door and slammed it shut. He stood for a moment, then turned and locked it. Just a few weeks before, he had never been concerned with his neighbors. Now, for the first time after seeing Mr. Masuko holding a knife and raising his voice in anger, Earl was scared.

He told himself that he hadn't started the war and it was not his to fight in. Wherever the war was happening, it wasn't coming to Omaha. Earl said under his breath, "Let the coasts worry about the enemy, and I'll only have to watch for my neighbors."

Chapter 27

Gerald had arrived exactly two weeks earlier. He had survived thirteen days of boot camp. They had been the hardest days of his life. He would much rather have been back in Harbitsburg, chopping wood and making cheese.

Every day started at 6:00 a.m. and didn't stop until 8:00 p.m. That went on six days a week, but just as with any new, physically demanding job, all it took was time to adapt. Gerald had been able to deal with the physical requirements. There was marching for miles each day. There were drills of bayonet charges and hand-to-hand combat. There were obstacle courses and ropes to climb. There was a rope bridge that had to be conquered to cross a small river. One soldier was not victorious on the bridge and fell in. No one was sure if he just panicked when he hit the water or was hurt, but he didn't come up. No one could get to him in time. Private Benjamin Schronce, aged eighteen, of Ohio, was killed in the line of duty after having served in the U.S. Army for nine days.

Gerald had decided that he wasn't cut out for military service. He had survived thus far, but he wasn't what a soldier should be. He didn't fit in. He was regularly yelled at. He stayed to himself while the others in the barracks drank booze that they had snuck in. They smoked, cursed and played cards.

There were some in the barracks who didn't participate in the unsavory activities. There was one young man from somewhere in New England who wore glasses and played the harmonica. There was a tree trunk of a fellow from the south who just sat back and read a lot.

A lot of time was spent on the firing range. This was the first time Gerald had fired a rifle. He was issued the standard M-1 Garand, and he hated it. He hated carrying it. It weighed about twelve pounds. The shoulder strap cut into him when he carried it. It made his arms ache when he carried it in front of him. It was large and bulky, and the stiff breach action sliced skin off his fingers on more than one occasion.

That afternoon the direct sunlight on the firing range was hot. The firing range was a field of about one square mile. It was divided in three sections. To the far left were beginning shooters and those who needed remedial weapons training. In the center was the bulk of the group, honing skills. To the right were advanced shooters and snipers. Sergeants and lieutenants walked up and down the lines yelling at the soldiers.

Gerald was to the left of the intermediate group and Sergeant Ashaul was nearby. Over the course of the previous two weeks he had developed the nickname of "Sergeant Asshole." A soldier in the beginner section stood up with his rifle and raised his hand.

Sergeant Ashaul responded with a typical scowl and stomped his boots. He walked directly to the soldier and stood within inches of his face. "What in the hell are you doing, soldier?" The young man had a look of sheer panic. "Do you stand up in the middle of a battle? Do you think this is a school room where you raise your hand to ask the teacher a question?" The sergeant never spoke in a normal tone; it was always loud.

The soldier half sat back down. The sergeant was in his face, screaming now. "This is war, Son! What is your malfunction that you have to stand up and cry for help?"

The soldier looked as if he were nearly in tears. He held out the rifle. "My gun jammed, sir."

"You hit the dirt and start giving me pushups until I say stop!" The soldier's response was immediate, and he fell to the ground and began pushups. "It's not a gun; it's a rifle, an M-1, Garand, army rifle, and I am not a sir! I am a master sergeant!"

Everyone within earshot sneaked looks. Sergeant Ashaul quickly scrutinized the rifle and tried to pull back the action. It wouldn't move. He put the butt of the rifle on the ground and pushed down on the action. Still no movement. The sergeant put his boot against the action and forced it open, then picked it back up and peered at it.

"What in the hell have you done, boy? Do you have shit for brains? Do you not have the sense that God gave a monkey? I could teach a half-witted dog quicker than you!" The sergeant turned the rifle upside down and began beating it on the ground right beside the soldier who was still doing pushups. The clip finally fell out. Sergeant Ashaul picked up the clip and snapped out a round. "On your feet now, you dumb ass, sad excuse for a man!" He held the round directly in front of the young man's nose. The soldier had a red face from the work, and he stared straight ahead with eyes as big around as a full moon.

"Please tell me what this is?"

The soldier's eyes darted back and forth as if he were searching for an answer. "A bullet?"

The sergeant lowered his voice and said in a sarcastic tone, "Very good, young man." He tipped his head to the side. "Now can you tell me which direction the bullet leaves the barrel?"

The soldier's eyes still darted. "The pointy end comes out first?"

The sergeant still had a tone of sarcasm. "That's very good." He moved to the young man's side and screamed in his ear, "Then why in the hell did you force the clip into the magazine backward, you miserable, damn excuse for a soldier?" Sergeant Ashaul threw the bullet to the ground. "I want you to run back to your barracks and stand with your nose in the corner just like in a schoolroom and don't leave from there until you're told. Move it!"

The soldier complied immediately, and the sergeant just shook his head in disbelief.

This was a good breaking point because everyone had stopped firing to listen to the sergeant's diatribe. The range master walked down the line from one end to the other, yelling for everyone to cease fire and clear weapons.

Sergeant Ashaul was still standing in the same spot. He yelled down the line, "Barracks D, fall in and line up with me! Barracks D, fall in!"

Soldiers ran from various places on the field. They didn't delay, knowing they could face the full brunt of the sergeant's wrath. "Line up and back to barracks." The sergeant started heading back toward camp as men were still running to fall into line.

Gerald slung his rifle over his already sore shoulder. It didn't sit there long before he shifted it and tried to take some weight off. The big, quiet, southern boy who was marching in line beside him apparently saw this wrestling match.

"That looks like a big gun for a little guy."

Gerald expected to hear a distinct drawl, but the man's speech barely revealed that he was from the South.

"It can cause a strain."

"Want to trade rifles?"

Gerald looked at the big man in surprise. "Trade?" He wasn't sure of the man's motive.

"Yes, trade. I have this little carbine that feels like a toy to me. What you have is more my size anyway because I had a bolt action thirty aught six at home. Let's trade."

Gerald looked ahead. There were two dozen men from the barracks in line in front of them with the sergeant.

The man beside Gerald continued, "No one is going to know or even care. We'll each have a rifle that's better suited to us."

Gerald slipped his ammo pouch off his waist and handed it over with his rifle. The southern gentleman reciprocated with his rifle and bag. The man threw the heavy rifle up onto his shoulder with one quick toss and carried the pouch with the few remaining clips of .30 caliber ammunition.

Gerald cradled the smaller rifle in his arms. It weighed several pounds less and was only about three feet long. It fitted him.

The group made it back to the barracks in a few minutes and stood to attention when the sergeant walked over and faced them.

When he began, his voice changed. He had always been loud and condescending until now. "Men, I can call you men now rather than children. I've had my concerns over the past couple weeks. I've wondered how many of you would actually survive."

Gerald asked himself the same question.

The sergeant scanned the line for several seconds, looking each soldier in the face. "You all have." He looked straight ahead at no one in particular and was quiet a moment. "I know that each of you will do what you need to do when you get to your duty. In my remaining two days with you my job is to get you ready to go kill as many Jap bastards as you can. On Sunday morning every one of you will head out to your assignments."

Gerald's heart sped up.

"You'll be rolled into B Company, assigned to the Sixth Mountain Army Division, and will head to central Oregon."

A noise of murmurs and movement rose in the group. Most were excited. They were ready for combat.

The sergeant continued, "This is a standing order. Stick together. Those little Jap bastards are mean and scary. I've seen them in the Pacific. When they get a piece of ground, they don't give it up without a fight to the death. You're fighting for our ground now. This is American soil and they will give it up when they're all dead. That's what you have to do. Go kill the bastards. Dig a hole and bury them. Get them out of our country." It sounded as if he sniffed when he finished. "Good luck and dismissed." Sergeant Ashaul gave a proper ninety degree turn and walked away.

The group started to break up, heading to the barracks. Gerald stood in place for a little while. He had believed he would never be sent to the front. By now he was just one man among millions in the army. He had to face his fears. He would have to continue to survive in the army and now it had to be in the face of the enemy.

Chapter 28

The president's head jerked, and he gasped deeply as he was awakened by the dream. He knew his eyes were open, but all he saw was pitch darkness. It took him a moment to gather his senses.

He rolled the covers off and dropped his feet onto the floor as he pushed himself up in bed. He pulled the chain on the bedside lamp, and as the bright bulb flashed on, he jerked back a bit in response. The light reminded him of his dream, a continuing dream of the land of the rising sun coming toward him.

He looked around the room and recognized everything. His wife was in New York overnight for a ceremony at the Brookline Navy Yard. The clock on the table read 6:15 a.m. It was still dark outside. He knew he wouldn't get back to sleep, but he did collapse onto the pillow in exhaustion. He hadn't slept well since taking office. He had slept even more poorly after the outbreak of the war in Europe, and more poorly still when the attack started in the United States. For the past several nights he hardly slept at all. He thought about living in the Executive Mansion for the previous nine years and how, even with what was probably the most comfortable bed that money could buy, he hadn't slept comfortably. He had brought the nation through the dark hours of the depression, and he had

had political battles of all kinds, but now, with the war in Europe and the Pacific having come to American soil, he was lucky to get four hours sleep per night.

He struggled with the war in his own nation everyday and didn't have all of the answers. In the darkness of the room, when he lay down at night, all he had were his thoughts. He was nearly ready to sleep with a light on. He even thought about having George sit in the room with him. George was always present for his needs, and sleep was now among them. He stared at the light beside the bed. When he closed his eyes, he continued to see the images of his dream.

It seemed that every night he had the same dream or something similar to it. He was torn from the safety of the White House and found himself in the field with soldiers of the U.S. Army. He was fighting with a rifle that he couldn't get to fire. Japanese soldiers were charging in his direction, screaming, and firing their guns. He knew they were the enemy even though he couldn't see them. They were attacking from a small ridge and the morning sun was at their backs. The president was frozen with fear, not able to defend the nation, not even able to save himself. The sounds of the battle were overtaken by the bright light of the sun. The rising sun seemed to be advancing with the enemy soldiers, coming directly at him. The whole war seemed to be advancing on him, and he couldn't do anything to stop it.

President Roosevelt lay in bed. He became anxious and started breathing more heavily just thinking about his dream. He asked himself what needed to be done to stop the advance of war in his nation. He swore to himself that he would do everything within his power to make sure the United States never fell. He was determined that his dream of the enemy sun approaching him in attack would never come true.

Chapter 29

Dinner had been on the table for more than an hour. Earl had never been this late before. When he was late, he would call ahead. Edith told the two boys to go ahead and have their meal. She was going to wait on their father.

There was probably nothing wrong with him. He just couldn't get to the telephone, she thought. What kind of emergency could come up at the bank? Dozens of scenarios ran through her mind. She thought about what she could do. Should she start walking to the bank to look for him? It was miles away, and if she took the bus, she would travel on a different route from Earl. Was it time to call the police?

She kept watch out the front window, and the shadows grew longer on the front yard as the sun set. Just before turning back toward the dining room, she caught a glimpse of him, walking down the street. He looked fine; he was just walking slowly. Edith headed out the front door to meet him. She didn't run up the street toward him, not wanting to embarrass him. She walked to the curb and looked up the street. They made eye contact. Earl looked tired. She still couldn't figure out the problem. There were no visible injuries, nothing about him that gave any indication of a problem, other than the car was missing. When he reached their yard, he turned across the grass and headed directly toward the front door. Edith wasn't sure how to respond to him. She walked up the steps behind him and through the doorway. As the front door closed, Peter walked in to greet his father with a warm smile as if nothing were wrong. "Where you been, Dad?" he asked, his tone completely honest and unassuming.

Earl smiled in disgust and shook his head. "I had car trouble."

"What happened?" Edith was still concerned.

"I walked." He was curt. "My car is up on Spring Street where it stopped when I ran out of gasoline."

"You walked from there?" Edith asked. "Why didn't you take a bus?"

"Why do I need to take public transportation?" He shot a glance at her. "I have a car." He headed toward the dining room. "And do you know why it ran out of gasoline?" he said flippantly as he continued walking.

Peter spoke up right away, "Because there was no gas in the tank."

Earl stopped in his tracks and turned his head to look sharply at him. "That was a rhetorical question."

Peter looked up with surprise. "I thought it was an easy one." He may have only had an elementary education, but he was still a smart young man.

Earl stared straight ahead for a second, then started walking toward the dining room. "I ran out of gas because I wasn't able to get any today. It's the wrong day of the week for me and my ration coupons are not good until next week anyway. So, because I couldn't get any gasoline, I ran out."

Peter continued completely seriously and innocently, "Maybe you shouldn't have driven without any gas."

"Young man!"

Edith jumped in and turned Peter's shoulders toward the stairs as she said, "It's time for you to head to your room." He dutifully complied, and Earl and Edith headed into the dining room. Christopher was still sitting at the table. He had heard everything and hid a smile but had no desire to talk to his father right then. He stood and headed toward the steps too.

"If you have some gasoline in the storage building, maybe Mr. Masuko can give you a ride to your car."

"No," he was quick to respond. "I will not get help from him."

Edith wasn't sure what she had said wrong, but decided to leave it alone.

"I'll take a taxi to work tomorrow and call a garage to go pick it up."

Edith decided she was still going to leave the subject alone.

"This nation has gone insane with rationing, and speed-limit changes, and car pooling, and buses and trains running everywhere with people. This nation is supposed to be about freedom isn't it?"

She wasn't sure if that were supposed to be rhetorical, but she replied, "People are sacrificing freedom to help insure freedom. We're in a fight that's threatening our freedom and by cutting back, we help with that."

"I'm not in a fight. It doesn't involve me. So, why can't I take my car to work?"

"Because the nation needs gasoline to fight." Edith had a bit of anger in her voice and she didn't care. "The nation needs the rubber. Others are sacrificing. I read that there's an air base in California where every person, from the lowest private to the general, rides bicycles everywhere. People are suffering and dying, and some have lost everything. You're mad because you can't jump in your car and go whenever you want. Some people in the country can't go anywhere at all."

Earl looked up in surprise. He wasn't sure where that had come from or what to say. They stared at one another for a bit before he said, "Is this about your eighth cousin in Oregon, or whatever she is?"

Edith was angry now. "It is about a human being other than you, whether they be related to me or not. If your walking for a few miles helps someone save a home, or another life, I'm in support of it." She walked toward the living room. Earl acted as if he were the only person in existence. She decided he could be alone.

After a few minutes Earl came out of the kitchen and found his wife standing on the front porch. The last light of day was upon this small part of the world. Edith was at peace for the moment listening to the sounds of the approaching night.

"I'm sorry," Earl said in a low voice. "I'm tired from the walk home and stressed from having to deal with the car, and I was already worn out from dealing with the bank examiner today."

Edith looked at him with a little sympathy. He saw this and continued, "The bank examiner came today along with some G-man from the Federal Bureau of Investigation."

Edith looked at him with some concern. "What was an FBI agent doing at the bank?"

"All day we went over the books, looking at names and accounts."

"What names?"

"Oh, nothing to be concerned about. It was just people with a Japanese name. The government wants to look at what money they have and what they're doing with it."

There was silence for a minute. Edith thought and looked at

Earl. "Why do you spend all day helping the government, but then never worry about anyone else?"

"Well . . . this was what they needed to help with the war."

Edith only raised her eyebrows.

Earl realized what he had walked into and he didn't like the questioning. "This is what I have to do as a manager. If the bank examiner wants these records, I have to provide them."

"You said it was for the war effort."

Earl's eyebrows were furrowed. "That's what they asked for; that's what I gave."

There was again silence for a time. Nothing had to be said, but Earl realized Edith had made a point. She was helping with the war, even though he didn't care to join any part of it. They both looked out across the landscape at the ever-darkening world. Both realized they had different views about what was going on in the nation. A fight in other places was turning into a fight here. No bullets were being fired, but the war seemed to be close to home.

Edith was the first to speak. "This war is involving everyone in America whether we realize it or not."

Earl fired back, "It seems to be involving our family."

She looked at him with a sincere expression. "You're right."

Earl thought about her response for a moment. "Are you ready to send your son off to war?"

"No. All I want is for my son to do what he feels he should do."

Earl looked at her with exasperation. "That is not his place. This is not our fight. We should fight when the war comes to us."

Edith sighed. "The war is here, and it is my fight."

Earl stared blankly and didn't say anything.

"I spoke to the hiring manager at Allied Canning, and I will take that job," Edith said. She walked inside without a word and didn't wait for anything else. Her heavy footsteps were her exclamation mark.

Earl couldn't make a response. He thought that the insanity elsewhere had now entered his household. Darkness was upon him, and he walked inside.

Chapter 30

They had joined the Sixth Mountain Division upon their arrival in central Oregon two days before. They had formed due east of Doris. The strategy to locate and destroy the invading Japanese was simple. Military units gathered all along the summit of the Cascade Range. This was as far as the Japanese invasion was thought to have penetrated inland. Additional special forces of the German and Japanese armies could have come in and spread out in various areas, but the Americans' immediate focus was on what had been observed: the Japanese army marching inland from the coast. Units gathered along the summit of the Coastal Range and the peak of the Klamath Mountains. The two flanks, now gathered into an immense military force, would sweep forward with such speed and strength that the Japanese army would be obliterated. The operation was called Bear Trap. Just as a bear trap snaps and traps its prey before the animal realizes it's in danger, the U. S. Army would trap and destroy the invaders before they could respond.

Gerald had accepted that he would be involved in a true military action. The fight was at hand. He was happy that he was one man in a force of possibly over a million men on the west side of the coming fight. He decided he would just find a way to move along with the activity and do what he could to fight and survive.

He was still finding his way around the company. The group from his barracks was the Fourth Platoon. Gerald knew everybody from his platoon, which ones to stay away from and which ones to trust.

On the second night in camp Gerald was put on sentry duty. Soldiers were positioned up to a mile east of the camp. Pairs of soldiers were spread out every two hundred feet. The citizens in the area knew where the military operations were taking place, and they knew to stay away. If anyone approached from the west, the soldiers were to shoot first and ask questions later.

Gerald was scared when he learned of his assignment. Everyone knew if the enemy approached these positions, the pickets there would probably be killed. The shots the pickets were to fire might kill one or two of the enemy, but more importantly, they would alert the soldiers in camp. The pickets would die to save the camp.

Gerald was cold as he rode in the truck. The temperature was about eighty-five degrees, but he still tried to prevent himself from shaking. The truck came to a stop and the new squad leader, Sergeant Merle Mast, pointed to the west. "Flaghart, Johnston, pace off fifty yards in that direction and set up post. Find a spot to see and not be seen. Don't leave that spot until you're relieved in three hours. The password is Sitting Bull."

Gerald jumped off the truck along with his partner for the next three hours, the same man who had graciously traded rifles with him several days before. Johnston dutifully stepped off at a quick pace, heading west. Gerald was happy to find he was partnered with an enthusiastic soldier, and a big one at that.

They walked through tall, dry grass and found a position in waist-high grass at the base of a single, scrubby-looking pine, which was typical of the area. Large areas of tall grass dominated the landscape. Single evergreens alternated with large areas of trees. The first twenty minutes passed with only the sounds of the night— crickets and night birds—and a light breeze blowing through the grass. Gerald was happy with his partner. Johnston had never done anything out of line in basic training. He was a big guy and didn't seem scared in the least. He was an expert shot and showed himself well at hand-to-hand combat. He was one of those Gerald wanted to stay near if they went into battle.

All he knew about Johnston was that he was from the South. Gerald thought that a person didn't have to be smart to follow orders. The two hadn't spoken a word all night and their stillness made Gerald uneasy. He wanted something to make the moment seem a little more human. He heard the other guys call Johnston by his first name and he decided to start a conversation, "How are you doing tonight, Hank?"

The big man turned his head and looked at Gerald with an expression of annoyance.

"Not the talkative type, are you Hank?"

Johnston turned to look ahead again, sat quietly for a moment and sniffed. "The name is Henry."

Gerald looked down in embarrassment. He was truly trying to be friendly and had seemed to mess it up. He spoke quietly, "I'm sorry. I thought I heard the guys call you Hank."

Johnston remained quiet for a moment longer, then said, "They did. I guess they thought it was a funny name for an Alabama boy."

A few more seconds of silence passed. "I like Henry better."

Gerald saw that the man he had just insulted by accident wasn't mad. "It's a name of royalty."

"I don't know about royalty. It was my grandfather's name and it's what my parents decided on when I was born." Now Henry looked at Gerald. "Where are you from?"

"Harbitsburg, Wisconsin. You?"

"I'm from Linville. It's not far from the Tennessee River in northern Alabama."

They sat silently for a minute, watching and listening. Gerald tried to find out where he stood with his newfound friend and continued, "What do you think about this whole mess?"

"What do you mean—the war?"

"Yeah. I don't know how I got here, but I'm not too happy about it."

Henry tipped his head, scanning the open expanse to the west. "War isn't a good thing, but sometimes it has to be done. Those Japanese and Germans are being run by madmen, hell-bent on destruction. If we don't stop them, they're going to try to take over the whole world. Somebody has to stop them and I might as well be a part of it. I'm here to do my duty. This is my country and it's my people being killed and my land being threatened. I'm going to do what I can to stop it."

It was almost a speech. Gerald felt ashamed. He had never taken the time to think about the others in this war. Already soldiers ahead of him had fought and died. Innocent people were being killed just because they were in the way. An evil force was at work in the world, and it had come to this country. It needed to be dealt with before it was unstoppable.

Gerald continued in a near whisper and a little embarrassment, "Did you volunteer?"

"No, I was drafted. I wasn't trying to avoid anything. It's in my blood. My grandfather, Henry, fought in the War Between the States. He was in the Fifteenth Alabama Regiment. Fought hard for what he thought was the right thing. I'll do the same. The army just decided to go ahead and call me. I had just finished my junior year in the engineering school at the University of Alabama."

Gerald looked at him with wide eyes. "You were an engineer?" Gerald was caught a bit off guard. He had made a judgment about this big fellow from the South and misjudged. "Why were you pulled out of college and put in an infantry unit? With your education you could have gone into the Seabees or the U.S. Corps of Engineers. You could have gone to OCS and been leading a platoon as a lieutenant instead of sitting here in the middle of nowhere all night."

Johnston just smiled a big smile. "I guess the U.S. government didn't concern itself very much with just another Alabama, redneck boy."

Gerald had learned a lot in a short period of time from Henry. "What'll you do when we go into battle and meet the Japanese?"

Henry kept looking ahead. "I'll do what I have to do to stop them and stay alive."

Gerald thought that even this big, brave man was a little scared. Gerald was definitely scared. If he could stick with Henry he might be able to do what he had to do and survive.

Gerald looked out over the blackness of the night to the west. Again, only the sounds of crickets and night birds could be heard. An occasional breeze would pass through the limbs above them and the tall grass in front of them. It was a peaceful night. Gerald hoped it would remain at peace.

Chapter 31

The meetings continued nearly on a daily basis. The business of the nation usually took place in the West Wing of the White House, but the president was comfortable letting the war counsel into the more private areas of the mansion. He would sometimes use the third floor, considered the private residence of the president and his family and completely off limits to others without the commander in chief's approval. In the mansion's treaty room the president was most happy to learn about the war's progress. The treaty room was in the center of the house on the ground floor and was the easiest room for visitors to find. Because this formal parlor with its Chippendale-style furniture and crystal chandeliers was frequently used and housed maps and documents, armed guards were stationed at each of its doors twenty-four hours a day.

President Roosevelt was already in the room for this day's midmorning meeting when the others arrived. He was comfortably seated in an oversized chair. A silver tea service and a porcelain cup and saucer sat on a tray beside him. Those arriving for the meeting were punctual and came through the front and back entrances of the mansion. They included top generals, the Joint Chiefs of Staff, cabinet members, and the vice-president, as well as government law-enforcement officials and intelligence agents. After many weeks of routine meetings these people came to be known as the war counsel.

President Roosevelt was always to the point. "Gentlemen, what news do you bring?"

General George Marshall spoke eagerly. "Mr. President, I believe it is safe to say the war in the west is contained." The others clapped their approval. Marshall continued, "Army divisions are heavily involved in actions all over the Pacific Northwest, and we are certain the Japanese have advanced no further than the eastern borders of Washington and Oregon. There have been no reports of invasion attempts in any locations other than those reported June 1. Enemy forces in Canada have not made it to American soil. The Japanese have done no better in Canada; they have progressed no more than a couple hundred miles inland. They've attacked, but not occupied any city in North America." Heads nodded in response and conversation became animated.

Admiral King jumped in. "It is safe to say the U.S. Navy has a secure hold on the western United States and no Japanese forces of any kind will be able to advance toward American shores." The men applauded briefly. "We have sunk two Japanese subs and three surface ships along with a half dozen zeros. Because of our sustained pressure on the Japanese navy, they appear to have withdrawn. Admiral Raymond Spruance is in pursuit of what he believes to be a sizable Japanese fleet."

Discussions continued quietly.

"Admiral King, how large of a fleet is Admiral Spruance responding with?"

King looked at the president. "It's a full carrier fleet, sir. That would include . . ."

"Admiral, obviously we have understood the immediate concern is the safety of this nation. Is it wise to have a U.S. fleet in pursuit of Japanese ships, when that fleet may be better utilized in the direct protection of this nation?"

Admiral Nimitz hesitated before replying, "Sir, we're happy with the response of the navy in the Pacific. We have ships along the coast to observe and respond to any possible further attack."

"How many ships are along the coast?"

The naval officers wore blank expressions at first. "Sir, ships are assigned patrol areas of a certain size, and they're patrolling from the Bering Strait to Central America. Any attempt at further action by the Japanese would be discovered immediately. War ships including carriers would be ready to move to the area, and the army would be notified to respond on land. Both coasts are fortified and have established very good early warning systems."

"Wouldn't more ships be even better for the defense of this nation? Wouldn't having those ships close to home make that barrier between the land and sea even more secure?"

King complied and gave a nod, "Yes, sir, it would."

The room sat quietly for a moment as the president continued, "How are things progressing inland? When are the last enemy invaders going to be rounded up?"

Marshall continued, "Mr. President, I believe the army has responded in spectacular fashion. Just in a few short weeks we have prepared and assembled a response of over a million men in the Pacific Northwest. Army units are easily handling the fractured invasion forces."

"How many Japanese soldiers were involved in this attack? Do we know how many are still fighting?"

"No, sir, we're unsure of how many made it ashore or how many are still present and fighting. We are now tightening the noose on those still here with Operation Bear Trap. We know the invasion force hasn't made it out of Washington or Oregon. We have forces under the command of Omar Bradley in the east, moving west. The forces on the far coast are under Mark Clark and moving east. The plan is simply to move forward, pushing and destroying the enemy until Bradley and Clark meet one another. Just as a trap surprises the bear with speed and force, our operation will catch the enemy before it can respond. The enemy forces are moving in disarray. Either they were not fully prepared when they invaded, or we responded with such strength that they recoiled and were not able to group for an effective attack."

"Why do you say that?" William Leahy asked.

Marshall spoke to him while looking at the president, "The Japanese don't seem to be moving on specific targets. When they came ashore, they left a path of destruction. Everything they came in contact with was damaged or destroyed, but they didn't go anywhere. They're moving in irregular patterns through the mountains as if they don't know where they're going. The forces seem to be avoiding contact with anyone now, military or civilian."

There were some puzzled looks in the room. There was no talking for the moment and a pair of fighter airplanes could be heard zipping over the White House. There were two airfields close by and a third had been newly constructed. The sound of planes over the city was now common.

The silence in the conversation was broken again by the president, "What about the eastern invasion that hasn't taken place?"

"We're unsure if our spotting German ships caused them concern that the invasion was compromised, and they didn't invade, or why they've held off. The military responded quickly and the navy and air corps has the coast well covered. German ships were sighted two days after the Japanese invasion. So, it would appear the timing was not well enough coordinated. Perhaps the Japanese were fast or the German forces were slow. Either way, the invasion didn't transpire and our defenses on the coast are well prepared."

Francis Biddle spoke up. "Mr. President, German spies and saboteurs are being captured. Military and intelligence personnel have rounded up a half dozen Nazi commandos. They were captured near military installations as well as oil refineries on the Gulf Coast."

Marshall leaned forward. "Defenses have been built not only at potential military targets, but also at essential civilian locations."

Secretary of War Henry Stinson leaned back and appeared completely relaxed. "Mr. President, the nation has responded very well to the war. In a few short weeks we have put over one and a half million men in uniform. Industries have not only survived the reduction in their work forces, but have begun to increase production for war needs."

The secretary of commerce chimed in. "The railroads are working at peak performance. Roadways are being built for the transportation of military equipment in an expeditious fashion. Physical defenses on the coasts are under construction."

Responses to the secretary of commerce erupted around the room as he spoke. "War bonds have already generated nearly three hundred million dollars. The price fixing established by your executive order has not had an adverse affect on the economy because war production has increased. Rationing is not causing undue hardship."

Some men looked around the room as if waiting for a turn to speak. There were smiles and looks of relief on faces all round the room. Marshall spoke again, "We do need to continue building our defenses even with no imminent threat of direct attack."

The president nodded his head. He looked reassured. "How are things in the Commonwealth of Canada?"

Stinson replied, "Canadian forces are responding to the Japanese in the west."

"That doesn't seem reassuring."

Stinson spoke a little more quietly. "The Canadians are returning to the Commonwealth and Great Britain has demanded they stay in Europe. There has been a state of near rebellion in London concerning those forces."

Secretary of State Hull spoke. "Of course, Great Britain and the Soviet Union are requesting we continue the physical support we've been providing."

The room was quiet a moment.

"Due to requirements here, the amount of supplies we have been sending has dropped by well over half."

Everyone realized the implications of Hull's words. The United States had been the lifeline to England and an enormous supporter of Russia. With supplies dwindling, their struggles would only worsen.

The president broke the silence. "We must first be concerned with our own war." With that the meeting was adjourned.

Chapter 32

The sea can do strange things to people. It requires strength and stamina to live on it. The small and often quiet confines of a U-boat can drive men to absolute madness. The boat had been at sea for months with little contact with friends. U-432 had successfully harassed the U.S. shoreline and sunk three ships, including a civilian fishing boat. Basically the same pattern prevailed day in and day out: surface at night and submerge during the day. Drills were common and attacks, few. The entire ship was tired. The boat itself was aging, needing more supplies and better maintenance. The men were tired and felt they had done their duty. They had put themselves in harm's way over and over in service to the Reich. Their captain had called on them to do more than what was necessary. Each man had appeared to age by years in the time frame of only months.

Captain Kurz considered himself a sensible and patient man. Members of his crew thought otherwise. Commander Gruber was friendly and well respected by the crew. He was a dutiful, career, navy man. He followed the direction of his commanding officer and the navy with utmost respect.

The sub, along with others, had sailed from Germany in early May. They had sailed without a specific directive and were told that they should stay on station for as long as possible. They didn't know what was going on in the world. They only knew of their own activities. Their supplies and contacts had been very few. The captain did not want to withdraw; he wanted to attack.

The two men spoke in the captain's small, simple compartment. "Captain, the Americans have responded in force," Gruber said. "Aircraft constantly patrol the coast and the number of ships increases more and more each day. At their current rate of growth, sailors will soon be able to walk from ship to ship across the ocean."

Gruber sat stiffly in a chair at the small table in the cabin. Captain Kurz lay on his bunk with his shoes off and his collar loosened. This was the only time and place that he'd appear out of uniform. "Commander Gruber, so many more ships means more targets for our sub to sink. Our duty is to attack the enemy at all costs. We will continue to attack."

"How will we do that?"

Kurz raised an eyebrow. Gruber had never questioned him like this before. Gruber was concerned for the boat and its men.

"We need fuel and food, or we can't survive. Captain, we are alone in the Atlantic."

"I have been trusted with a very important mission. I will not fail; the crew will not fail, or we will not return!"

The captain stood and stepped to the table. He shot an evil glare at the commander. He then grabbed a map, unrolled it and pointed at a location. "Plot a course to here."

Commander Gruber peered at what the captain was pointing at: Charleston. Gruber was startled, but said nothing. Charleston Harbor was a large naval base on the eastern seaboard of the United States. It would therefore be one of the most heavily defended locations. What could possibly possess this trusted officer of the German navy to attempt an attack on a naval base? After a long and successful mission, the captain seemed to be losing touch with reality.

Chapter 33

The Sixth Mountain Division had been in the field for three days after leaving Doris. The further west they traveled, the more evidence they saw of the Japanese army. Some sections were completely untouched. Then there were areas of complete devastation. People and animals alike had been killed and left lying on the ground. Most had been found and buried. Some citizens who had attempted to flee and hide from the invaders were killed and left to rot where they had fallen. The heat of summer made the army's discoveries grim in the remote areas where it traveled.

Some small towns and villages had been burned to the ground. Crops and orchards had been destroyed. The Japanese army could often be found by following its path of destruction. Veteran soldiers who had been in the area for more than a month had faced the enemy and told stories of their tenacity. Most of the Japanese soldiers would flee further into the forests and mountains when faced with a large force. Some small groups would make vicious, suicidal Banzai charges with fixed bayonets. Running forward with evil expressions on their faces and screaming like maniacs, they would try to stab their enemy, but most were unable to reach their targets.

The stories were told by scared, tired men who wanted to frighten the rookies to help keep them alive.

S.D. HILDEBRAND

It was a bright summer day in the thick woods of the Pacific Northwest. The sun was high in the sky, but in the mountains and under thousands of leaves Gerald was quite comfortable. His unit had stopped for ten minutes at midday. He took the time to remove his boots and socks and rest his feet. He also grabbed a quick bite from a can of meat and some crackers. He would eat small amounts all day in the field and then eat as much as he could in the evening. A little would get him through the march. He might not get another rest for another two hours.

He emptied the can and put the last two crackers in his pocket. He pulled his socks and boots back on and laced them in a hurry when he saw Lieutenant Delgardo moving forward. "Let's move out. We've still got a war to fight." The platoon leader led from the front.

Gerald didn't know where they were. The last town they had passed was a little community named Regal Summit. The residents, the ones that hadn't left, were happy to see U.S. soldiers. When troops passed through, the residents felt more secure. They knew enemy forces no longer occupied their land and they could begin to recover. The American soldiers were tasked with advancing inland and rounding up all enemy forces.

The advanced forces, including Baker Company, were well into the wilderness of the Oregon Mountains now. The rugged terrain prevented tanks and trucks from supporting their moves. Airplanes kept vigil overhead, but the weapons that Baker Company carried were all that were necessary for small forces to fight in close combat.

Marching all day was monotonous, nothing but step after step of pounding dirt, crunching leaves, fighting bugs, trying not to fall in the rough terrain, and always looking and listening for the enemy. Gerald felt pretty safe in his group. He hadn't been called on to be a flanker, a soldier who walked at the front or sides of the group. He always kept to the middle of the lines, a few people in front, a few people behind. All he worried about was not twisting an ankle going over rocks. There was no sound of talking, just the sound of men moving over uneven ground and through tree limbs and leaves.

The silence was abruptly shattered by gunfire. Multiple shots rained down through the trees from ahead and to the left. Gerald froze in his tracks when he saw Lieutenant Delgardo fall where he stood.

Sergeant Mast yelled, "Hit the dirt! Take cover!"

Shots flew forward in response to the enemy gunfire. Gerald felt something grab his shirt from behind and pull him hard backward. He fell backward and hit the ground hard. His hip landed on a rock and he winced in pain but didn't make a sound. He was surrounded by the noise of hundreds of bullets being fired. He took a breath and rolled on his side. He looked up and saw Henry beside him. Henry was on one knee in the firing position and already had his rifle to his shoulder, slowly and calmly squeezing off rounds. The shots sounded louder than when he had fired the same weapon at the firing range just a week before. He squeezed off the eight rounds and the clip snapped out of the action with a clink. He quickly reached for another clip. The platoon was in full response now. A private with a BAR fired bursts of automatic gunfire beside Henry. A few Thompson submachine guns rattled away.

Gerald's arm felt like mush. His heart pounded and he concentrated on drawing in each breath. He pulled his carbine off his shoulder and rolled into a prone, firing position. He was afraid to even raise his head in the heated gun battle. He looked ahead under the brim of his helmet. He could see dozens of flashes coming from a rocky ridge fifty yards to the northeast. He moved his rifle up from his side toward his shoulder. He put the butt into a good position and moved his hand toward the trigger. He was about to shoot. He couldn't see any faces, just flashes of light from enemy rifles, visible in the light of the bright afternoon sun, which shone behind the enemy troops. When his finger found the trigger, the metal felt cold. His finger tensed.

"Sergeant Vogel," Sergeant Mast shouted, "keep your squad here and keep it hot for the Japs! My guys with me!"

Sergeant Mast stood, but stayed low. He moved back to the east. Gerald thought for a moment that this was a retreat but quickly realized that this wasn't the case. Nearly a dozen men followed the sergeant in the same manner. Without realizing he was reacting, Gerald rolled off the ground and ran along at the tail end of the line, which was already quickly moving down the hill to the east. The gunfire behind him still pounded away, and he nearly fell from fear that he was going to get shot in the back.

His squad moved fast and hard down the hill. They crossed the ridge going south and headed back west directly toward the enemy. It was uphill, but no harder than what he had experienced in boot camp. Even with a sprint of no more than a couple hundred yards, Gerald gasped for air. He wasn't out of shape; he was terrified. He fought to get each breath when they stopped short of the Japanese position.

The sergeant squatted and lowered his voice. It was still intense. "Hansen, Branch, be ready with grenades. Peters, Fregeolle, twenty yards over my shoulder and be ready with the BAR. Everybody else on my ass, and we don't stop until those sons of bitches are dead." The sergeant turned. "Full mags and clips. Let's move!"

Two men headed up the hill. Two men pulled pins on grenades and threw them in long arches. Two simultaneous explosions caught the line of Japanese attackers off guard. Before the dust had settled, Sergeant Mast moved forward with the rest of the squad only a half step behind him. Privates Peters and Fregeolle opened up with automatics as the sergeant opened up with his carbine on his right side and his Colt pistol on his left. It was a quick seesaw with the sergeant squeezing each index finger back and forth on the two triggers. He wasn't even aiming well, just putting out as much fire as possible. Men fanned out around him and began with their own firepower.

Gerald began pushing himself forward, struggling to lift his feet. He could hear his heart beating even over the gunfire, which was coming closer and harder. He thought he could make himself move. The charge that soldiers made toward the enemy was so contrary to the human instinct of survival. They had been taught in basic training to not think, just react and this was one of those situations. Every soldier needed to do his duty to defend himself, his fellow soldiers, and his nation. Gerald had to act too. The small group of men in front of him disappeared into the smoke and blaze of the attack. He saw Japanese soldiers falling. Those left were screaming like lunatics, lunging at the green fatigues that flowed into the position like floodwaters saturating dry land.

Gerald had his rifle to his shoulder as he moved onto the rocky ridge. A man from his squad fell in front of him. Another fell. Soldiers were now fighting hand to hand, stabbing with bayonets and swinging rifles. A dark-green, foreign uniform ran toward him and he jerked the trigger. The man fell in front of him, and the steel blade of his bayonet brushed Gerald's leg as it hit the ground.

There was less movement now and no more shots. The sergeant

was still yelling at the men to move up the hill. The man who had run into the attack like some cowboy with guns blazing had survived.

Gerald looked around. Men lay dead and wounded all around. Medics were being called. He sat down and looked at the sky because he didn't want to see anything more. He had killed an enemy soldier who had attacked his nation and probably killed Americans and helped destroy property—a soldier who had tried to kill him. Gerald wondered what his father would think of him now. He had survived boot camp and gone into battle.

He could draw a breath now, and when he exhaled, his jaw quivered. The battle was over, and he had survived.

Chapter 34

Seaman Nagami believed he was doing well with his duties aboard the *Okhotsk*. They had been in two engagements, and they were praised by the commander for their hard work and diligent efforts. Morale was very high in the crew. Each man was proud to serve and was eager to do his duty. All were prepared to go through many fights and wanted to achieve glorious victories for themselves and for their homeland. They considered this a fight against the evil of America, and a fight for their nation's liberation and prestige. With each confrontation every man was prepared to fight to the death, if necessary, to achieve victory. He would sooner die than lose the fight and live.

Below decks none of the low-ranking men knew what course the war was taking. They knew they had fought twice and suffered no casualties. They had been praised for their actions. They didn't know if they had fought naval ships or fired on military emplacements on shore. All they knew was they must continue to do their jobs and trust in their leaders.

Hashani wrote of his actions and the victories of the *Okhotsk* in his journal and in letters home. He wrote of his hopes and dreams during this war and after the great win. As an enlisted man he would not have had the arrogance to dream of becoming an officer, but his dreams took him to great places. He was a lover of the sea and the great naval power of Japan. He believed the greatest service to his emperor was at the bridge of a mighty warship, contemplating strategy that would lead to greatness for the empire. He dreamed of directing the movements of the awesome vessel and ordering his men to fire its mighty guns at the enemy. He had his thoughts and dreams and was happy with his humble job. During his time off duty he was happy to be lost in his own writings.

After the great war against the villainous United States, he would celebrate victory with his shipmates. He had been told that Japan and Germany might occupy the United States for a time. He didn't want to do that. Why would anyone want to live in such a repulsive land? Japan would have its place in the world and he was interested in exploring the newly acquired lands of the empire, but his deepest desires for happiness took him no farther than his boyhood village of Ujimon. He thought he would probably work in the fishing industry, hopefully on a boat, and he wanted to try his hand at writing novels. He thought that was a noble and intellectual profession. He could continue to lose himself in stories.

A voice interrupted Hashani's thoughts. Directly beside his bunk was Sanka Haas, a sailor from his compartment. The young man, embarrassed to disturb the peace, cast his eyes down.

"Nagami, sir, I am sorry to be a bother. May we speak?"

"Of course." The two had not sat down to talk to one another before; they had only spoken to each other in passing. Hashani closed his journal with the pencil inside and threw his legs out over the edge of his bunk. He lowered his head to look at the sailor.

The young man spoke very softly. "I was wondering if you could help me with something?"

"Yes, I will try in any way."

The young man's eyes darted back and forth and he moved his head forward, again speaking in hushed tones. "Would you help me, please, to write a letter to my wife?"

Such a simple thing, Hashani thought, and the man seemed embarrassed. Perhaps the man knew Hashani enjoyed writing, even on behalf of someone else. Perhaps he knew that Hashani, with his calm nature, would not make fun of a young sailor who could barely read the letter that had been sent to him.

Hashani smiled warmly. "I would be most happy to help you, Haas. Come."

Hashani folded his legs back inside his bunk, and Sanka sat down on the edge. He took a folded and well-worn piece of paper out of his pants pocket and handed it to Hashani. Hashani was at first hesitant to open a private letter, but his shipmate was not ashamed and trusted the bright young man. Hashani unfolded the letter and read a very neatly written note.

'My dearest, darling Sanka: I hope that my letter has found you well. I am fine here and your older sister comes to see me daily. She always has some type of food in hand for me and your daughter. When she comes, she plays with Tahmie, sometimes for hours. She allows me to get much of the outside work done while she is here. She insists that soon we will travel to a place to have a picture taken of Tahmie. Your daughter is very big now. The first steps that you saw have now turned into a constant run. She laughs often, and waits for your return, as do I. The emperor has said that the battle is near the end for your force and that the victors will return soon. I am proud of your duties and your bravery for our nation. Please fight with honor and return to your family. Your devoted wife, Lapta' Hashani was moved by the simple words and envied the man sitting with him.

Sanka looked at Hashani and asked, "Can you write the words

that I would like to say to my wife?"

Hashani raised his chin and straightened his back as much as he could in the bunk. "I will do my best to help you."

On the bridge Commander Hatsoto was under stress and duly vigilant. He only had contact with Japanese ships in close proximity to his own. All of the ships in the fleet he had sailed with to Vancouver Island had sailed their own ways after the first invasion. They were all under orders to attack the enemy at all costs, harass the mainland of the United States, and fight to the death if necessary. The *Okhotsk* was one of them. Many of the captains were arrogant to the end. They truly believed they could destroy any American ship or installation. Hatsoto was a bit more pragmatic. He was a longtime navy man, trained in the ways of the Imperial Japanese Navy, and he knew he had a great fighting vessel. He also knew that the U.S. Navy could be a powerful adversary, especially when directly attacked in its homeland. Hatsoto put on a strong image in front of his men. They never saw his concern, and he continued to push them in the dutiful attack against America. He believed in all that his nation did and he would continue the fight. He knew fights were taking place on land and in the great expanse of the Pacific. The *Okhotsk* had attacked two land targets: cities on the coast. Hatsoto was taking the fight to the very people who produced the vileness. He would attack whoever stood for America and stood against his own people. The only contact his ship had had with an enemy ship had happened the day before as the *Okhotsk* continued its trek close to the coast. The previous evening it had encountered a number of American ships traveling north at top speed. He wasn't entirely sure why they hadn't attacked his ship, or why he hadn't fired on them. The encounter happened so quickly the *Okhotsk* crew hadn't even been called to battle stations. Only a handful of men knew about it. He wondered what the bridge crew thought. He knew no man would question him. He knew that not one word would be spoken of the contact. Each man knew his place, and it was not to second-guess the commander.

The orders had changed for the *Okhotsk* and the entire Japanese fleet that had sailed for the assault on America. They had been at sea all summer and the Japanese heavy cruiser commanded by Meki Hatsoto had sailed entirely on its own. Hatsoto had met a supply ship once and had refueled twice some thousand miles from the Pacific coast of the United States. Hatsoto knew that the imperial fleet had suffered many losses. The U.S. Navy had mobilized and responded with enormous strength. The Japanese fleet was slowly being decimated. Hatsoto knew that the forces that had landed in the northwestern United States were probably suffering the same fate if any were still alive.

The order given to the fleet still attacking the western mainland of the United States was to cease attacking the Americans directly, stay in contact and avoid confrontation. The order was given directly to the ships' commanders and known only to the highest military commands. It was not repeated through the ranks. The commanders questioned the order from Supreme Military commander, General Tojo. Why would this great weapon of war that had been sent to assault the American nation now be ordered to avoid the Americans? The commander of the *Okhotsk* would follow the commands given to him to the letter, just as every other naval commander would be expected to. Loyalty was expected, but the order to cease fighting would raise a lot of questions. Hatsoto, like every other commander, realized that if this order became known to his crew, each man would take it upon himself to fight without direction. The enlisted navy men would rise up in mutiny and take the battle on themselves. The Bushido code taught that a glorious death in battle ensured great respect and brought peace to a fighter's spirit. The order would not last long. Commanders would take it upon themselves to act.

The ship was approximately one hundred and forty miles off the cost of California, nearly directly in line with San Francisco. Hatsoto had half thought of ignoring the orders. He could sail into San Francisco Bay in about five hours. He could make a heroic charge directly at the enemy and destroy as much as possible before certain death.

Commander Hatsoto followed his orders, continuing to put his trust in the determined military leaders of the Japanese Empire. The fight continued.

Hatsoto's record of failure to engage a U.S. ship was to change that evening. At approximately 1940 hours a lookout spotted smoke rising in the east. Commander Hatsoto arrived on the bridge in a matter of seconds. He directed the large binoculars on the port side of the bridge in the direction of the contact. The smoke came from an American battleship. It was leading a large group of smaller war ships, headed west at high speed.

Hatsoto took a step back. No matter what his orders were, there was no avoiding this fight. He took a breath of contentment knowing that this would be the first and only naval battle this ship would see. He would lead and fight as a true warrior. He would show inspiration to his crew through his final actions.

"Multiple enemy contacts, eighteen miles, bearing two five zero, speed in excess of twenty knots." His voice was calm. He had found his resolve. "Order all crews to battle stations. Prepare for attack." Bushido dictated an attack even when certain defeat was at hand. Possibly hundreds of thousands of tons of U.S. warships were bearing down directly on his position and this was to be an attack by the *Okhotsk*. He would continue the fight until the very end.

The horns over the ship began a mournful blast, as if they were aware of the deadly situation. The entire ship seemed to jump in response. Every man on board ran to his assigned place. There were no discussions and no questions. Nothing was said, just silent obedience. Most on board didn't know what was happening and were unaware of their fate.

In the forward quarters the games that the men commonly played during their hours off duty were dropped and thrown across the floor as dozens of boots skidded in several directions. It took Hashani several seconds to realize what was happening. He had found some paper and was sharpening his pencil. He looked up to see Sanka was gone and the compartment was nearly empty. He recognized that his ship was being called to service and his heart grew warm thinking of his duty. He was the last out of the room, but like a locomotive building steam, he moved faster as he went farther. He slipped the small pencil inside his journal and was about to put the small book in his hip pocket when it fell out of his hand and slid against the wall as he turned into the corridor. He slowed and turned but, knowing he would be punished by the turret chief for again being the last to arrive, he continued running to his station. He told himself the book would be there when he returned.

Within minutes the ship was on station. Shells and gunpowder were hoisted from the magazines below decks. The CAC plotted their targets and there were a lot to choose from. This was the first time some of the men had faced enemy ships, and they were scared. Commander Hatsoto began battle tactics, altering the ship's speed and direction, but he continued south, taking the enemy fleet on the port side so that all of the *Okhotsk*'s big guns could be fired.

As the CAC gave the first range and bearing coordinates to the turret chiefs, the *Okhotsk* came under its first barrage of enemy shells. Tons of high explosive shells from the U.S. battleship fell all around the *Okhotsk*, sending seawater over the deck like a downpour of rain.

On the bridge Commander Hatsoto looked through his binoculars at the increasing number of ships approaching from the west. He was disappointed that his ship had not fired on an enemy ship until that moment. He believed he could have done more for the war. He was disappointed with himself and hoped his family would not be shamed by his failure. He was also sad that thousands of young men would not see the sun rise over their homeland again.

Someone standing behind Commander Hatsoto handed him his helmet. He turned and looked at the young officer who wore a brave expression. Hatsoto then looked back at the sea, not taking the helmet.

Hashani worked with his fellow crewmen, coaxing the fourteen-inch diameter shells into the breach of the guns. They could hear the whistle of the enemy shells sailing over their ship. They knew for the first time they were being fired on. The heavy shells fired at their ship made the crew think of death, but they were not afraid to die for their nation. They concentrated on their jobs. The powder bags were shoved in behind the shells. The turrets had been turned, the barrels raised, and the guns were ready to fire when another salvo from the American fleet sailed toward the *Okhotsk*. Inside the turret the men knew at least one of the shells had hit its target because the ship shook and the metal rang from the strike.

The low-ranking sailors were not aware of a battle's progress. They just kept working and responding mechanically to their jobs.

As quickly as the next shells and powder bags arrived from the magazine, the guns were loaded.

As the American fleet fanned out, more big guns fired on the *Okhotsk*. Just as lions work together to quickly take down their prey, the American ships surrounded and took down their target. The orders from the CAC stopped. It had been destroyed by a direct hit. The ship slowed significantly because the engine room was flooding and out of commission. There were no orders. It was every man for himself now because the bridge had been destroyed.

Inside turret number two the men continued tamping the barrels with shells and powder. They would continue their duty even without orders. A Samurai attacked by himself if required. The turret chief decided his shots after viewing the targets through the scope.

Firing from the *Okhotsk* had slowed. The shells and powder arriving from the magazine had slowed. The guns facing the *Okhotsk* quickly put an end to this once proud vessel of the Japanese Imperial Navy. In its short life, the crew believed it had never had an opportunity to prove its worth. No one on board realized his part in the war. The crewmen weren't told of their strategic role and their sacrifice.

With their ammunition coming up from below decks more slowly, the crew of the number-two turret realized the ship was listing. Inside the dark confines of the gun turret they didn't know which way they were pointing, but they still had a sense of gravity and they knew they were leaning. The ship was taking on water and sinking quickly. Each man thought about the end for the first time. Hashani had never thought about his own death before, only victory and glory.

The men in the gun turret knew that some crewmen remained in the magazine below them because more shells arrived. The cargo elevator made a screeching noise because it tilted as it rose. Knowing water was coming in below, the gun crew realized that the men in the magazine were trapped. Those men were now in their watery tomb and still doing their jobs.

The gun crew found strength in the pride of the brave men below them. They quickly rammed the shells as powder bags were hoisted from below. The ship continued to tip and the turret chief adjusted the elevation of the guns. The number-two turret, the last operational guns on the *Okhotsk*, fired its remaining rounds. The ship sat so low in the water that the shells, traveling at several thousand feet per second, made wakes in the water as they passed across it like a plow in a field. No one saw whether the shells hit their target.

The stern of the ship began to slip under the waves as the lights went out. Hashani struggled to keep on his feet. The only sound was that of water pouring in. No man made a sound, fearing their fellow crewmen would judge them to be cowards. Hashani pushed his way through the water trying to find his way to the hatch. He moved in the direction he thought it was. He was in complete darkness. He floated, but didn't know which way was up. The water surrounded him and he heard the last of the air spewing out of the turret. He heard a gurgling sound as the water rose over his ears. After that came silence. The ship was entirely under water now and there was no way out. The water pressed harder against Hashani's body and was pushing the last bit of breath out of him. It pushed into his nose and he forced his mouth closed. Struggling to keep his sanity, he understood that death was at hand. His mind was a complete haze. With no physical feeling left, he had no more understanding. He held his breath, but the water pressure pressed the last air out of his lungs and ruptured his eardrums. There was only darkness. Everything faded to nothingness.

Chapter 35

Commander Gruber was concerned about his captain. He had seen great energy in the man, but now he saw feebleness. His actions, once spontaneous and brilliant, had turned into calculated acts of desperation.

Johan Kurz had been a trusted U-boat captain. He was now a megalomaniac who seemed to barely be holding onto reality. He didn't know where any of his fellow naval vessels were. He didn't know what his current orders were and continued with his orders from months before. He didn't know where his quickly dwindling supplies were going to come from, but he was continuing with his duties. He said that more ships blockading the coast of the United States meant that there were more targets for U-432. There were fewer civilian ships on the ocean. The risk would be great, but Kurz believed he could overtake a U.S. Navy ship. He had mistakenly led himself beyond his own skill and beyond the capabilities of his fragile crew and weakening vessel. He believed his destiny was to be a war hero capable of destroying the entire American fleet.

The job that the captain now directed was to attack and overrun an American ship to resupply his own. No supplies were known to be available from the German navy. Kurz had been resupplied, but that had been long ago. He had no ability and no desire to return to his home port. Withdrawal from the Atlantic was not what he wanted. Withdrawal equaled retreat to Captain Kurz. In the face of the enemy, retreat was the same as cowardice.

Commander Gruber knew that the captain was planning an attack on a supply source. It was necessary for their survival, but it could lead to their deaths. Gruber was a pragmatic man and he offered his opinions to the captain. His statements were summarily ignored. Kurz was determined to get another kill and find his supplies. He found his target about forty miles east/southeast of Charleston: a supply ship, leaving under cover of darkness with no escort vessel. Reality did find its way into Kurz's head for a moment. The target on first appearance seemed perfect. Perhaps it was too perfect. The rapid build-up of the American navy had been done with such regard for detail that this situation seemed odd. A warship by itself on a patrol mission would not have aroused his suspicion in the least, but an unarmed supply ship was out of place in the lonely waters of the North Atlantic. Was it a trick? Was there a trailing American submarine? Had the ship been sent to draw unsuspecting German U-boats into a destroyer trap?

If this ship were loaded, it would supply everything U-432 needed for months. It was sitting deep enough in the water to suggest it was carrying cargo, which would allow Kurz to continue to cruise the U.S. coast and quietly target his enemy. He was too cunning, and too determined. "The ship is mine," he said to himself.

With that, Captain Kurz set a course to the port stern of the southward traveling ship. He would fall behind, but would never give up on his prey. Like a hungry wolf after a swifter animal, he would catch and kill and take what he wanted.

Chapter 36

It had been about twenty-six hours since U-432 had spotted the supply ship, USS *Fort MacPherson*, moving south. The supply ship had stopped twice in its short travel to provide items to a cruiser in a large group of warships, and a destroyer, which then headed quickly south. Kurz was happy that the U-432 had performed spectacularly after first finding the ship. His ship had been submerged for most of the journey. It sailed slowly, quietly, and undetected just a thousand yards away from the group of enemy ships. Even though U-432 had stayed in contact with the supply ship, it had only been able to travel at a top speed of eight knots. The two stops made by the *Fort MacPherson* had given the sub the opportunity to pull ahead. It hurt Kurz to have to pass by such prime targets as the war ships, but he needed supplies, and he needed to allow time for his boat to recover before roaming the waters of the open Atlantic to look for more prey.

The American ship was now some four hundred yards off the starboard bow. Captain Kurz needed to muster all of his ability to pull off this mission under the dark sky, lit only by a crescent moon. During the entire pursuit he had discussed the attack with Commander Gruber. Many ideas about how it would be carried out ran through his head. Every one of them was of victory. Defeat was never an option for the little man. He knew that he would need to disable the American ship without destroying it. A tired German crew would have to climb aboard the enemy ship, overrun the crew and quickly offload what they needed. Kurz knew it could be done. It would be done. He demanded it.

"Commander Gruber, call the torpedo crew to battle stations and prepare the boarding crew for their attack."

Commander Gruber had aged just as the crew had. He was afraid for the men about to be sent to their likely deaths. He was afraid to speak to the captain but knew his words needed to be said although they would probably be in vain.

"Captain, I must strongly urge you to reconsider this attack. The men are not commandos, prepared for a supported blitz. They are U-boat marines."

The captain stared coldly. "Commander, do your duty and expect my crew to do theirs! These men are well-trained members of the *unterseeboot* corps. They are trained to do great things or they would not be under my command. They are expected to overcome adversity and they will do the duty that I commit them to."

"Captain, they will literally be fighting an uphill battle. They'll have to climb onto an enemy ship at sea, surely under fire. They will have to fight their way through the ship—that is, if they're able to get onto the ship to begin with. They must sling grappling hooks and rappel. I don't believe the sailors of the American ship will throw rope ladders over the side as a welcome."

The tension building in Kurz's face was palpable. Probably no one else had heard what was said, but Gruber knew he had gone too far.

Kurz had never heard such opposition from the second in command. He was disappointed but very angry. Gruber's sarcasm could easily have been considered insubordination.

His voice was no more than a whisper. "Commander Gruber, if you choose not to participate in the activities of this ship of war, you may feel free to leave at any time." He pointed to his left. "Your homeland is about eight thousand kilometers in that direction. I'll see you when my boat returns there."

Gruber hurt inside. He knew the attack was a mistake and some of his crew would die. His words to the captain were met with a response that made him feel like a schoolboy whose schoolmaster had just harshly corrected his misbehavior. There was nothing he could say or do. Franz Gruber literally looked down at his boots when he spoke to the captain, "I humbly ask for your forgiveness, Captain Kurz. I've always been cautious and have concerned myself with the crew. I am sorry." Gruber wasn't sorry for the words he had spoken, just for not being able to do anything about it.

Kurz looked back through the periscope. "That, Commander Gruber, my senior in age but not in rank, is precisely why I've been given command of a ship and you will remain a subordinate."

Gruber still couldn't look up, partly out of shame, but mostly out of disgust. He had no control, even of himself, within the small confines of the German boat. He had learned that Kurz was arrogant and now decided that Kurz was completely mad.

"Commander, this is an American supply ship. It's armed with a small group of sailors, the last weak part of an inferior navy. Our abilities and superior fire power will overcome whatever they may be able to muster." Kurz spoke again in a normal voice. "Prepare the attack."

Gruber quietly responded to the directive, "Aye, Captain."

Kurz checked the periscope again. He was having difficulty seeing the ship in the dark waters of the night. As he focused, he could

see that the USS *Fort MacPherson* was moving just as he had pre-
dicted. It was traveling at a top speed of about fourteen knots. Its
course was steady. There was nothing else known to be in the immediate area. Even so, the crew of the U-432 would have to work
quickly. When they hit the enemy ship, they would have probably
thirty minutes—forty-five minutes maximum—to board and get
what they could. No matter the amount of time, Kurz believed
he could submerge and avoid anything the Americans could attack with. He was drunk with power after sailing for many miles
over the Atlantic Ocean to within just a few thousand yards of the
coastline. He had traveled around and under U.S. Navy ships. He
dreamed the impossible.

He had calculated in his head how to fire on the unsuspecting
ship. He had consulted his plotting charts and rules. He now gave
orders to turn his boat toward the *Fort MacPherson* and called the
sub to a stop. He would have a difficult shot, firing on a vessel that
was moving nearly directly away and from an odd angle. It was to
his advantage that the *Fort MacPherson* was a fairly large and slow
moving ship. It would be a difficult shot, but he believed it would
be magnificent.

"All stations ready?"

"Aye, Captain."

Kurz began the grueling mental process of deciding on his shot.
He must calculate precisely when to launch the torpedo to catch
the moving ship at the right location. He decided the best way to
immobilize the ship was to hit the stern. It would be like shooting
out the eye of a badger, but he would do it. No matter what the
point of contact was, he only needed to break the rudder or shatter the propeller. Even if the ship started taking on water, it would
be confined to a small area of the watertight compartments. That

would be when the crew of U-432 would make its move. The crew
on the American ship would be concerned with damage control
and would never suspect a boarding attack.

His eyes ached. His hands worked constantly to adjust the periscope. He squinted for all his might to see the departing ship. He
became more confident as the sub came within firing distance. He
was no longer anxious. All emotion left him. He counted down out
loud, *"Funf . . . vier . . . drei . . . zwei . . . eins ...feuer!"*

The boat lurched in response as the torpedo was spit out of the
tube. Within seconds of Kurz's order the projectile had risen to the
surface of the water and was directly on its way to its target a few
hundred yards away.

The captain was so confident that he gave the command to
move ahead at three knots. The boat moved toward the ship that
was about to experience a huge explosion. Commander Gruber was
powerless to question the captain. He could only repeat the order.
"Aye, Captain, ahead three knots."

Kurz looked at the supply ship, squinting in anticipation of an
explosion that would light up the night sky.

The torpedo found its mark. Only inches in front of the rudder
it struck the hull of the ship at the waterline. The resulting explosion dislodged the rudder and destroyed the propeller. The big ship
staggered in the water and continued a bit further under its own
momentum. Sailors on the American ship jumped from their bunks,
knowing immediately what was going on. They rushed to firefight-
ing stations and manned guns. Most of the small crew in the engine
compartment were killed by the explosion. The remaining men fled
the rapidly rising water. Two men were not able to move because
of injuries. Kurz had thought little of the men delegated to a supply ship, but there was as much bravery there as anywhere in the

U.S. military. The two injured men made it out with the assistance of fellow crewmen. There was no question of duty. There was no need for thanks. There was just action in time of need. With every man safely out of the engine compartment, the hatch was dogged. The water that made it out could be pumped from the ship. On the deck men had taken up positions along the sides in addition to those already in lookouts.

U-432 moved behind the *Fort MacPherson* and was squarely aligned on the starboard side when it surfaced. As soon as the boat leveled, the hatches came open on the front and back of the conning tower. The German sailors struggled to get up the ladders and onto the deck as quickly as they could. Their first efforts were met with a hail of gunfire from the half dozen or so M-1s held by the sailors on the deck of the *Fort MacPherson*. Thirty-caliber ammunition cut down German sailors where they stood. The rounds bounced off the steel deck of the submarine like small lightning strikes. One or two rounds found their way inside the hatches on the top of the deck and bounced around the interior of the submarine for several seconds. No men screamed. They died bravely, or they were too tired to react to their pain.

Two German MP machine guns were able to return fire, with one gunner hanging over the side by his fingernails and the other firing blindly from an open hatch. Three hundred rounds per minute of nine millimeter ammunition only hit metal on the side of the supply ship or sailed over it but did cause the American sailors to duck. This gave the Germans an opportunity to advance from the hull of the submarine.

New clips were fed into Garand rifles on the deck of the U.S. ship and aimed over the side down toward the sub. When a gun and head appeared from above, a German MP opened up another burst of fire. All of the shots back and forth were blind reactions.

Captain Kurz found his way to the top of the ladder in the conning tower. He stayed low against the side. Commander Gruber never made it to the top of the ladder because Kurz blocked the hole. "Captain, our men will never make it to the deck of the American ship."

"Superior fire from superior sailors will get them on deck."

Kurz had a Luger pistol in his hand. He didn't use it. He quickly poked his head above the side and looked down to the deck of his boat. He motioned the men on the deck to move up. Ropes with grappling hooks were thrown up and snatched the side railing on the USS *Fort MacPherson*. Guns from the deck of the submarine kept heads above them down. Smoke from the hundreds of rounds fired, hung low against the water. Sailors on the deck of the submarine had to watch their step so as to not roll on the spent cartridges from their guns. With machine guns slung over their shoulders, they jumped and swung over, hitting the side of the supply ship with their boots. When the ropes were tight, hands holding knife blades appeared above. Just a few quick slices and the couple men trying to make it up fell into the water. They flapped in their uniforms, struggled back over to the submarine and were met by the outstretched arms of their fellow crewmen. With no way up, sailors on the submarine's deck were ready to fall back.

Kurz stood up. He said to himself, loudly enough for Gruber to hear, "Imbeciles." He yelled down, "Shoot the enemy off the deck and get up there!"

Bewildered sailors looked up at the captain in confusion. They had always followed his direction without hesitation, but now they questioned his mental soundness. How could they possibly make the ten meters to the deck? Men just stood, unsure of what to do.

Kurz was still standing when something came over the side of the American ship. Everyone on board heard two small splashes, then the sound of a metal object hitting the deck of the submarine. Kurz ducked for dear life. Before the item bounced, it exploded, knocking two sailors into the water, dead. One man nearby had most of one arm torn off. There was no noise; no sound of orders. Sailors jumped into the open hatches, preferring the possibility of broken bones to mutilated bodies. Men grabbed for the ladders and fell the rest of the way. One scared young seaman, the last man on the deck, got a foothold on the ladder and had begun to pull on the hatch for all his might when he heard a muffled gurgling. It took him a moment to realize where it was coming from. He climbed back far enough to look over the side of his boat. He could see a fellow crewman in the water, struggling with one arm. As the young sailor on the ladder started to help the man, he saw the left side of the man's face. The man appeared to look up at the submarine, but one eye looked forward and one eye dangled from its socket. The side of his head looked like ground meat. The young sailor on deck gasped and dropped back into the boat, closing the hatch.

Kurz stepped on Gruber as he made his way down the ladder back to the bridge. "Submerge the ship!"

"Captain, our men!"

"Better be on the ship. Submerge it! Dive to thirty meters, heading zero one five, all ahead full," he said, gritting his teeth. "Get us out of the area at top speed."

Commander Gruber was already turning around when he asked, "Captain, permission to check on the crews?"

"Denied."

Gruber was taken by surprise. "Captain!"

"Your request is denied. Your job is to get my boat safely out of

the area. Had those men made it onto the enemy ship and extermi-
nated the crew we wouldn't have to worry. Because of this failure,
the supply ship has surely contacted help from destroyers heading
in our direction." He looked around the room coldly. "This failure
has cost me too much."

The sailors in the room looked back at the captain.

Operations on the bridge continued as usual, but the thoughts
in the men's minds had changed.

Kurz told himself that he would not be beaten. His ship would
continue and succeed.

Chapter 37

Earl had had another long day dealing with inspectors at the bank and he was ready to be home. He thought about nothing but what was on the table for dinner and a warm bath. He wasn't sure about the dinner because Edith had taken the job in the cannery. Why she wanted to do such things with a household to deal with was beyond him. Earl thought that he made all the money they needed, and she concern herself with the house and children rather than canned food going to who knows where.

The days were getting noticeably shorter. Earl hurried to get home before they called for the next, silly, air-raid drill. He would either be stuck where he was or have to attempt to drive home in the dark with no headlights. No danger of that tonight. The sun was beginning to set, but in the future he would have to concern himself with Jake, the crazy air-raid warden on his block. He couldn't legally arrest Earl, but he was just nuts enough to shoot out the car's headlights as it came down the street.

Earl slowed and made the turn into his driveway. He had to come to a stop just off the street and pull slowly forward to the left. He wasn't sure what disaster had taken place, but there was a pile of junk in the driveway. It was obviously out of the garage building because he recognized the old, rusty, metal lawn chair; the broken radiator out of Peter's bedroom; some old car parts; an inner tube; and a little pile of scrap metal. "What kind of craziness is going on now?" he said out loud.

He came to a stop and shut the engine off just as the dog ran to greet him and Peter emerged from the building with a metal pipe in his hands and a smile on his dirty face. Earl stepped out of the car with a completely disgusted expression on his face. "What in the world are you doing?" Earl asked, as Jake nuzzled his hand. "Go away, dog."

"We're collecting scrap metal and rubber for the drive on Saturday." Peter was beaming. "We're doing our part to smash the enemy and run those SOBs back to Germany and Japan."

He sounded like some war poster.

"Watch your language and who exactly is 'we'?"

Peter stopped for a moment. "'We' is the family. Me and Jake are cleaning up the junk in the garage and getting it ready to take down to the Wayman Park tomorrow at noon. The city is sponsoring a drive. There's going to be a band and army men there." He threw the pipe on the pile and started back toward the garage. He turned his head to say, "Pots, pans, and movie fans. Any old steel will help grease the wheels."

Earl huffed. "Enough with the poster language." His arms were folded in front of him. "Where did you get the idea to just start throwing away our stuff?"

"It's old junk. We're not using it and Uncle Sam can."

Earl threw his hands up. "Oh yes, I'm sure Uncle Sam can use a broken radiator."

"No, Dad. They melt it down and re-use it. Just think. That radiator could become a bomb that sinks a Jap battleship." Peter nodded his head confidently.

"You let Uncle Sam worry about the bombs and clean up our driveway."

"But, Dad, it's for the drive!"

"You don't concern yourself with that and clean up."

Peter looked disappointed, confused, and maybe a little bit angry. Earl wasn't worried about that. He thought that Peter was just too young to understand everything in the world. Earl may not have been able to decide what was best for his own wife, but he could decide what was best for his sons.

Earl was just about to go inside when he saw crazy Jake headed down the street. Just like a policeman walking the beat, Jake made his rounds almost every night. Earl decided to say hello so as to not be rude. The man was strange, but he seemed mostly harmless and dedicated to the job.

Jake gave a sort of salute. "Good evening, citizen."

Earl nodded his head in response. Peter stopped and stood straight. He always looked at Jake with reverence. Jake was the closest thing to a soldier Peter ever saw and the young man had heard the war stories about Jake.

Jake walked to the corner of the drive and made a quick ninety-degree turn toward Earl. Peter stood watching. Jake came to a stop at the back of the car and clicked his heels together. Maybe he was showing off in front of Peter, or maybe he was just caught up in the whole character, but he was trying to act like some serviceman on parade.

The dog walked over to the block captain. Earl noticed the dog wasn't wagging his tail. That seemed odd because the dog had never been unfriendly to anyone before. Jake held out his hand. The dog stood in place and moved his head toward the man's hand. He sniffed for a second and backed away. The old man's eyebrows creased. He looked at Earl and asked, "Anything to report?"

Earl was caught by surprise. "Uh, nothing, sir. All is well."

"You know that we're holding an air-raid warning tonight. It'll soon be time to go inside and extinguish all lights. No smoking outside; all windows covered." He spoke as if this were the first time Earl had heard the orders although the drills had been going on for months. "Any questions?"

Earl hesitated a moment and looked down. "I do have one. Why are we still having air-raid drills every couple of weeks? This has been going on for some time now."

Jake tipped his head and looked at Earl with a look of surprise. "We always have to be prepared for any enemy attack."

Earl looked up now. "Do you really believe that some German or Japanese bomber is going to fly over probably the dullest street, smack in the middle of the country, and bomb us? We're thousands of miles from the enemy and there's nothing here to bomb." Earl spoke in a tone of sarcasm. "Do you believe we're going to be attacked here?"

The old soldier looked squarely at Mr. Frankton and gave a low, sturdy response. "Not on my watch."

Earl just stared. What can I say to that? he thought. He laughed inside when he realized the old man and his youngest son were so much alike in their thoughts about the war. Both were zealous. Both had a certain innocence.

Jake continued unfazed. "Attacks can come not only from the air, you know. The Japs and the Jerrys have people in the country."

Earl looked over at Peter who was still standing in the same spot. Peter had an awestruck expression on his face. Jake didn't scare him, but Earl didn't like the talk in front of his son. Peter already had exaggerated thoughts about the war. He didn't need to hear anything more.

Jake said, "Saboteurs can cause as much damage as a five-hundred pound bomb."

"I really don't think there are any enemy saboteurs on McCabe Avenue in Omaha."

"What do you know about your neighbors?" Jake pointed to the Masuko house.

Earl looked. "It's a quiet family that has lived in this country for a long time."

"That's what they've said. What do you know about them?"

Earl's face took on the same expression as his son. He had never stopped to think about his neighbor. They had met and spoken a few times, but they never socialized. The only thing Earl knew about them was what they said about themselves.

Jake continued. "I've watched them. I know they're concerned about us because I've seen them watching me. I keep an eye on them and report what I see. I know the government is finding out about them."

The old soldier turned toward the neighbor's house with a scowl. "We won't have to worry about them for long."

Earl continued staring at Jake.

Jake turned back. "They've been told already. They're going to one of those camps."

"They're being relocated?"

"Yeah. They've been told already. We're trying to make this city safe." He was acting like some fanatic. "Don't turn your back on them."

The streets are supposed to be safe, Earl thought. The enemy is not here; it's hundreds of miles away. Everyone is acting crazy.

"Blackout begins at 2030 hours. That's 8:30 p.m. You be sure and be inside and secured by that time."

It would be a night of fun for Peter. It would be nothing but a useless inconvenience for Earl.

Jake started down the driveway to continue his rounds. As he turned, he said, "Be sure and report anything odd to me immediately."

Earl tried to hold back his sarcasm. "Yes, I'll let you know about the war raging here in Omaha. We'll not worry about something happening somewhere else."

The dog walked in front of Earl and pushed against his leg. "Jake, you dummy!"

Jake was at the end of the driveway and turned. He had an evil look on his face.

Earl realized what he had said and was embarrassed. He looked up. "Uh . . . the dog." It would be better just to leave things as is, he thought.

"Mr. Frankton, if you don't prepare to meet the war, the war might find you." Jake continued down the street.

Earl spoke to Peter and told him to get inside. Peter headed toward the door with the four-legged Jake and its wagging tail in tow. "Peter, leave the dog outside."

"But, Dad, if he's out at blackout, he'll have to be out all night."

"That's where he belongs." Earl thought Jake, the dog and Jake, the man. Both needed to be on a leash. Nothing seemed to be getting any better around there. The danger in the rest of the country seemed to be decreasing, but in Omaha the war seemed to rage on.

Chapter 38

It was the day of the big recycling drive at Wayman Park and Peter still wanted to go. He decided he could at least show up with old newspapers and the stove grease his mother had been collecting. "That would make a decent wagon load," he said to himself. He could still take pride in the fact that he wasn't showing up empty handed and could see the activities.

It was breakfast as usual at the kitchen table, and then outside he went to begin his day. He left through the side door and jumped down the steps, hitting only one step on the way down as usual. He turned toward the garage to dig out his wagon. He wouldn't be able to carry much on his bicycle, but he could still ride down a couple hills inside the wagon.

Just as he reached the edge of the house, he glanced out of the corner of his eye. His dog was lying in the back yard. Something didn't look right about it, and he immediately wondered why Jake hadn't greeted him at the back door, wagging his tail and jumping with paws extended. He froze in his tracks for a moment. He knew something was wrong, and he was scared.

"Jake?" Peter felt a chill, even standing in the sun. "Jake, what's wrong, boy?"

Peter was stuck somewhere between boyhood and manhood.

He seemed to have grown so much just that summer. No longer would he run. The ten-year-old made his legs step forward as he went to check on his friend, lying behind the house.

He could see the bright red covering the dog, and some in the grass. He stood over Jake and looked down over his longtime companion. The dog had a small hole on the side of his chest, and his neck was cut. Peter stood motionless, as motionless as the dog on the grass. There was no sound from either of them.

Edith was at the kitchen sink, looking out the back window. All she could see was Peter standing still with his head down. She watched for a moment, and when Peter didn't move, she walked outside to see what he was doing. As she came around the back corner of the house, she could see what her young son could see. She walked up beside him, not sure of what to say or do. Her son wasn't crying; he was just looking over the body of his dog. This was Peter's closest friend. They had come to the house at about the same time, and a younger Jake had watched over the infant Peter like a mother. As they grew up together, Peter would do anything for his friend. Jake was there even when friends from school or the neighborhood were not.

"Peter, I'm . . ." Edith couldn't say a word.

"Jake is dead." Peter's voice was steady and distant.

Edith still couldn't speak. She held back tears. She didn't want to cry in front of her son who appeared to be stronger than she was. She just walked away quietly to the house where she found Earl.

When Earl heard the family dog was dead, his first reaction was fear. He ran to his son's side. Who would do this? he wondered. Why would any human being do this? His fear suddenly turned to anger. This was just a family pet that had threatened no one. This was his son's ever-present companion. Killing Peter's dog was barbaric.

Earl kneeled beside his son and wanted to help him understand, but he didn't understand himself. This was hatred, and destruction, and selfishness.

"This is about war, Dad." Peter looked up for the first time.

Earl raised his eyebrows in shock. "No, Peter, this isn't about war. This is about a mean person wanting to do something bad."

"This is war. War is when somebody wants to take something from somebody, or make somebody else be different, or hurt or kill."

They locked eyes with one another. Earl realized that was exactly right. It was spoken in simple terms, short and sweet, and it was correct. Peter had learned, just as Earl had, that war didn't only exist on the battlefields of Europe and the Pacific. It existed here in the United States and even in Omaha. Peter and Earl were learning about the mean and changing world. They stayed still for a few moments.

"Peter, we'll go bury him."

Peter looked back down at Jake. "I'll bury him. I'll take him to the woods and find a good spot." He looked back up at his father and shook his head. "He was my dog and my responsibility. I'll bury him."

This struck Earl every bit as hard as seeing the dog dead. His ten-year-old wasn't crying. He didn't seem upset. He was taking the death of his friend like more of a man than Earl had been. Peter had grown so much, right before Earl's eyes. He was becoming wise beyond his years and learning the harsh realities of the world. In burying his dog, he was doing what he thought he should, just as other people in the house were doing what they thought they should.

Earl was the adult and he was learning from his child. For the first time he realized how small and selfish he had been for the past several months. He realized that he should be proud of his wife for doing what so many other women were doing. She took a job not for herself, but to help others. He should be proud of Christopher and supportive of his son's decision to join the army like so many millions of other young men. Christopher was prepared to fight for his nation. Earl was definitely proud of his youngest son who seemingly could do the least but taught the most.

Earl stood up. He was a couple feet taller than his son, but they seemed to look eye to eye. "Peter, you take whatever time you need to bury Jake. When you come home, we'll load up all of that scrap that needs to go to the drive today." The two looked directly at one another. "And since it's at the park, we'll give your mother a day off and pack a picnic lunch, and we'll take Christopher along. Those soldiers you were talking about can probably help him get recruited into the army."

They turned away from Jake and walked toward the garage side by side. Earl thought Peter seemed the most concerned and sincere person he knew. Earl thought about the comments he had made so many times about this not being his war. He regretted ever having said them and realized the war belonged to those who were in the path of it. The war had found Earl, even in the middle of America, and it was now his war also.

Chapter 39

Their mission had dragged on for months. U-432 was floating blind in the Atlantic. They no longer had contact with any friendly ships. The crew was near starvation. They had only enough fuel to maneuver, not to travel any distance. To the best of anyone's knowledge, all other vessels of the German navy had returned home. Captain Kurz's boat could be the only one left near the coast of the United States, and he was okay with that. Kurz regularly expressed his disappointment in the crew for their—in his words— "lack of proper response." Since the debacle with the supply ship, his words and demands became harsher and severer. His actions seemed more and more desperate.

The crew was in discussion with Commander Gruber about their future. They all realized they wouldn't be able to return to Europe under their own power. They weren't sure if they would live long with their small stocks of food and water. They were driven to near insanity by their long confinement in the small boat. Their captain continually pushed them close to the breaking point. The crew trusted Gruber to lead them, not knowing how powerless he was. Gruber no longer knew how to speak to the captain. He tried to talk about survival. Kurz's response was that as long as they could fight they would stay and do their job no matter what the cost would be. Gruber wondered if Captain Kurz was prepared to receive his war decorations posthumously. He knew that surrender was not an option for his captain. Their future was bleak and would probably be short.

Life on the small bridge of U-432 continued. The area was always silent as the captain expected it to be and as the men focused on their duties. Now the mood was somber. The room was very dark because batteries were weak and systems were failing. The men on board became frail and ill as the long journey continued with no successful end in sight. Each man had volunteered for this duty and had been proud when he sailed, believing in himself and his nation. Now each man was ready to give up. There was nothing left to fight for, not even one another.

Captain Kurz didn't stop. He was also tired, but stubborn and proud. Even though he was becoming thinner because of the growing shortage of food supplies, he didn't show it. He would always appear in front of the crew with a shaved face, polished boots, and a pressed uniform and cap. This mighty weapon of the German military—U-432—would continue. The captain sat staunchly in his chair on the bridge, unwavering and unmoving. He seemed content to allow the hours to pass by. He had sat in silence and completely still for well over an hour when his voice cracked, "Commander Gruber."

The commander turned. "Aye, Captain?"

Kurz breathed deeply before clearing his throat. "Surface the ship."

Things started running through Gruber's mind. It was daytime. They would be easy targets to the wall of U.S. ships, but he complied without question, "Aye, Captain. Surface the ship."

The ship had also aged, and it seemed slower in its response to commands. It rose directly until water splashed off the conning tower and over the deck on the front and back of the ship. Lookouts went to their respective posts. A petty officer climbed the ladder in the conning tower and opened the hatch. He slid back down the back of the ladder just as Captain Kurz moved up the front. Commander Gruber climbed the ladder after Kurz.

On top, the sea breeze was a welcome change to the acrid air of the ship. Kurz enjoyed it for several seconds. Gruber thought the crew deserved as much. He was sure he had known what the captain's intentions had been. Was he now considering surrender?

Kurz lifted his binoculars and began scanning the horizon. The U.S. Navy had responded with such force that it was a surprise they hadn't surfaced beside an American ship. One was surely nearby. Kurz stopped and directed his glasses toward the southwest. Gruber focused in that direction and could see the smoke from a steaming ship. Kurz continued looking in that direction.

Gruber wondered what was going through Kurz's mind and what would happen next. He thought for a few seconds; he could get a flare gun and signal the ship. The war could be over in the next few minutes for U-432.

Kurz put down his binoculars and stood for a minute. Gruber could see a second column of smoke. There were surely many more ships.

"Submerge the ship." Kurz climbed back down the ladder. He reached the bottom and looked up at Gruber who was still at the top. Gruber was ready to collapse in disbelief, but retreated.

The room suddenly became more active with the captain's commands. "Submerge the ship. Dive to five meters, heading two one zero; ahead at four knots; man battle stations."

Gruber was on the bridge now and repeated the orders. The

men at their posts on deck came back inside. Sailors moved to their stations, unsure of the ship's activities.

"Captain, what are your intentions?" Gruber asked directly.

Kurz was surprised. He didn't believe his second in command had questioned him in such a manner. He didn't know whether to give him a response or order him to be arrested. He was still the ultimate authority on the ship and he would not be questioned like this. "Commander Gruber, there is an enemy ship within our reach and we will attack it and sink it. There will be no failures this time. Go to your station and await my orders."

"Captain, there are surely a number of ships. By firing on the ship we would reveal our location and be attacked. Captain, there is entirely too much risk."

Kurz's nostrils flared. "This is a warship. It is my duty to bring the war to the enemy. We will do that and we will be successful without question or hesitation." His voice had risen to a scream. "Commander Gruber, go to your station and await my orders!"

There was dead silence on the bridge.

"Up periscope, load torpedo tubes one and two."

The men on board hesitatingly complied. U-432 had slowly and quietly moved to within fifteen hundred meters of the enemy ship, BB-52, the USS *Kansas*. Captain Kurz eyed the big battleship through the periscope and concerned himself only with the target in front of him. It was a modern battleship, over nine hundred feet long, displacing some forty-four thousand tons of seawater. The ship wore its measure twenty-two, camouflage paint to confuse the enemy as to its direction of travel and speed. Kurz laughed inside. He would only need to watch the ship for a short time in the mid-day sun to decide on its direction and speed. He gave no thought to being spotted, either visually or by sonar. His only concern was to sink an enemy ship—a big one.

While focusing through the periscope, he began giving his directions. "Range, fourteen hundred fifty meters; bearing, one one zero; speed of target, sixteen knots."

Gruber didn't repeat the orders; he only acknowledged the captain with an aye and nodded at the seaman at the controls. Kurz didn't look away from the periscope.

"Come left, three degrees," Kurz continued. His breathing was shallow. He so wanted a kill mark for sinking a battleship. With two, well-placed shots into the side, he could do it. He began his mental countdown.

All was quiet on the *Kansas*. Its crew, as young as every other crew in the navy, was proud, frightened, and lonely in the big North Atlantic. They were happy to be guarding the waters of the United States and they had not yet been in combat. Little did they know that was about to change.

Seaman Third Class Matt Rosen was a lookout. He was bored with his duties but did as he was told. He had been on duty for about twenty minutes, scanning the horizon for enemy ships. He had not seen one in his brief navy career. After a couple months at sea with nothing going on, his boredom had turned to complacency. It was a warm, sunny day on the ocean and he was as happy as a cloud in the sky, or one of the dolphins that so commonly raced along with the behemoth ship. Through his binoculars he could see two of the happy animals, apparently jumping in competition with one another. There appeared to be only two, jumping back and forth in a small area. He had seen a lot of dolphin activity, but this seemed odd. He moved to the larger, mounted scope and zeroed in on the area. The dolphins seemed nervous. He knew they were intelligent creatures and could even be human-like. What were they doing? Near them he saw a thin, dark object sticking straight up in the water. It was not moving, just sitting still in the water. It wasn't a piece of floating wood. He had not seen one in real life, but his heart hit his stomach when he recognized the periscope of a German U-boat. He lunged for the telephone headset. It rang on the bridge the moment he picked it up.

Lieutenant Commander Mick Frailey was in charge of the bridge at that moment. He was sitting in the command chair, relaxing with a cigarette, when the lookout phone rang. Frailey was a dutiful sailor and had the receiver to his ear in one second. Without acknowledging the man on the other end, he listened to his intense voice. "Enemy sub, port side, fifteen hundred yards!"

Commander Frailey jumped out of the chair and yelled in a single breath, "Enemy sub, port side, all ahead full, hard to port, battle stations!" The sailor at the wheel started turning as hard as he could. He was joined by a nearby officer and they turned the rudder as far as it would move. Hand over hand they turned, painfully long seconds, until the wheel wouldn't go any further.

Horns sounded all over the ship and sailors responded to their duty. The engines responded and began spinning the propellers faster. The rudder turned and began moving the back of the mighty warship toward its right, sending the front of the ship in the direction of the enemy sub. Commander Frailey's concern was to avoid any torpedoes that might already be on their way toward the ship's huge side. He wanted to spin the back of the ship out of the way and make the *Kansas* as narrow as possible to the enemy.

Captain Kurz made his countdown and gave the command to fire two torpedoes. Within a second of his command everyone heard the powerful rush of air in water as the first torpedo was propelled from its tube. This sound had not faded before the second torpedo tube responded in the same way a few seconds later. The projectiles were on their way to their target several thousand feet away.

Moving millions of tons of warship in the ocean was no quick or easy task. In the short time that it took the sailors and officers on the bridge to respond to the orders, they were sweating, both from fear and from the burst of energy they had had to exert. The two men were still pushing against the wheel, which was turned all the way to the left. Anyone on the rear of the ship could have seen the action. The wake increased in response to the speed and began to shift behind the ship. The seaman on the lookout strained his eyes as he peered into the water until he saw something even scarier than the periscope: the trails created by two torpedoes, headed directly toward the *Kansas*. Rosen, still holding onto the headset so hard that his knuckles were white, screamed so loudly his words were barely understood by Commander Frailey. "Torpedoes in the water!"

Captain Benjamin Karr was on the bridge now. Frailey quickly gave him the information: "U-boat, three quarters of a mile to port. Torpedoes in the water." The captain didn't need to ask for any more information. He trusted his number-three man of the ship and felt the ship turning toward the left. This was all the battleship could do for the moment. It could not easily maneuver to avoid a sub, and it had no particular defense against a torpedo striking the hull. Sometimes a ship just had to take the hit and repair, if it could. Turning toward the sub was safe for the battleship. It put the submarine at risk of colliding with the larger-surfaced vessel. If the ship collided with the U-boat, there would be very little, if any, damage to the ship. A collision could cause the U-boat to stop operating, founder, or split into pieces.

Captain Kurz could see that the battleship was turning. He

waited, wanting to see his shots.

The ship did its best. It was turning to face its enemy when the first torpedo found its mark. The nose of the torpedo struck the side of the ship at the water line about three quarters of the way back. The ship had turned on the torpedo at just enough of an obtuse angle to make the torpedo ricochet off to the right. The explosive didn't detonate. It floated toward the back of the turning ship and into the path of the second torpedo. They struck one another and exploded simultaneously. The explosion sent plumes of water as high as the ship's smoke stacks, but did no damage.

Captain Kurz witnessed this through the periscope. With his blood at a boil he slammed the handles of the scope against its sides. Now he must run with no victory to show for his efforts. "Down periscope. Dive the ship to thirty meters, course of one nine zero, all ahead full."

Gruber responded immediately. He knew an attack would bring an instant and bitter response from the American fleet. He knew the Americans and British had developed tactics with their destroyers in the North Atlantic convoys. Each nimble ship could carry hundreds of depth charges and torpedoes and would saturate an area until they ran out of ammunition or were positive the U-boat was sunk.

The U-boat began its dive and the propeller began spinning to move them out of the area as quickly as possible. They could not afford much maneuverability. The ship was low on battery life and very low on fuel. They had to move away from the area before the submarine killers arrived.

The *Kansas* had already been in contact with nearby ships. The U.S. Navy was entirely prepared for anything the German and Japanese military could throw at it. There were torpedo planes stationed on each coast that could be on their way to a target within minutes. There were rigid airships armed with depth charges and constantly patrolling the shores. The fleet of warships was large, powerful, and ready for a fight. Within seconds of the call from the *Kansas* several destroyers were on their way to the area. They had drilled and practiced for this. Thousands of American sailors were ready for the fight to defend their nation.

U-432 was moving at top speed away from the area. Unfortunately, top speed for the German submarine was about a third of the speed of the destroyers, which could move on the surface of the ocean like well-trained quarter horses and could avoid torpedoes fired by a U-boat. The U-boat could not surface to fight the destroyers because the surface ships had several bigger and more accurate guns than the sub. The submariners knew the sub could not outrun the surface ships, nor could it outmaneuver them. They could only hope to be deep into the ocean before the destroyers arrived.

On the bridge of U-432 the tension was high. Kurz was livid about what he considered a retreat without a victory. Everyone was fearful of an attack. Only the sound of their own ship could be heard, churning out to sea as hard as it could go. When they heard the distinctive ping of a destroyer's active sonar, the crewmen gasped collectively.

Kurz said in a hushed, even tone, "All stop. Maintain thirty meters." Commander Gruber repeated the orders and the ship quieted in the water. It was best not to be moving. If the destroyer's sonar man were to see something that large moving at eight knots, he could be sure it was a submarine.

The destroyers in the North Atlantic convoys had worked well against the German wolf packs. The more destroyers that arrived, the easier it would be for them to ping away with their sonar and triangulate the position of the sub. What the U-boat heard was behind them and at a distance. The farther away they were, the less likely they were to be seen by the destroyer. The U-boat sat there, still in the water, hoping to be invisible. After several seconds they heard the destroyer ping again, still searching. After a short time they heard a sonar ping from another destroyer, this time from far to their starboard. One sonar man could mistake a single target, not moving and at a distance, but two sonar men could compare their scope information and be better informed. The U-432 could only stay still and silent.

The pings from the ships continued and even more fear built on U-432 when a ping was heard very close on the port side—another destroyer. This was surely the beginning of the end. There was nothing that could be done. The submarine could not hide from sonar contact. The three ships could compare contact information and precisely locate the U-boats location down to a square yard.

The sonar pings from the approaching enemy ships were constant now. It was only a matter of time until they would begin their attack on the stationary U-boat. It was time to begin weighing options. The propellers of the ships above could be heard, and then came the sound that would make even the most war-hardened sailor nearly collapse in fear: the sound of splashes. Gruber and Kurz looked at one another.

Kurz yelled, "Dive to sixty meters, full speed ahead!"

Gruber had just as much tension in his voice. "Aye, dive to sixty meters, full speed ahead!"

The destroyers had the location and depth of the U-boat and Captain Kurz could only try to stay ahead of the depth charges. The charges were set and fired into the water at a precise location.

The U-boat needed to be out of the area where the depth charge would sink before reaching its exploding depth. The captain would continue as long as possible, changing speed, direction, and depth in an attempt to avoid the charges.

The first charges detonated with a huge shock. The entire ship shook from the explosion only yards away. This was the first time many of the crewmen had experienced this type of attack and they were terrified. This young crew had gone to sea with fearless pride, and now they felt numbing horror.

The explosions continued at a tremendous rate. Kurz could only hope the ships would run out of ammunition before his sub was damaged. That was not likely. The destroyers could sustain a lengthy attack, and then be relieved by another nearby ship. The explosions were coming closer. The U-boat was being deluged with charges. The close explosions threw men to the floor and bounced them off walls. Quick vibrations passed through the metal boat, causing violent shaking. The older crew knew to stay put and not touch anything. Jolts could break bones and knock men across the room. With each explosion ears ached inside the pressurized tube because the sides of the sub were being squeezed and released. Men were shocked and shaken into madness. They knew their deaths could come at any moment.

Gruber yelled as loud as he could at the captain, "Sir, we should surface the ship."

Captain Kurz had strapped himself tightly into his chair. He looked straight ahead. He had heard his commander, but refused to respond.

"Captain, we will not survive!"

Kurz remained unresponsive.

Other ships had apparently arrived because the rate of

explosions had increased almost to the speed of a machine gun. Thrown around the ocean like a rag doll, the U-boat could barely continue to function. It began to make a noise. The damage it had sustained had allowed water to seep into several areas. It could go down quickly.

"Captain!" Gruber screamed. "The ship is taking on water. We may not be able to blow the ballast tanks. We need to surface now!"

Kurz had blocked everything out. He was calmly deciding what should be done. He was proud of his boat. It had served well and was a fine product of the fatherland. It was not able to do any more. His crew was weak and starving. If he continued, everyone would surely die. Explosions continued around them as Kurz sat quietly. The small boat could no longer fight. He would surface the ship and surrender with all due dignity. The war could continue, even without his diligence.

The captain uttered the simple and reserved order: "Surface the boat."

Gruber yelled to the dive officer, "Emergency blow of the ballast tanks!" The men on the bridge reacted immediately and began turning several large wheels as hard as they were able.

The tanks around the ship that held the seawater to submerge the boat began forcing out water. With air replacing water in the tanks, the boat should have begun to rise, but it didn't. The captain had contemplated his options for about twenty seconds. Had he made a decision in fifteen seconds, the crew could have been saved. The once quick witted and brilliant sub skipper had delayed and failed. Failed for the first and last time.

It was quickly known that the ship was not responding.

Gruber continued, "Begin all pumps; have crews check the hatches and valves!"

Water was entering the boat too fast. The U-boat was too heavy to rise to the surface. With more water coming onboard, it would continue to sink. That reality passed through the ship. They could not rise. They could not get out. They would sink to their deaths. The end was approaching.

No one knew how far the U-boat could sink before it broke apart. The farther down it continued, the greater the pressure against it. The crew could only think about what their final moments would be like. Would the boat be broken into pieces, or would it continue to collapse on itself until everyone was crushed?

Gruber stared at his captain. He had feared and respected the man; now he pitied him. The man had been a great military leader at one time; now he could do nothing.

All over the ship grown men cried. They could not see or have one last contact with their families. Men said prayers in silence. Some men panicked and ran in circles. On the bridge Captain Johan Kurz sat in silence, staring blankly.

The boat sank faster. The sounds of exploding depth charges were overtaken by the sounds of the ship dying. Metal moaned and screamed as it warped. Small components snapped and broke. Everyone onboard could feel pressure against their bodies as the tube was squeezed ever tighter. The depth gauge had passed the two-hundred-meters mark and broke. The needle stuck and the glass flew out like a bullet. The boat rolled and sank faster.

After several more seconds that seemed like agonizing minutes, somewhere near the engine room the power of the ocean found its weakest link. The water had pushed so hard against a seam that it completely folded in. Water rushed in at an unimaginable rate. The submarine submitted to ocean pressure in less than one hundredth of a second.

No one on board was aware of his death. Every man was obliterated almost instantly. The only evidence of destruction was the enormous bubble of air that flew out of the ocean above them.

Chapter 40

The meeting of the war counsel was held in the Oval Office because it was expected to be brief and the president could continue working there afterward. The news of the past couple weeks had been good.

The top brass entered the room at the same time and found their places. There was no particular pecking order. Some sat on the comfortable, upholstered couches and others sat in wooden chairs. President Roosevelt was seated in a chair in front of his desk, facing the sofas. He took the time to personally greet everyone by name or title.

"Well, everyone, how have things progressed?"

The men looked pleased and glanced around to see who would speak.

Secretary Henry Stinson spoke first. "Mr. President, America's war machine has responded to every need in fine fashion. The work force has increased and is more productive than at any time in the history of the nation. All efforts are being put forth for the direct defense of the nation. Special effort is being made with our coastal defenses." He nodded confidently. "No further invasions will take place now. Civilian contractors responded quickly with the production of fast, short-range vehicles for the rapid deployment of troops."

Secretary of the Interior Ickes chimed in. "Mostly, civilian contractors have answered the need for roadways. The railroads are operating very efficiently."

People all around the room began talking.

Hap Arnold said, "We've already produced hundreds of airplanes of various types for close patrol of the coasts. These planes can advance on any ships that may venture toward the coasts or they can directly attack troops on shore. They can provide close support for our troops."

Stinson spoke again. "We have mobile, antiaircraft batteries for any airborne attempts, and we have large guns and rocket platforms for seaborne invasions. Sir, with the air force and naval patrols we have on each coast, no enemy can approach within a hundred and fifty miles without being spotted."

Roosevelt nodded. "It sounds as if we are well prepared for anything in the future. What about the current fight in the west?"

General Marshall who always began with troop updates said, "We are rounding up the last of the Japanese invaders in the mountains in Oregon. Those that came ashore near the Columbia River attempted to move directly inland. They were stopped quickly. Those that attacked in Oregon moved inland, but then wandered through the mountains for weeks without attacking." There were some looks of confusion in the room. "It seems they have been avoiding contact with military or civilians for the last few weeks. Few Japanese soldiers have been taken prisoner; that's just the tenacity of the Japanese. We know from the few who have been captured that they apparently weren't sent with an objective."

The room was quiet as this odd information sank in.

"The big invasions that appeared to be looming from the west and the east never transpired. From all intelligence gathered, there was never a significant number of troop transport ships in the Pacific. We don't know how many Japanese soldiers came ashore, and we don't know how many came in the invasion force. Of the German ships that were seen in the Atlantic, no transport ships were ever spotted."

Everyone sat in silence for a few moments.

President Roosevelt ended the day's events. "Thank you, gentlemen, for the continuing good news."

Everyone left and the president picked up a folder from the table beside him to continue his work. He thought about the information from the meeting. He was happy the nation seemed secure, but the future was still unknown.

Chapter 41

The few Japanese soldiers who had survived the many weeks of the war were only shells of their once proud selves. The Tenth Regiment had not joined others of the invasion force. They had not received the support they had been promised. Just as each man marched slowly forward, so the war moved on.

Lt. Hato was in charge of less than two dozen young soldiers of the Imperial Japanese Army. They had not made a significant attack, and the small unit would have to avoid the ever-growing American military forces. Yoshi was confused by his unit's tactics. He had been trained by the army in rugged fashion to never give up the fight. He had taught himself the Bushido way of tenacity in battle. Now the soldiers fled any encounter.

The day of marching had taken its toll on the small unit. Everyone was nearly spent from the invasion. There was little food left; they took from wherever they could find, but now they avoided all contact with Americans. The men no longer picked up weapons and ammunition from American soldiers and civilians. Some of the men were out of ammunition and carried empty rifles. They could use them only as clubs.

The small force reached the top of a peak along the Cascade Mountain range. The top of the knob had nothing on it but rocks and boulders, some the size of cars. The rocky area was completely flat like a table. Rocks jutted up out of the soil below this flat area like the parapets of a castle. The areas to the north and south were too steep for anyone to climb up or walk down safely. The only approaches were east and west. Corporal Iwanami was an inexperienced, noncommissioned officer, but he believed this was an area where they could stay for a long period of time.

Lt. Hato paused on the top and men began falling to the ground from exhaustion. Yoshi stood, wanting to be the proper leader. Hato took out his binoculars and surveyed the area. They were well protected and could see for miles. It was a warm, wonderful day with a breeze on the top of the ridge. The area surrounding this unknown spot in the mountains of the northwestern United States was gorgeous. Yoshi had not compared the mountains of his homeland to that of America before. The sight was beautiful, much like home.

Lt. Hato came down from the ledge where he had been standing and said they would stay the night. No one bothered to move.

Yoshi was still standing. "Lt. Hato, what is our next mission? When do we charge to the enemy?"

Lt. Hato had tired eyes. He looked around at the men before responding. "Corporal, we have no ability to charge, or directive to do so." He moved over to an area in shade, sat and leaned back against a rock without bothering to take off his pack.

Yoshi stood a moment longer, then sat near his lieutenant. He didn't realize how weak his legs were until he sat down. They hurt as he stretched them out in front of him.

"Corporal, do you take pride in your duties?" The lieutenant spoke in a relaxed tone.

"Yes, sir, I do very much."

"I have heard it said of you that when you joined the military, you had found your purpose. Do you believe that is true?"

Yoshi wondered if he were being tested. "Yes, sir. I do not know how this invasion will turn out, but when I return with my forces to Japan, I would like to apply to officer candidate school. With my determined duty in foreign service here in this force I would hope I might receive recognition for my actions and a possible recommendation."

Lt. Hato looked at Yoshi. "You have performed your duties well, Corporal, but you have much to learn before becoming an officer. You do not yet have an understanding of the mission."

Yoshi sat up straight and bowed his head. "I am sorry, sir. I believed we were to strike at the heart of the enemy."

"We were to strike at the enemy directly." Hato nodded. "We caught the enemy asleep and we put fear into the nation, but our force was no more than a pin prick at the giant's heart."

Yoshi thought about the statement. As a simple soldier, his job was just to charge and fight. He had never put thought into how they were to do their mission, or why.

"Corporal, we caused pain and bloodshed, but we angered the giant and we . . ." he looked into Yoshi's eyes, "we will be stabbed by the giant."

Yoshi paused and stared blankly. He thought military leaders were always supposed to think about victory. He questioned why his lieutenant was so doubtful. He thought about the many weeks since his first fears of coming ashore. His army had caused a lot of destruction; they had killed many of the enemy, but to what end? They stayed alive and the war continued. He questioned his military for the first time. He wondered if the Imperial Japanese Army would fail and be destroyed by the giant.

He made himself stop thinking about such things. He would

not let himself question his leaders or the purpose of his duty. He wanted to continue to work hard for what he believed he should do. He wanted a last glorious battle to prove his worth to Lt. Hato and to prove it to himself.

Chapter 42

American soldiers continued tracking and fighting the Japanese. There had been no big battles, just skirmishes that were quickly fought and won. Where was the big invasion force?

Gerald had made it through a couple battles. He had been shot at and had fired in return. He had become war hardened in the short period of time. He was not like veteran soldiers, not like men who had fought through weeks of long engagements on the battlefields in Europe and the Pacific, but he had become more calloused. The northwestern United States had not seen the years of destruction that other nations had seen. Millions were not dead as they were elsewhere, but Gerald had witnessed hatred and death.

This morning his company was moving forward with the division. It was advancing on a rocky peak. U.S. Army Rangers had been tracking the dwindling Japanese invaders. Gerald's company had been told Japanese soldiers were in that area. The company commander, Captain Curt Manegin, had said the peak would be the perfect defensive position. He had delivered his words of motivation. "The enemy is on American soil and we are tasked with defending it. We will do whatever necessary to dislodge them."

Gerald knew that meant a hard fight and more death.

The unit was moving slowly into the forest undergrowth when

Sergeant Mast, leading the line, came to a stop. Looking through the trees he pointed to the rocky heights ahead. He turned to the group behind him and made motions with his hands to listen and look. At that moment a shot rang out, and Sergeant Mast fell dead.

Chapter 43

The night was as restful as any other. Breakfast consisted of a small piece of dried beef and an apple. Yoshi had only one swallow of water from his canteen, which was now empty. He watched the sun rise in the sky on another day of the continuing war.

He thought about his duties as a soldier and leader of soldiers. There was little to do. He folded his bedroll and sat down to clean his rifle.

No one had thought about bringing gun oil. Every rifle was dirty and becoming harder to operate. Yoshi thought he would at least clean the dirt off with his shirt. His shirt was dirty too, but could probably take off excess grime.

Private Sakamoto noticed Yoshi cleaning his rifle. He sat down near Yoshi and began cleaning his own rifle.

"Private, it is good that you continue with your duties. You should be prepared at all times for battle."

"Thank you, Corporal Iwanami. I will keep my rifle ready, but I only have two more bullets."

Yoshi looked up in surprise.

"It does not matter, sir. I will use my hands to kill the enemy if that is all I have left."

Yoshi looked down. He had seen much dedication and strong

will in the many who had died. He believed this young soldier would die like all before him.

"Corporal, where will you live?"

Yoshi looked up again. "What do you mean?"

"When we occupy this country, where will you live? I like the mountains here, but I would like to see the wide, open area in the middle of the country. That is where the Indians hunt the buffalo. I would like to see the country before deciding where I will live."

Yoshi saw himself in the young private. He had been idealistic. He had thought that the invasion force would destroy so much of the nation it would no longer be a threat to Japan. After this annihilation he would return home. Those were his thoughts when he sailed with the fleet. After the protracted fighting and his conversation with the lieutenant he began to believe they had been sent there to die.

Yoshi said nothing more. He sat in silence, wiping his rifle.

A breeze blew over the rocks and the temperature was perfect in the sunlight. Yoshi heard the screech of bird and looked up to see a hawk float out over the valley from the peak. It must nest there. It probably didn't like the soldiers on its mountain. His moment of solitude was interrupted by a shot fired from a Japanese rifle, which was answered by a barrage of gunfire. The hawk drifted away quickly as if flying from an approaching storm.

Private Sakamoto jumped to his feet and ran to the west. As he ran, he shoved one of the two bullets he had into his rifle chamber and slammed home the bolt. Men scurried in the direction of the shot, which had come from a Japanese sentry who had not retreated to warn his unit but had fired a shot to kill an enemy soldier. In doing so, he had exposed himself to sure death.

Lt. Hato was standing on the west side of the rocky area,

giving the order to take cover and prepare to meet the enemy. Yoshi casually walked over and kneeled behind a rock. He took out the two clips of ammunition he had left. He fastened his bayonet to the rifle barrel. He was determined that this was to be his last glorious battle. He would decide his fate.

Lt. Hato knew the desperation of the situation. There was little ammunition left. There was little chance of escape. There was most likely a formidable enemy force assembling around the rocky knob. "Hold your fire until the last moment! Make each shot a kill! When you have no more ammunition, show your gallantry and sacrifice for your nation!"

Yoshi looked below and could see movement in the woods. He could not identify individual soldiers, but he could see the leaves move. Below, a wider and wider area moved. Yoshi thought that the hill could be quickly surrounded.

A soldier to Yoshi's left fired a round into the abyss of green below. This brought a violent conflagration of muzzle fire from the American soldiers. Rounds hit all around. Dust and small rocks were thrown up into the air. Rocks rolled down behind them. The shots from below slowed, and two more soldiers popped up above their protection and fired more shots. The gunfire opened up again from below with the same effect. The shooting stopped and all was quiet for a moment. Yoshi thought that the army group moving up the ridge was smart. Charging up a steep, rocky hillside with the enemy well entrenched on top would be suicidal. "That sounds like something a Japanese force would do," he said to himself. This group of Americans knew that even though they were in an inferior position, they were in charge. They could surround the mountain and wait; they could call in artillery from miles away and blow the top off of the mountain; they could set up mortars and lob in rounds or call in airplanes to shoot anything that moved with a hail of unavoidable gunfire. This battle could be quick or slow, but it would end the same way.

Lt. Hato apparently also realized this. He jumped onto a rock with his pistol raised above his head and yelled to open fire. The remaining men of the Tenth Regiment stood and began firing into the woods below. The sound of the gunfire reverberating off the rocks surrounding them was overwhelming. The woods around the ridge became bright with returned gunfire.

Lt. Hato quickly emptied his sidearm and threw it forward, knowing it would never hit anyone. He was just responding to the desire to strike at the enemy. He screamed and reached down to pick up a rock when the first round hit him. He was hunched over and wobbled. He tried to pick up a rock but was weakened by the gunshot wound. He rolled the rock forward so it would fall down the hill. He turned to find another rock and was struck again. He went to his knees and weaved when a round struck him hard in his left side. He didn't react other than to twist and fall forward out of sight.

Other soldiers followed suit. As they ran out of ammunition, they threw their rifles, their canteens, rocks—anything they could use. When they stood up, they were quickly cut down.

The gunshots from the American soldiers pelted the rocks like a summer downpour. Rocks were knocked loose and thrown around. Dust and gun smoke made a haze in the battle zone. Yoshi had mechanically fired one clip as he had with hundreds of rounds before. He couldn't see the soldiers. He just fired in the Americans' direction, trying to stay low. When the first clip was fired, he ducked behind his cover to load his last one. He slammed the bolt forward and was about to emerge from his cover when the soldier to his right convulsed and fell against his leg. Blood poured out on Yoshi's leg from several wounds on the young man. He pushed the body off and reached for the trigger. As he raised his right hand, he saw the blood on it. The blood was the same color as that of the Americans he had killed. It was warm and flowed the same way. He was fixated by the liquid on his hand.

The sounds of the battle were all around him, but he wasn't aware of them. He looked around. Maybe ten men were still alive. They stood with rifles raised above their heads and evil expressions on their faces. They all jumped on the rocks and pointed themselves and their bayonets toward the enemy below. Each man was ready to take one last stab at the enemy and find his eternity.

Yoshi looked over the rocks and saw American soldiers running up the hill. Their faces were dirty and weary and determined like his. He stood and stumbled over the rocks.

The young privates, the last of his unit, charged forward. They were shot and fell. Two met the advancing American line and stabbed at the enemy. They drew their last blood, only to be knocked to the ground and killed.

Yoshi gripped his rifle and stepped forward. His legs were heavy, even going downhill. His heart felt heavy and pounded inside his chest. Soldiers were running up from all over. He met a small man with enormously bright, blue eyes who pointed a rifle at him. Yoshi stopped. There was nothing to go on for.

He dropped his rifle at his feet, raised his chin and stood to attention. Tears poured out of his eyes, a release of the emotions that had built in his body. The last few days had been a complete haze. He had been so sure of his mission and duty and ashamed that he had questioned them. His part was over now.

Chapter 44

After the barrage of American gunfire answered the shot that killed Sergeant Mast, Henry Johnston moved up and called out for the men around him to advance. All guns were ready.

Gerald was ready along with his fellow soldiers. He thought this would surely be the last battle.

Men spread out all through the woods, and more units quickly moved forward behind them. Everyone was ready for the end and ready to meet a hard battle with overwhelming force and determination.

The American soldiers advanced quickly through the woods but had only gone a few yards when a single shot was fired down from the bluffs. The men opened up on the Japanese position. The gunshots slowed and the men maneuvered for better firing positions. There were more shots from above and another large return of fire.

The captain was near the front of the force that was growing and spreading out farther. He called out for a ceasefire. The guns were silenced and the last sounds were those of metal shell casings striking one another in the leaves. Everyone stood motionless with guns poised. The area was completely silent for a moment—no birds, no wind, only the sounds of pride and determination.

Captain Manegin spoke in a calm voice. "Be smart. They have the hill. That's fine. They won't have it for long. We'll surround the peak and move slowly."

After he had spoken, all that could be heard was the sound of dozens of troops rapidly pushing through the vegetation, their boots pounding the ground.

A Japanese soldier stood up on a rock on the ridge above. This was what Gerald had seen Japanese soldiers do many times. They appeared without fear, and stood up so all could see their courage. The battle began again with gunshots now fired from each side.

Gerald was secure behind a thick oak. He had his carbine rifle tucked against his shoulder, squeezing shot after shot. He was steady and precise now. As he fired away, he could see the green-shirted men above beginning to fall under the curtain of steel flying up from the American fighting men. Fewer and fewer men were left above; possibly a dozen stood with rifles raised and bayonets fixed. They ran over the rocks and charged screaming down the hill.

The line of men around Gerald had seen this before. A last-effort, spirited Banzai charge. The men around him had apparently had enough. They also charged forward like rams running at one another. The battle was about to come to a vicious end.

Gerald moved forward without hesitation. The head-to-head conflict was short. The Japanese soldiers fell like cut blades of grass. One last man with two stripes on his sleeves stumbled toward Gerald. The man was gaunt and confused. Gerald realized this would be a bayonet fight. The young Japanese soldier stopped a couple feet in front of him. He dropped his rifle. The two men stood face to face. The Japanese was crying and Gerald saw the human side of this once vicious fighter.

There had been enough killing. The battle here was at an end.

Chapter 45

It was now well into the summer and the German high command was happy with the course of the war. Adolph Hitler and the imperial leadership of Japan still had questions. Neither Hitler nor Tojo believed in holding back against an enemy—gain at all costs. Goering was to deal with the führer. To help allay the concerns of the Japanese, he sent a trusted friend, the sturdy general Kristoph Meiner who would travel to the Pacific Rim to meet with General Tojo.

It was a miserably humid day in the Philippines. Meiner was accustomed to the cooler climate of the Allgau Alps where he had grown up and where he had returned between the wars. He enjoyed traveling and wanted to see the world after the war. He decided he would have to get used to the varying climates. His trip had been long and tiring. He had traveled for nearly three solid days, starting in Berlin, flying to Rome, then over to Cairo. The trip across the Indian Ocean was lengthy. It began on the eastern tip of the African continent and went to the western tip of Indonesia. From there he had made the last leg to Manila where he would meet Tojo for the first time. He had rested for an entire day in anticipation of the meeting.

Meiner met his compatriot, Major Burkhalter, on the morning

of the meeting. Burkhalter entered the dining room of Meiner's hotel suite. He stood at attention, clicked the heels of his well-polished boots and gave the compulsory "Heil, Hitler." Meiner was impressed by the young major. He had heard and read much about the officer and his appearance was just as pleasing.

"Sit, please, Major Burkhalter."

Burkhalter moved to the table and sat in a formal fashion, placing his hat in front of him.

"Please enjoy a cup of coffee with me," Meiner said, motioning to the butler.

"General Tojo will be here at ten o'clock. Is that correct General Meiner?"

"Correct, Major."

"Are you prepared for your meeting, General?" Burkhalter looked anxious.

Meiner wore a confident smile. "Major, I have dealt with the highest ranks of the German command, the leaders of the Italian forces, and numerous world leaders in my career. I do not fear this simple, Japanese soldier."

"With no disrespect to the general, sir, this simple Japanese soldier is a powerful and influential man. He is now considered the leader of the entire South Pacific including the area where you are sitting."

Burkhalter's comments seemed a bit condescending, as if he were a student talking back to a teacher.

"I have no intention of insulting the man." The general's comment was curt. "We are allies. I intend to offer appropriate support, offer advice, and insure that our mutual goals are met. The Germans and Japanese will soon enough be the rulers of this earth. We should start getting comfortable with one another."

Meiner stood and walked over to Burkhalter. He acted the part of the teacher again and put his hand on the major's shoulder. "I'm sure you have a close friendship with all of those in the Japanese military command. I'm not here to destroy anything but to strengthen."

Meiner moved to the living-room area of the suite while Burkhalter stayed in the dining room. They sat, separate and silent, until the arrival of General Tojo.

At ten o'clock on the nose they heard a distinct knock on the door. A captain on the general's staff went to meet the Japanese visitors. As he opened the door, he was all but physically pushed to the side by two Japanese soldiers in full dress uniform. The men were dressed in light colors with ribbons and shoulder braids, and they wore tall hats. They made a bold entrance, their boots striking the floor and their hands holding their rifles close to their chests. They moved in and slid to each side of the door. Tojo walked in slowly and powerfully, followed by an entourage of men, some in uniforms and some in well-tailored suits. The Germans expected trumpets to sound on such an entrance. Tojo surveyed the room as if he were expecting a large welcoming party. Meiner had not expected to be involved in such pomp and circumstance.

Tojo was a small-framed man. Meiner couldn't help but feel superior to a race that only produced fully grown men of less than six feet tall. Tojo's uniform fit well and was heavily decorated. Meiner knew Tojo was in his best uniform for the meeting of such high caliber. The two allies were trying to impress each other. Tojo grew up the son of an army officer in Tokyo. He was educated at the Imperial Military Academy and had dedicated his life to a strong, military career.

The two met in the center of the room and greeted one another in their own military style, with Meiner snapping to attention and clicking his heels, and Tojo slowly bowing.

"It is a great pleasure to meet with you, sir." Meiner was not sure how to address Tojo. He was the ranking general, leader of all the Japanese forces and prime minister.

"Welcome to your newly acquired province of Japan, General Meiner."

Burkhalter approached and bowed to Tojo in true Japanese style. Tojo returned the gesture.

"I believe you have met the distinguished Major Stephen Burkhalter."

"I know the major very well."

"I hope he has been of as much service to the Japanese Empire as he has to the Reich."

Tojo looked at Burkhalter with a friendly smile. "He has been most impressive in his duties. I feel great confidence that his abilities will provide much in this war."

General Meiner gestured to the room, "Please make yourself comfortable."

Everyone found a seat except for the lowest-ranking officials who remained standing.

"Would you care for a beverage, General Tojo?" Meiner asked.

"I do not care for a drink."

Formalities were only going to slow down the meeting. Both men were aware of their power. Decisions affecting the war and the future of the world would be made. Each represented their nation and had their own opinions as to how things should take place. Millions of lives hung in the balance with this conference.

Meiner had been sent with the agenda of making sure the Japanese continued their course. He knew that Tojo was an extreme militarist and advocate of total war. Tojo was the designer of the attack that was to have taken place at Pearl Harbor. Meiner was sure it had been difficult to call it off. He was sure the Japanese, if given the opportunity, would commit to a full assault on the United States.

"General Meiner, the emperor is saddened that young men have been sent to die in the land of the enemy. The Japanese Empire has committed thousands of soldiers, hundreds of trucks, tanks, cannons, and ships to a minor effort." Tojo had contempt in his voice and anger on his face. "Perhaps the nation of Germany does not believe in the military might of Japan."

"That is far from true, General Tojo." Meiner spoke in a calm, even tone, just like a diplomat. "The military prowess of Japan is well known to the world. That is one thing that will ultimately work against America."

"It would seem that our reduced efforts at attack have done nothing but allow the United States to strengthen its national defense. Had we attacked the American naval fleet at Pearl Harbor, we could have crippled their ability to sail the Pacific and they would have been of little threat to us. We were told by your government," Tojo looked at Burkhalter, identifying him as a representative of Nazi Germany, "that we could undertake a better course against the United States. We reluctantly agreed. We again coordinated with your nation to undertake a two-front attack on the mainland of the United States. The nation of Japan was fully prepared to attack with all diligence, yet this attack has been nothing more than the sacrifice of valuable resources and young, brave fighting men. Had we taken steps for a total, planned attack, Japanese forces could now be occupying a significant portion of the western United States and driving east, with German forces occupying the east and moving west."

Tojo was beginning to raise his usually calm voice. "Please explain to me, General Meiner, how the slaughter of a small Japanese force and a token response by Nazi forces will work against the United States.

Meiner bowed his head slightly in response. "General Tojo, I realize that Japan has sacrificed much. I know it's difficult to send men to their deaths with little to show for their loss."

"Young men dying in service to their nation is a great honor to themselves and the emperor, but death should come from striking at the enemy, not hiding from them."

Meiner looked directly into the eyes of Tojo. "General, it would be wise to continue with our course. The deaths of these men and the loss of materials is an investment."

There was a pause. Tojo thought an investment involved money, not souls.

Meiner continued, "General, does it not feel good that a small part of the Japanese army and navy is distressing one of the greatest world powers? This small force occupies the entire Western Hemisphere. The men who have fought and continue to fight within the borders of the United States—both Japanese and German forces—are sacrificing themselves for future victory."

The room seemed more relaxed now. General Tojo leaned back into the sofa. Meiner continued in his diplomatic voice. "General, German forces have fought and won spectacular victories for three years. Your expansion in the Pacific and Southeast Asia has gone on constantly for more than a decade. General, to be frank, we need to control our advance."

Tojo looked offended. This was not how he or the Japanese people felt about warfare. A true Samurai warrior would never yield. He would never consider slowing an advance.

Tojo spoke. "Why should we not strike now? War has raged over the world for years and America has been in isolation, asleep."

"Because a sleeping giant poses no danger."

Meiner's words reverberated through the room. No one had spoken like this before. No one had spoken with such candor. "The United States is a nation that can press millions of men into service. They are a nation of wealth and nearly unlimited resources. To stir them would bring about an awesome fight." Meiner moved forward to emphasize his words. "If the giant is allowed to sleep so that strength can be gained for a fight against it, then even a giant can be beaten."

This was still hard for General Tojo to accept. It was contrary to the nature of the Japanese fighting man, but Tojo could be pragmatic.

"General Tojo, the code name given to the operation is Two Swords. I learned of that name from Field Marshall Goering. He has studied your history and has some understanding of the Bushido code. Two swords does not necessarily mean that a soldier must use two swords in battle. One sword with two strikes can be effective."

Tojo looked at the man using Japanese culture to make his point.

Meiner continued, "The second strike of a sword can be even more devastating than the first. You believe the first attack against the United States was small and weak. The second attack will be complete annihilation. If we continue our course of putting pressure on American shores, the Americans will return to protect themselves. England will quickly fall without the Americans. We can continue against Russia. Sir, Japan can control the entire Pacific up to the American shores. You are enjoying your conquest of the

Pacific region. You can conquer Australia when you choose. You may finish China at your leisure. As your area of control grows, so will your military strength. You will have growth through the natural resources you gain. America will lie idly by, watching its own oceans and borders, while your nation and our nation will grow into the greater giant. When the United States stand alone, they will be irrelevant in the struggles of the world."

Meiner had a subtle smile on his face. "General Tojo, when the Imperial Japanese Army and the German Wehrmacht meet in the middle of Russia, you and I will meet again. Our meeting at that time will be to decide on the division of the Eastern Hemisphere. There will be millions of acres of farmland in the Soviet Union and China along with the labor that comes with them. There will be more than enough oil in the Middle East for both of our nations. We can mine precious metals in Africa."

Tojo was now sitting more comfortably and had no arguments against Meiner's rant. The room seemed to have energy even though the Nazi general was the only one speaking. He continued, "General, my führer can walk on the Great Wall of China, while your emperor can rest on the sands of a Mediterranean beach."

Tojo actually smiled.

With General Tojo in line with the plan, General Meiner's speech came to an end. He was prepared to enjoy the remainder of his trip. Knowing the meeting was coming to a conclusion, he stood. "General Tojo, you spoke of the pains of war. Pain now will lead to pleasure later. With the United States occupied, we will continue our victories. When most of the world is in the control of the Third Reich and the Japanese Empire, then we can decide on how to handle the lonesome United States."

This had been an unusual meeting for Germany and Japan.

Their national cultures were so completely different that they made odd allies. Moreover, because neither nation had shown much restraint in its assault on its enemies, the generals' agreement to hold back a full attack to gain control later seemed odd.

Chapter 46

The meeting was called on the third floor of the Executive Mansion. The president had decided that because the war had begun while he was in the treaty room in the upstairs living quarters of the residence, it should end there also. The day had been greatly anticipated and the president prepared his speech to Congress, this time to say the war was over.

Today was the formal meeting to announce what was already known: that the invasion was contained and America had repelled the attack. After the meeting of the war counsel in the treaty room, they were to sit down for lunch, after which President Roosevelt would talk to reporters in the West Wing.

The president was seated at the small conference table as the counsel arrived. The room was a tight fit for the large number of people, but the meeting was going to be brief and afterward, guests would move into the large, center-hall, living-room area where lunch would be served.

The faces of those entering the room were filled with expressions of joy, relief, satisfaction, pride, and so much more. These men were experienced leaders and were bringing an apparent end to a difficult task.

Everyone found their seats and the president began. His voice sounded different when he gave his customary, "Gentlemen, what news do you bring me?"

There had probably been discussion ahead of time as to who was going to make the statement. Secretary of War Stinson, seated on the president's right, spoke in a loud and clear voice: "Mr. President, it is our duty and privilege to announce to you that the war in America is over."

Everyone broke into applause. It was a small meeting of military and political figures with no audience, but men clapped and rose to their feet.

Stinson continued, "The invasion force of the Imperial Japanese Army has been destroyed. The nation has been completely fortified and there is no fear of future invasion. The war is over and the nation is safe."

The president spoke lightheartedly, even as he talked about war. "How did the end take place in the west?"

General Marshall was comfortable for the first time in months when he spoke. "The last few Japanese soldiers were tracked by U.S. Army Rangers to a rocky ridge in Oregon called Hawks Nest. They had an excellent location for a defensive battle, but they were overwhelmed by army units. Their last desperate actions brought an end to the fighting."

They continued around the room with Admiral King speaking next. "Our navy has put an end to any threat in close proximity to the United States. We've sunk ships and subs on both coasts and no other ships are within striking distance of the country."

Stinson completed the address. "Mr. President, all of America is safe."

President Roosevelt continued, "I believe much praise is to be given to the army and the navy. They have performed spectacularly in the defense of the nation, and that is no small feat, considering the history of the Japanese and German armies."

The men in the room nodded, admitting that the enemy forces were formidable foes.

Roosevelt continued, "It seemed the Japanese were unstoppable in taking areas of the Pacific. The Germans have moved freely over Europe and Africa."

Marshall responded, "They just didn't seem prepared for an attack on the United States. They were not prepared to occupy our country as they were able to do in so many other areas. It would seem that Germany did nothing more than demonstrate against our eastern seaboard." There were some questioning looks in the room. "The Japanese were so ill prepared that it appeared those who did make it ashore were sent on a suicide mission."

The chief of staff, always at the president's side, spoke. "We believed both nations were brazen enough to attack the United States even with their other actions all over the globe. Why would they not attack as they have historically? The United States was vulnerable. It had a small force compared to the military forces of the enemy. The Nazis blitzed Europe with no fear. The Japanese army and navy overwhelmed areas of the South Pacific in fanatical fashion. Why did they attack here with such hesitation?"

Men looked around the room, apparently seeking answers and asking themselves the same questions.

Secretary Stinson spoke. "They knew they could not attack and occupy us as they've been able to do in so many other places. The Japanese would have needed much more in resources from the South Pacific than what they have now. The Germans have to control their enemies before dealing with us. This nation is seen as a world power that can't be overlooked. The Japs and Germans surely have to realize we can't be easily defeated; we need to be dealt with separately and at a later time."

As Stinson ended his statement, the men in the room seemed to sink simultaneously. The once happy faces seemed to age and show fear again. Stinson dropped his head as he concluded, "And that is what they have done."

The crowd that had been ready to break into a humble celebration now sat quietly.

The president shifted uncomfortably in his chair. "What is currently going on in the rest of the world?"

The mood of the room suddenly changed. Eyes darted around when Secretary of State Cordell Hull finally spoke. "Sir, the Germans and Japanese are still advancing in other parts of the world and now even more forcefully. Great Britain is again under day and night attacks. The Germans are flying with many more and larger bombers, and a large force of deadly fighter planes. When planes are not flying, long-range artillery is used, and they are experimenting with long-range missiles. German ships are now attacking throughout the English Channel." He looked at a file. "The ships include the battleship *Sheer* and cruiser *Hipper*."

It took only a moment for everyone to realize these were the same ships seen on June 3 and believed to be leading the East Coast invasion of the United States.

"The Germans are also advancing east. They have begun attacking Stalingrad and are moving on Moscow."

Heads began to bow in the room as Hull picked up another file and continued. "The Japanese are bombing Darwin, Australia, in apparent preparation for invasion. They're continuing into China and are even advancing on India. With the Nazis moving southeastward around the Caspian Sea and the Japanese moving northwestward through India, the vanguard of the two armies could meet by early spring."

Roosevelt asked, "How could this have taken place without our knowing?"

Hull replied, "The advances began about six weeks after we cut supplies to our allies."

What had happened over the summer was sinking in.

"What about the heads of state in these nations? How are they responding to the continuing war in their nations?"

Hull tipped his head to the side and raised his eyebrows. "Resiliently, sir. England has vowed to fight to the death. The people have demanded King George and Queen Elizabeth leave the country. Both have refused and it's said King George is taking target practice with a revolver inside Buckingham Palace. Chairman Stalin regularly visits the front from Moscow. Generalissimo Chiang Kai-shek has fortified the capital and is prepared for a defensive battle there. General de Gaulle has left England and fled to Iceland."

President Roosevelt struck the table with his hand. This was the first time this dignified and generally reserved leader had shown his anger with physical force. "We cannot allow this to continue. We must immediately send planes to England. We can support Russia with tanks and guns. We need to move men into the Pacific. We have to act now!"

Everyone recognized the president's frustration. They began to understand the implications of what was happening in the world.

Secretary Stinson spoke up. "Mr. President, sir." His voice became quieter. "Great Britain is the Alamo." The room went silent for several moments. "We can't send planes because we don't have planes that the Brits can use and there is no place to land them. We can't send supplies to the Soviets because the Germans moved to within only a few miles of their last port at Murmansk. Australia is the last finger hold we have against Japan, and we would have to sail our men through extremely hostile waters to even reach it."

The president had a distant look on his face. The pitch in his voice never changed as he tried to understand, "You're saying the other nations of the world are lost?"

No one answered or even looked at the president.

His voice became quiet and his head went down. "We have sat here concerned only with ourselves while the rest of the world has withered away and fallen under the control of evil." His voice fell nearly to a whisper as if he were only questioning himself. "My God, what have we done?"

His head was bowed as he wondered what the world had become.

Chapter 47

President Roosevelt sat in the garden with his manservant, George. It was a comfortable Saturday morning in the nation's capital. Roosevelt was relaxed in the quiet and attractive setting. He was at peace while the rest of the world was in turmoil.

George carried a cutting from one of the trailing rose bushes and handed it to the president. The two roses on the cutting were white, signifying purity and innocence. "Here you go, sir. The roses still look mighty good." George turned and surveyed the area. "And the mums are coming along nicely."

The president took the roses and gave a perfunctory smile.

George knew his place. He never discussed issues with the man; he just attended to the president's needs. "Yes, sir, shaping up to be a mighty fine day, wouldn't you say so?"

The president made eye contact with the modest and trustworthy old man who was ever present. He nodded his head. "Yes, George, it is a lovely morning." Autumn was fast approaching. The productive season was ending and it was time to start storing for the winter.

The war in the United States was over, but at what cost? The country prospered while the rest of the world died. The Axis powers seemed unstoppable and the United States stood alone. It had fought off attacks, but what of the future?

President Roosevelt sat in the large, beautiful garden of the Executive Mansion and thought to himself how small the country seemed. On each side were large oceans and although the American continent was vast, it was a small place in a large world threatened at every turn.

It was still chilly as the morning fog was burning away in the sun. This was a new day in a new world. The president sat enjoying the moment. A cool breeze blew in from the east. He turned toward it and faced the ever-rising sun.

Chapter 48

The winter had passed painfully for the president. It had been long, cold and weakening for the feeble man, physically and mentally. He had always made what he had thought were sound decisions for what was right for the nation, but now he thought that he had failed. He believed that he had cost his nation and the world a great toll.

President Roosevelt sat in the third-floor treaty room, which had been a contemplative place of refuge. Still only a select few were allowed to enter this small, peaceful office. It faced south and he could look out and see the shadows on the expansive, manicured lawn growing shorter as the sun rose. It was still many weeks until summer, but the longer days with the sun moving north helped to push out the cold weather and the fear of a world held hostage all around him.

He had spun his wheelchair around and had rolled forward to the table when he heard the first sounds of the admirals and generals approaching. The war council meetings began promptly at 8:00 a.m. and the military men were regimentally on time. The meetings were generally grim. He witnessed the blank faces, which he knew hid fear. Everyone knew that the Axis was on the cusp of controlling the entire world.

General Marshall entered the room with a hearty, "Good morning, Mr. President."

President Roosevelt returned the good morning. Each of the ranking commanders followed suit with proper greetings.

The actions of each man in the room were quick and deliberate. Lower-ranking officers set up an easel and were ready, as always, to put up the map before being told to do so. Others plugged in telephones near the doorway and a secretary was always present to put the content of the meeting on record.

Once everyone was seated and still, President Roosevelt silently surveyed the room. All of his trusted military leaders were present, and he looked for a glimpse of anything on their faces.

"Gentlemen, what news do you bring?" His voice had grown tired over his long presidency and strained by war.

As was the custom, the general chief of staff, George Marshall, began. "Sir, it's my humble belief that this war is turning."

With that he was silent for a few moments, only shuffling papers in front of him. Officers put a map of Western Europe on the easel. It was already marked with circles, lines, and arrows. "Sir, it would seem that the German invasion of England will not transpire. Their bombing and shelling of the coast haven't yet resulted in anything that would indicate they're trying to cross the Channel. Perhaps, Hitler's knowledge that an American expeditionary force has arrived has made him hesitate to attempt a landing, and with the arrival of a large part of our Atlantic fleet augmenting the Royal Navy, we are starting to take control of the English Channel."

Roosevelt knew that the fight England had put up, nearly entirely alone for some time, was intense and devastating. He felt ashamed that the United States had not done more. He questioned his own importance in the whole scheme of the things. He felt horrible that the country had worked to build its own nation, only to lose the world.

General Marshall continued speaking and pointing to the map, but the president wasn't paying attention. The general got his attention again when the map was changed to one of the Soviet Union. It too had markings, with Moscow nearly obliterated by pen marks.

Marshall went on. "Sir, the Nazi's couldn't hold onto Moscow through to the spring. They occupied it for a hundred days, through a hard winter, trying to keep their troops supplied by the Luftwaffe."

That caught some by surprise and made them think about an air force flying supplies into a city to support its troops.

"The Germans couldn't maintain their hold on the city," the general continued. "Over sixty thousand German soldiers were captured, and there are over one hundred thousand in retreat."

Those numbers sank into the men in the room: Armies of millions; battles costing the lives of tens of thousands of people, millions of civilians—those who happened to be in the way, those hated because of who they were—all trampled and eliminated in a moment of time. Over sixty thousand German soldiers were out of the fight for the remainder of the war, but there were still over a hundred thousand able to carry on the war.

The warmth of the sun started to seep more directly into the room and onto the back of President Roosevelt. He rarely made facial expressions during conversations or speeches. He continued listening to General Marshall intently.

"Sir, General McArthur has gathered his forces in northern Australia and his headquarters is now established in Darwin. From that location he is capable of moving almost anywhere between Indonesia and the Marshal Islands. The navy has established a shipping lane through the Coral Sea, which is moving an average of thirty thousand tons of supplies per day." There were many looks of satisfaction in the room, but the president sat expressionless. "The Pacific Fleet has had only intermittent contact with the Japanese navy without a major confrontation in months."

A single sentence was spoken concerning top secret activities taking place in several locations around the nation, "The Manhattan project is well underway, but is estimated to be ten months to two years away from any practical testing."

Those who knew about the project knew not to speak about it. Those who were not privy knew not to ask. The president was both excited and horrified. The pain of his duties ran in tandem with his own physical and emotional weaknesses.

There was a lot of anxious movement in the room. These were soldiers and sailors ready for a fight. The winter was one of no fighting for the American forces, just support of other armies and preparation for a large confrontation ahead. After the room was silent for several seconds, General Marshal looked directly into the sullen face of the president. He spoke with a confident voice, "Mr. President, we have the strongest navy and air force in the history of mankind. There are over six million men in uniform, prepared for any eventuality."

President Roosevelt continued to sit quietly. He knew all the men in the room were doing their duty, preparing plans for attack and defense, and he was ready to leave them to their tasks. All were dismissed, leaving the president alone with his duty to lead a nation in war as best he could.

As each man filed out, George walked in. He usually offered coffee, which was available to the president twenty-four hours a day. Today, with the changing season, it seemed appropriate for the stately old gentleman to offer the president some iced tea.

"I'd be happy to have a glass, George, perhaps with some cookies." President Roosevelt's face turned up toward the man and showed warmth and a slight smile. "Thank you."

George dutifully left the room. He would be back from the long walk to the kitchen in several minutes.

The president did his best to keep Congress and the American people informed about the war, just as he was kept informed by his staff. He pulled a file from a nearby drawer and continued work on a speech.

He tried to form his thoughts and wrote quickly. "We believe we have felt the blanket of security in our nation, but as others in this world toil under the violence of fanatics and the heinousness of tyrants, these terrible acts have crept closer, shaking the very foundations of peace, prosperity, and happiness for which this nation stands."

President Roosevelt felt remorse for ignoring the rest of the world. Millions had suffered while the United States stood by, preparing to defend only itself. The sun shone brightly and directly into the room. The day was becoming warmer, and the president sat in comfort with his back to the window. He continued writing. "As long as truth, justice, and righteousness exist in the hearts of men, evil will never completely overcome us, and freedom shall not perish from this earth."

Breinigsville, PA USA
29 December 2010
252355BV00003B/2/P